The Triplets
and
Cryptic's Revenge

An Old Schoolhouse Mystery
Book Three

The Triplets and Cryptic's Revenge—An Old Schoolhouse
Mystery—Book Three
Copyright © 2018 by Tim Tweedie

Credits

Cover art & illustrations © Tim Tweedie

LCN   2018906094
ISBN   978-1-945539-26-8

The Triplets
and
Cryptic's Revenge

An Old Schoolhouse Mystery
Book Three

Tim Tweedie

Dunecrest Press

This book is dedicated
to my six exceptional grandchildren
who are avid readers and the inspiration behind
the Old Schoolhouse Mysteries.
And to my wonderful wife, Judy and my amazing
brother, Jim, for doing so much to help me put
the story together for publication.

Contents

About the Story

After settling into their new home in the small, Sierra foothill town of Opportunity, Mikaia, Jonathan, and Nicholas, born into the world as triplets, find themselves caught up in a dark and dangerous struggle for the future of the town. Armed with hidden powers given to them by an old schoolhouse, they survive an attack by the mysterious Cryptic and struggle to find a way to outwit his evil Followers. But Cryptic wants his revenge. Will good win over evil? Will love win over hate? Or will the future of Opportunity be lost?

Chapter One

Premonition

The trail wound through the woods. Blue light was reflected down through the tall pine trees hitting the trail as dancing light between the shadows.

"Do you smell smoke?" I asked Mikaia.

"Yeah, I do. It's probably just some camper's camp fire."

"Hey, Jonathan, don't get too far ahead!" I yelled as he seemed to bound up the trail even faster.

A gray haze appeared above me and soon filtered down through the trees. I felt a slight irritation in my eyes as my nose sensed that the smoke was coming from more than a campfire.

"I think we ought to get out of here!" I advised.

Now even Jonathan was heading back towards us looking up into the sky and watching the blue change to a large charcoal colored cloud.

As we turned and faced back down the trail, I could see tongues of orange flames begin to climb above the trees. The crackling of burning wood

1

began to fill my ears as a hot wind blew across my face.

"No, Mikaia, Jonathan, we'll need to go back up the trail! The fire's burning fast!" I shouted.

We began to run but the fire seemed to be coming towards us from all directions. The heat was intense.

"Quick, let's use the time-slide sign and pop out of here!" I screamed. But my arms wouldn't move. My hands would not come together to form the sign.

An icy coldness filled my head. My body felt numb. Where was the heat? All I could feel was ice, like I was suspended in a large cold cube. I tried to move my arms as I felt the ice begin to melt into water. I still couldn't sign! All I could do was thrash my arms around trying to swim, trying to keep from drowning!

A voice! I hear a voice! "Did you come to save us?" I yelled.

"Fire and ice are my friends, Nicholas. I use them all the time! You three need to be much more afraid of me and my powers. I demand your respect or you will simply disappear in the smoke and ice. You've been warned. Be very careful how you use your powers. Don't interfere with my work!"

Nicholas found himself sitting up in his bed. Beads of salty sweat were burning his eyes as they ran down his face. His heart was beating fast. Slowly he began to realize that he'd been dreaming, or was it one of his premonitions? Had Cryptic gotten into his

2

mind? Was it a message? A warning from him?

Nicholas sat still for a moment but soon got up realizing there was no way he'd be going back to sleep. Besides it was almost six in the morning so he might as well.

As Nicholas sat in the kitchen buttering some bread he'd just toasted, Mikaia walked in.

"Good morning" she said, smiling and sitting down next to him. "You couldn't sleep any longer either?"

"No. I guess I had a lot on my mind and woke up early. The last few days have really got me thinking...and worrying."

"Me too. Matter of fact I had this strange vision last night that had something to do with fire and ice. I didn't know what it was, but it seemed almost sinister, like some kind of warning."

"Then it wasn't just me!" Nicholas replied.

"What do you mean?"

"I had a dream or premonition that the three of us were trapped in a forest fire and couldn't escape. Then I was surrounded by ice and almost drowned in its water. Then a voice warned me to be careful how I use my powers and not to interfere or else."

"Do you think it was a message from Cryptic?" Mikaia asked very seriously.

"Probably. I don't know anyone else who has the power to enter my dreams and threaten me."

"I see what you mean by the worrying part. I just had a small piece of your dream but I'm sure it came

3

from Cryptic. He's obviously interested in getting rid of us as soon as he can after his humiliation at the old school, especially since we embarrassed him in front of his Apprentices and Followers."

"Yeah, as though Sam Hawkins stayed around long enough to see how it all turned out...great Followers!" Nicholas said as he and Mikaia managed a smile.

"Hey, what are you guys doing up so early?" Jonathan asked, heading over to the cupboard and taking out the pancake mix.

"I guess we both had trouble sleeping last night," answered Mikaia.

"Not me, after all we'd been through this last week, I slept like a log!"

"We both had weird dreams that woke us up," Nicholas added.

"I only dreamt about a big plate of pancakes! Do you want me to make some for you too?" asked Jonathan.

"That would be nice, thanks!" Mikaia said softly.

Jonathan paused for a moment and looked over at his brother and sister. He'd just added an egg and milk to the pancake batter but stopped his stirring.

"Wow! You both did have a bad night, especially you Nicholas, a real downer of a dream!"

"You could tell?"

"Yeah, I could read the pain you were feeling in your mind as you thought about it," Jonathan said as he sat down next to them.

Both Mikaia and Nicholas shared what they'd seen in their dreams, especially Nicholas, with the warnings he'd received.

"I was just feeling pretty good about how we were able to stop Cryptic in his tracks and chalk one up for good over evil and now this. Seems like we don't get any slack," Jonathan said. He stood up and continued stirring.

"We do have more powers to help us now, and we do know the Master Inventor and Halo are helping us, not to mention Mom and Dad!" Mikaia declared.

"That's all fine and I'm really glad we don't have to hold things back from Mom and Dad anymore, but we're still the custodians of the old school and Cryptic's targets. We're the ones he wants to stop and get rid of," Nicholas replied.

"Are you going to tell Mom and Dad about your dreams?" asked Jonathan.

"Probably not," answered Nicholas. "They, especially Dad, already know about Cryptic and his evil and how he tried to kill us at the old school. This will worry them even more. Besides they really can't help us much with this problem."

"You're right," agreed Mikaia.

"Right about what?" their mother, Cathy, asked.

"Oh, good morning, Mom," Mikaia said. "Right about the three of us needing to be very cautious with Cryptic not liking us and our powers"

"That's for sure. You know how much your Dad and I trust the three of you. We respect your powers and the trust Halo and the Master Inventor have in you. That still doesn't stop us from worrying, even though we know you have some powerful people looking out for you. You also know that we're willing to help and support you in any way, don't you?"

"We know that, Mom. We're just glad that all this is out in the open now and we can count on you and Dad to support us," replied Nicholas.

"Well, I guess it's about time we hit the tunnels," Jonathan said.

"Hit what tunnels?" their dad, Nathan, asked.

"Good morning, Dad," Jonathan replied. "Do you want some pancakes too?"

"Sure, that would be great...a Jonathan special! Not bad."

"The tunnels and cavern where Sam left all those explosive charges," replied Jonathan.

"I was wondering when we were going to get around to that. They are dangerous and we definitely don't want any more explosions and cave-ins especially on the machine," Nicholas added.

The triplets could hear a soft sigh coming from their mother as she put plates on the table.

"I know this hasn't been easy for you, Cathy," their dad said, "but the triplets do have a lot of responsibility now. I'm afraid picking up the explosives is just one of them whether we like it or not. If you like, I'm willing to help."

"Thanks, Dad, but we'll have to use the time-slide sign to pop into the cavern where most of the explosive charges are so you wouldn't be able to help us much," Mikaia replied. "But thanks for asking."

"By the way, I was talking to Bill Peters yesterday afternoon and he mentioned that Terry's brother, Bo Flanders, has been in town a couple of days taking care of her effects and business. Bill didn't know much about him other than he was a tall, athletic looking man in his late forties."

"I'm glad to see Terry had some family who can take care of things for her. I sure hope he's not a Follower too," replied Mikaia.

"I'm full!" exclaimed Jonathan, "and those were great pancakes if I do say so myself."

"They hit the spot. Good job, Jonathan," his dad said just as he finished off his first pancake.

"Are you guys ready to go? I'll get a couple of burlap bags to put the charges in and two of Mom's small garden shovels to help us dig some out of the tunnel walls, if you don't mind, Mom," Jonathan said.

"Anything that will help, but I would like them both back, Jonathan," Mom replied.

"No problem," returned Jonathan. "See you outside."

"We'll be there in just a minute," Nicholas said as he gulped down what was now going to be his last pancake. "Man, Jonathan's always in such a hurry."

"Once he's full he's ready to move on quickly to the next thing on his mind," Mikaia added. "I guess that's a kind of gift?"

"Sometimes," Nicholas said with a mouthful of

pancakes, as he headed out the front door with Mikaia close behind

"How do you want to travel?" Mikaia asked when they all met on the front porch.

"Since we have to get the charges out of the mine tunnels on our way to the cavern, we might as well climb down through the Creekside Mine Tunnel entrance in our barn and walk there," answered Nicholas.

"Good. Let's go!" Jonathan said, as he quickly headed off towards the barn.

"Are you sure he didn't drink caffeinated coffee this morning?" Nicholas asked while he and Mikaia hurried to catch up.

Once they arrived at the junction of the Hole in the Mountain tunnel, they started gathering the small explosives with the antennas they had clipped a few days before. They figured Sam had placed about forty altogether.

When they got to the invisible curtain which had hidden the opening to the cavern, they found that it had caved in. The debris partly blocked the tunnel and had sealed off the cavern.

"Wow, what a mess! I guess it's for the best. Now no one can get in through there except us," stated Nicholas.

"Unless they reinforce the ceiling and work for a few days with a lot of equipment," Jonathan added.

"Are you ready to use the time-slide sign and pop in?" Mikaia asked.

"Let's go!" Jonathan said.

Mikaia counted to three and they all made the signal thinking about where and why they wanted to travel inside the cavern. After three pops they reappeared inside.

"Everything looks fine in here and the time machine hasn't been touched, just as you foresaw in your vision the other day, Mikaia," Nicholas said.

They started looking for explosive charges.

"After this I'd like to take a random field trip, just

Using their flashlights, they searched
for explosives.

to see where we'd go to learn something new. We could also say 'Hi' to Hither and Yon, if we travel more than fifty years forward or back in time!" Jonathan suggested.

"You are full of energy," replied Mikaia as she took two charges out from under the invisibility curtain that covered the time machine.

"Hey, Nicholas, do you want the radio signal jammer you placed in here?" she asked. "By the way, it was a great move to think of that."

"No, let's leave it by the machine just in case we missed a charge or two. With it jamming, they'd be less likely to go off if something happened to trigger them," Nicholas replied.

"It's still sad to think that Terry is under that messy cave-in that leads up to the old school," Jonathan said.

"I don't feel too bad since she ran down here so Cryptic could kill all of us," Nicholas replied.

"When you put it that way I guess we were lucky she didn't make it," agreed Jonathan.

"Is the tunnel into the old school completely blocked, Nicholas?" Mikaia asked when she saw that he was in the cavern looking at the rock and dirt pile in front of it.

"It sure is. It would take several weeks to get through this," he replied.

"Let's get out of here and go back home. This place still has bad memories for me," declared Mikaia.

"For all of us," added Jonathan. "Let's bury these charges up at the tunnel's end and head home."

After popping back out into the tunnel and digging a hole as deep as their mother's small shovels

10

allowed, the triplets dropped the burlap bags into it, and covered it over.

After three popping sounds, the triplets reappeared in Mikaia's room.

"Mom, we're back!" Mikaia called down the stairs.

"Did everything go all right?' she called back up.

"Just fine, Mom," answered Mikaia.

"When you were gone, you received two calls. One was from Marie reminding you of her birthday party at Mariposa County Regional Park tomorrow at noon. The other was from Calvin Hill for the boys. He said that football practice begins on Monday morning at the Middle School."

"Thanks, Mom!"

"By the way, Marie said to tell you to bring your dancing shoes!"

"Shoot!" Jonathan said loudly.

"I guess you guys heard all of that by your response," Mikaia said with a quiet laugh.

"Yeah, we got it," replied Nicholas.

"I don't think the two of you have danced since they made us folk dance at school in San Francisco for the May Day celebration!" mentioned Mikaia.

"You're right. And I don't think we'll be dancing around a giant pole with long ribbons on Saturday either," replied Nicholas.

"At least we get to play a little football on Monday," Jonathan added.

"It will probably be a week or more of

conditioning before we actually play, if you like running and sweating," said Nicholas.

"We should keep in shape. You never know where we might end up when we travel on field trips," added Jonathan.

"Good point," Nicholas replied.

"I want to go into town and poke around. I'd especially like to check out this Bo Flanders guy and see what he's up to," suggested Mikaia.

"I'm game," said Nicholas.

"Me too," added Jonathan.

Chapter Two

New Faces and New Dangers

As luck would have it, the triplets found that their mom was headed into town to pick up some supplies for their dad so they were able to hitch a ride.

"I'll meet you back at the car in an hour," she said as she parked in the grocery store parking lot.

The triplets nodded, jumped out, and walked to the antique shop. Jonathan was the first to get to the front door.

"See you later Frank!" said a stocky man in his late thirties as he strode out the door nodding to Jonathan.

"Who was that?" Mikaia asked when she and Nicholas caught up.

"I don't know. Someone named Frank," Jonathan replied as they entered the shop.

Standing behind the counter looking over what appeared to be some financial records was a tall, handsome man in his late forties.

"Good day to the three of you," he said when he noticed them walk in.

His voice was pleasing and his smile appeared to be warm and natural. This caught the triplets off guard.

"Oh, good morning to you too," said Mikaia.

"How may I help you today?" he asked.

Mikaia decided to test the waters right away. "We're the Frazier triplets. I'm Mikaia, and these are Jonathan and Nicholas. We did a lot of business with Terry before she passed away. We were very sorry to hear about the accident. She was always very nice to us...when we came into the store."

"Well I'm glad to hear that. I miss her too. By the way, I'm her brother, Bo Flanders. I've just been organizing her things and dealing with a lot of details."

"Do you plan on keeping the shop open?" Nicholas asked.

"Actually, I had just made up my mind to operate it myself."

"Oh, do you live nearby?" asked Jonathan.

"No. I'm from Los Angeles. I was a police officer there for many years until I left the force to open a Tae Kwon Do school five years ago. I've always liked the California foothills. Every time I visited Terry I told myself that someday I should settle here. I guess some good can come out of even bad situations. So, here I am to stay, and how about you three?"

"We're from San Francisco and have only been here since the summer began. We really like the community and we start school in a week," replied

Mikaia.

"That's nice, some other newcomers. Now I won't feel like the only new guy in town," Bo replied. "What kind of business did you do with my sister?"

"We collect things," said Nicholas. "I like old bottles, Jonathan likes old documents and Mikaia has an antique doll collection."

"Well, I just hope that I can keep you three supplied with items you like."

"It was nice meeting you, Mr. Flanders," Mikaia said, turning to leave.

"It's just Bo now, Mikaia," he replied as they went out the door.

"He sure seems like a nice man," Mikaia said. "What did you think, Jonathan?"

"I tried to pick up on his thoughts, but I couldn't get any kind of reading at all. That's sure strange because now, when I concentrate, I can usually read someone's mind," Jonathan said as he shook his head. "But with Bo, I didn't get anything!"

"Then maybe he's all right and not a Follower like his sister," Mikaia added.

"I don't know, Mikaia. It seems that evil unfortunately seems to run for generations in some families around here, at least that's been our experience so far," Nicholas said.

"You're right about that," agreed Jonathan.

"Let's not judge too soon," said Mikaia.

"And let's not be too careless and miss something because someone seems super nice. Just remember his sister," replied Nicholas.

All of a sudden Jonathan took off down the street.

"Hey, where are you going?" Nicholas shouted.

As they ran down the street after him, Mikaia declared, "I know. Don't bother asking. We'll just follow him to the Ice Cream and Candy Shop. I think Jonathan has double chocolate chip on his brain again."

When they got to the ice cream shop, Jonathan was already in line. Several other people were in front of him. Right away Mikaia noticed that one of them was Sam Hawkins!

"Man, what luck. We get to have ice cream with Sam Hawkins," she said.

"This could be awkward," replied Nicholas when they walked in and got in line behind Jonathan.

Jonathan was so busy checking out all the ice cream flavors that he apparently hadn't seen Sam in line in front of him.

When Sam spotted the triplets, he turned away quickly and his face became a bright red. He shifted back and forth uncomfortably and spoke with the man next to him. After they received their ice cream and began to leave, Jonathan finally spotted him.

"Oh hi there, Mr. Hawkins. We haven't seen you since, oh yes, now I remember," Jonathan said.

Mikaia and Nicholas almost wished to be invisible.

"It's you again. I'd hoped I wouldn't bump into the three of you for a long time since you're the source of most of my problems!" he grunted back.

Jonathan didn't seem to want to back off. "I'd say you're the source of most of your problems and if you acted like a responsible adult you'd be much better off!"

Sam merely snarled and looked away... then smirking he announced, "I want you to meet a friend of mine. Mitch Steffini, these are the Frazier triplets."

Mr. Steffini's piercing eyes caught Jonathan by surprise as he just nodded back at him.

"Mitch is my attorney, the best defense attorney in the county. No thanks to you I have to engage his services. Fortunately, he's also my friend and not lost a case in five years."

As he and Sam walked towards the door, Mr. Steffini ominously said, in a low, slow voice, "I've heard a bit about the three of you, and I look forward to seeing more of you."

"That guy is creepy," muttered Jonathan.

"He looks like the kind of attorney Cryptic should have on his defense team," added Nicholas.

"Maybe he is," Mikaia replied as they all looked at each other.

"Next please," Willow, the tall slender girl serving the ice cream, stated from behind the counter.

"After looking at your extensive menu, I'd like to have two scoops of your double chocolate chip, please," said Jonathan.

"Jonathan, why do you study the menu so carefully each time then still order the same thing?"

asked Mikaia.

"I like to make the servers feel that their ice cream is so good that each flavor deserves special consideration...at least until I order my double chocolate chip cone," he said.

A smiling Willow handed him his cone and he took a big bite off the top.

"Sometimes I think I'll never figure you out," Mikaia said. Then she asked for her usual rocky road, and Nicholas followed with his mint chip order.

As they sat at one of the tables enjoying their ice cream, in between big bites, Jonathan declared, "That Mr. Steffini knows a lot about us. Probably more than Sam should have told him... unless he too is a Follower."

"Do you think he is a Follower?" Nicholas asked.

"With what I could see in his mind I'd have to say yes, he probably is, and that's one more person we're going to have to watch out for. Cryptic said he'd have more Followers and I guess he wasn't lying."

Nicholas let out a little chuckle.

"What's that about?" asked Mikaia, as they got up and left the shop.

"I found what Jonathan just said paradoxical, that Cryptic probably wasn't lying. That's all evil can do! Cryptic lies about everything, if it serves his purpose."

"Hi guys!" Larry said. "What are you three up to?"

"Hi, Larry, we're checking some things out in town and of course, as you can see, just stopped at the

18

ice cream shop," Nicholas answered as he took a lick of his mint chip.

"Yeah, that's what we plan to do too! My dad and I are going there right now. By the way, this is my dad, Tom Vidali. He works for the forestry service in land management and fire protection. Dad, Nicholas, Mikaia, and Jonathan, are some new friends of mine."

"It's nice to meet the three of you. Larry has mentioned your names several times. You helped find Ashlee when she got lost in Yosemite. Good job," he said with a big smile. "I hope you like our little town and plan to stay here."

"Yes, we do," replied Jonathan.

"And the way things are going, we will be here a long time," added Mikaia as she smiled back.

"I have to go. See you all at Marie's birthday party," Larry said, heading for the ice cream shop.

"His dad seems like a nice man," said Mikaia.

"Maybe that's where Larry gets his outgoing personality," Jonathan added.

"I for one think we should meet Mom and go home. From what I've seen you've both got lessons to take," Mikaia said as she stood up.

"Lessons to take, what are you talking about?" asked Jonathan.

With that Mikaia did a little two step and spun around.

"Dancing lessons?" Nicholas asked.

"Or you can go to Marie's birthday party

tomorrow and fill your hands with pizza the whole time, like you did at Ashlee's, so you won't have to dance," she replied.

"I like pizza, but not that much," Jonathan said. He looked down and shook his head. "You're right. A little practice would be good."

"Mark my words, Jonathan, someday you're going to love to dance with girls, especially the slow dances," said Mikaia as they neared the car.

"Right now it's way below a couple of good pizzas."

"I know you like Marie, Jonathan," added Nicholas.

"Okay, I'll do it...for Marie that is."

When their mom drove out of the grocery store parking lot, a large sixteen-wheeler almost cut them off. Mom quickly applied the brakes.

"Hey, what's that guy doing?" Nicholas asked. He looked out the window at the large silver truck with two red lines down the side.

"I don't know, but he's following us very closely," Mom replied.

When they turned east the truck followed, but at a greater distance. When their mom turned left up their roadway the truck slowed, then sped on up the hill.

"What was that about?" asked Jonathan.

"Who knows? Just a guy with some kind of problem, I guess," replied their mom.

"Okay you two, to the barn!" Mikaia said, jumping

out of their Odyssey. "I'll get my laptop and boom box and meet you there.

"I can't wait," said Nicholas slowly getting out.

"I can," Jonathan replied, staying seated.

"Sooner or later we're going to have to practice, so it might as well be sooner," Nicholas said.

"I'd much rather go on a field trip somewhere. The chance of us having to dance when we do that is slim," said Jonathan as he finally started moving towards the barn.

"Maybe we'll have time after our lesson."

"I hope Mikaia knows what she's doing," replied Jonathan.

"You know how much time Mikaia and her friends spent dancing to those music DVDs. By now she must know what she's doing. Besides, girls always seem to know about that kind of stuff," Nicholas said as they entered the barn.

Mikaia was just behind them. She set up the laptop and pushed in a DVD.

"I'll try to keep this simple. Now, I want you to watch this first one. Watch how that guy and his partner are moving their feet with the music," she said pointing at the screen. "This move you can use for most dance music."

"It looks to me like they're just jumping randomly around," Nicholas said and bent down to get a better look at the screen.

"That's often part of it, but if you look there is a pattern," replied Mikaia. "Now watch my feet and do as I do."

Both boys watched then tried to follow Mikaia's lead.

"Not bad guys, keep moving."

"This isn't so hard," Nicholas said as he bounced around kicking up some dust from the barn floor.

"Man, I don't know about this," said Jonathan spinning around. "I think I'd better take some pizza along with me tomorrow just in case."

"Actually, Jonathan, you're not bad," Mikaia said, dancing next to him.

After a few spins with both of her brothers Mikaia put in a different DVD.

"Now this is the way you hold and lead a girl when you're dancing to slow music. It's a lot more romantic."

"Wow," said Jonathan, "I can see if you don't like the girl you're with when the slow music starts, you'd better grab a slice or two of pizza...fast!"

"Yeah, but if you do like her, it could be a lot of fun," Nicholas added as he took a closer look.

"Okay, Nicholas, take hold of me like that."

"But you're my sister!"

"You don't have to hold me that close. Friends and family dance together all the time. I'll show you both a couple of basic two and four step moves," said Mikaia and she pulled Nicholas's arm around her waist.

After about an hour's practice Mikaia felt that both Nicholas and Jonathan could hold their own if

Marie ran out of pizza.

"Why don't we head over to the old school now and give the merry-go-round a spin and see where we end up," said Jonathan.

"I'm game. We haven't taken a random field trip following someone's Essence since our trip to Independence, Missouri in 1846!" Nicholas said.

"Since the main reason the Master Inventor has given us these powers is to learn and grow in knowledge so we can help others, let's go," added Mikaia.

They picked up the laptop and boom box and headed back up to the house.

"How'd your brothers do, Mikaia?" her mother asked.

"Actually, not too bad, at least they won't embarrass themselves or me," she replied.

"That's good. What are you going to do now?"

"We decided to go over to the old school and take a random field trip."

"Oh...well be careful...I think it's actually harder on me when I know you're going to do something like that than when I wasn't always sure. But I know those trips help you to learn...so see you back soon."

The triplets met in Mikaia's room and decided to hike over to the old school instead of use the time-slide sign to pop over. They had agreed to use that power only when it was absolutely necessary.

"We may have to do a bit of weeding around here soon," said Nicholas when they approached the old

23

school.

"They sure do grow fast," replied Mikaia.

"I'd say about as fast as Cryptic's Followers," Jonathan added, "and I sure hope we can keep up on the weeding in that area."

"That's also what we're being trained for," replied Nicholas.

Mikaia jumped on the merry-go-round after pushing it around a couple of times. Then Jonathan hopped on next as Nicholas pushed it even faster. Nicholas kept right on running and pushing until Jonathan told him to grab his hand and jump on.

As Nicholas jumped and was pulled on by Jonathan, Mikaia yelled, "Think of Midst!" They all let go and spun off into the swirling white cotton candy like fibers that meant they were on their way to Midst. Within moments they found themselves landing softly on the clouds of Midst.

"Welcome strangers," a deep voice said when they looked up and saw Yon.

"Hi Yon," replied Mikaia. She noticed that Yon's hair and eyes seemed bluer than ever in contrast to his white round cloud-like body.

"Haven't seen you three around these parts for a while," he continued.

The triplets stood there for a moment trying to figure out what was going on. But knowing Yon it could be anything. Just then Hither appeared.

"Howdy partners! What brings you three to this neck of the woods?" Hither asked.

"Why you know what we're here for. We're on a field trip," Jonathan said looking curiously at both of them.

"I figure the three of you are on a cattle drive and on your way to...Abilene, yes sir, probably Abilene!" Hither replied.

"I guess we could let you bunk down here for the night and share some vittles with us," Yon added.

Nicholas caught a glimpse of a box with an antenna on it partly hidden in the clouds.

"Is that a television I see over there?" Nicholas asked pointing.

"No, sir. Can't be. We ain't allowed to watch no television," replied Yon.

"It sounds to me like you have been and you're linked up to the western channel," Nicholas said as he walked over to the television.

"Well darn, partner, we sure hope you ain't going to say anything to Halo about this. Since we haven't seen you folks for quite a spell, we have to keep busy doing something," said Hither.

"Where did you get that TV?" asked Mikaia.

"Sorry, little lady, we can't tell you that," answered Yon. "Besides, as long as we do our chores and send you on your cattle drives, who's it going to bother?"

"Hey Jonathan, look at this. It only seems to get the western channel," Nicholas said as he tried to change the channel. "No wonder they're talking like that after a couple of weeks of hearing nothing but this!"

"You mean that television is supposed to show other things?" Hither asked.

"Of course," said Mikaia. "Our satellite system at home gets over a hundred different channels."

"Really?" Hither said. "I thought it was a strange kind of entertainment. I gotta talk to that guy who sold it to me!"

"You're the one who felt we could use that thing," said Yon.

"That's only because I get tired of hearing nothing but you," Hither replied.

"Hey, it gets one other channel!" exclaimed Jonathan.

"What is it?" asked Mikaia.

"I'm not sure, but it's all in Spanish," Jonathan replied.

"Oh man!" Nicholas sighed. "Let's get on with the trip."

"Well hombre, I guess you'll need my help then," said Yon.

"Then we're going further in time?" Jonathan asked.

"I'd say back about a hundred and sixty years, partner," replied Yon.

"You're not supposed to tell them how far they're going, Yon," said Hither.

"Why not? They're going to find out in a couple of earth time minutes anyway."

"Cause it ain't in our log!" a frustrated Hither

replied.

"These hombres did help us with the television so we now have another channel. It's only right," Yon replied as Hither said something about heading off into the sunset and quickly disappeared between two clouds.

"Then you're all ready to go?" asked Yon.

"Let's do it!" Jonathan replied.

"Okay now, hold hands, close your eyes, and..." The triplets felt a strong wind and heard the time machine's electrical current sparking and hissing. Then everything became silent.

"Boy that's cold," Nicholas said standing up. "What is it?"

"I think we're on a concrete sidewalk somewhere. But it's hard to tell since it's rather dark," replied Mikaia as she stood up and patted the dust off her jeans.

Close by they heard an engine hum. They made out the shadow of an old pickup truck pulling up near them. Someone threw a big pile of tied-up newspapers off onto the corner as the truck sped off.

"What was that all about?" Jonathan asked. "Hey, look up at all the tall buildings."

"I can make them out now," Nicholas said. "We're in a large city and it must be early morning since the newspapers are being put out for the newsboys to pick up and sell."

"How'd you know about that?" asked Jonathan.

"I read a story about newsboys in a big city once.

The newspaper prints them up at night after the reporters have finished writing. Then they spend the early morning hours delivering them all around town where the newsboys pick them up and sell them."

"That sounds like a cold, hard, and too early job for me," stated Jonathan.

Mikaia slowly walked over to the stack of papers.

"Where are you going?" Jonathan asked.

"We need to find out where we are and what year this is, don't we? What better way than to look in the morning newspaper. What great timing!" said Mikaia as she reached down and pulled out a paper.

"From what Yon told us a hundred and sixty years from today would make it about 1847, but they didn't have trucks driving around back then," a puzzled Nicholas said.

"Then how about April 18th, 1906!" said Mikaia.

"1906, that can't be right, Yon distinctly said back a hundred and sixty years," Nicholas replied.

"I heard him say that too," added Jonathan.

"Then I have one more surprise for you...we're in San Francisco!"

"We just moved from here!" Jonathan exclaimed. "Hey, I can make out that street sign now... 'Market Street'...I know where that is!"

"Something isn't right. 1906 is only a hundred and one years away. We didn't end up where Yon thought he was sending us," Nicholas said excitedly.

"1906, it says," Mikaia said pensively. There's something about that...Hey, do you remember when

28

our class took the Muni bus to the San Francisco Museum and we saw that display about the time San Francisco had a massive earthquake, and then burned down?"

"Oh man, I remember now!" said Nicholas. "That was in 1906 and I think it happened on April 18th in the early morning! What is today's date again, Mikaia?"

"April 18th!" read Mikaia.

At that very moment the ground began to move and shake as the awning on the building next to them collapsed onto the sidewalk. Then the shaking ended and there was complete silence.

"We've got to get out of here!" yelled Mikaia.

"Is that the end of it?" asked Jonathan.

Nicholas grabbed his arm and pulled him and Mikaia through the door behind them. "Quick, into the basement! There's no time to waste. We can time travel out from there."

He threw open a second door that led down under the building. "As I remember the biggest quake came right about now!"

Just as Nicholas finished speaking the floor began to sway violently back and forth. Loud explosions and vibrations from falling buildings joined the deafening volley. The triplets tried to join hands but kept getting thrown apart. Finally, they crawled together on the basement floor and joined hands as Mikaia yelled out. "Think of what you were doing and thinking the very moment you slid off the merry-go-round!" As she finished they saw the first mortar and bricks start crumbling loose around them along with what appeared to be the white cotton candy stuff...

After what seemed like forever, Jonathan found himself sitting in his desk in the old school. He looked over at Mikaia and Nicholas's desks but they weren't there. He yelled their names as loud as he could...but there was only silence...Then he heard Nicholas's voice shouting, *Where's Jonathan?* A moment later they both appeared in their desks, covered with dirt.

"Man, I thought I'd lost you two," he said as he quickly moved over by them. "I heard you yell my name, after I yelled yours, and a moment later you appeared!"

"I never yelled your name, I was just thinking of where you might be," replied Nicholas.

"I could have sworn I heard you call out," said Jonathan.

"Somehow we got hung up," Nicholas said.

Mikaia looked up as she tried to wipe the dust off her face. "We weren't hung up, we were stopped!" Mikaia said angrily.

"What do you mean, stopped?" asked Jonathan.

"Cryptic!" she said. "He grabbed me for a moment and since I still had hold of Nicholas's hand he stopped too."

"Why'd he do that?" Jonathan quickly asked.

"He was in my mind, my vision. He said 'fire and ice, and, oh, earthquakes too. Too bad you three weren't trapped so you could have hung around for the flames...They were beautiful!' That's when I was able to pull my mind free from his."

"That answers why we ended up sixty years away from where Yon was supposed to send us. I guess Cryptic became the Essence we were forced to follow once Yon let go of us. He was trying to crush us in our home town of San Francisco!" said Nicholas angrily, wiping dirt off his shirt.

"Sounds like you just had a harrowing experience," Tique said.

"Tique, it's sure good to see you! Yeah, I hope we never have to take a field trip like that again," Nicholas said.

"We were tricked, and then almost crushed!" said Jonathan.

With a soft popping sound Halo appeared.

"Halo, do you know what happened?" asked Jonathan.

"Yes, I was afraid Cryptic would try something like this. He's become very brazen and now wants to interfere personally. You've really got him worried."

"He almost stopped us on the way back when he appeared to me," said Mikaia.

"I know. It took my mind to help you break free," Halo said quietly.

"Then I didn't do it by myself?" Mikaia asked.

"Not this time. But you're constantly strengthening your powers and will soon be able to match his. That's why I needed to help a bit."

"Thanks! It looks like we need all the help we can

get," said Mikaia.

"You're going to have to continue to be very careful. Whenever you time travel any distance, take into consideration all possible outcomes. I'm sure Cryptic will try again. From now on I'll have Hither and Yon team up when they send you on a field trip. Together their powers will get you where you're going. They're too strong for Cryptic to override again."

"Did you know that Terry has a brother named Bo Flanders who is going to take over her shop?" Nicholas asked.

"Yes. You'll see a few new faces in town," Halo replied.

"Is Bo a Follower too?" asked Mikaia.

"I'm not sure, although his past history as a police officer and all, doesn't seem to indicate that he is. We'll need to keep an eye on him."

There was a 'pop' and Halo was gone.

"Man, I wish he'd at least say 'good bye' when he was finished instead of just popping away," said Jonathan.

"Since I can see that you never got to your field trip destination, and that you've already discussed what you've learned about Cryptic with Halo...class dismissed!" Tique said.

"Thanks, Tique. We'll see you later," Mikaia said.

"That you will," Tique replied.

The triplets peeked out the windows before leaving the school.

"After all of that, I think I'm about ready for a good party. You know, have some safe fun!" Jonathan said as they walked back home through the apple trees.

"I don't know how safe our dancing is but it will be nice to be with Marie, Ashlee, and some of our friends," Nicholas added.

Chapter Three

The Party

When Nicholas, Jonathan, and Mikaia got home, both their mom and dad were in the kitchen.

"Where did you end up on your field trip?" asked Mom.

"We're not sure exactly where we were supposed to go, but we ended up in San Francisco in 1906!" answered Mikaia.

"Not a good year to be in San Francisco," replied Dad.

"You don't need to tell us that! Cryptic diverted us there just as the earthquake began. I don't think he likes us anymore," Nicholas said with a smile.

"Are you three all right?" their mom asked as she stopped peeling a potato and looked at them closely.

"Yeah, but we're going to have to be even more careful when we travel from Midst from now on," replied Mikaia.

"I just picked up the mail and there is a letter for each of you from the Foothill Unified School District," said their dad. "I tossed them all on

Mikaia's bed since you seem to spend a lot of time in her room."

"Thanks Dad," Mikaia replied as they headed up the stairs.

"I got a letter!" Jonathan said. "First one since we moved here."

"I bet it tells us what we're supposed to do at school a week from now," Nicholas said, quickly tearing his own letter open.

"You're right," Mikaia replied reading through the letter. "My home room and first teacher for social studies and language arts is Mr. George."

"Hey mine is too!" said Nicholas.

"Me too!" Jonathan chimed in. "Then I have Ms. Trudeau for my Science and Math classes.

"I think we're all in the same classes!" said Mikaia.

"Check out your P.E. teacher, Mikaia. Looks like Jonathan and I have Mr. Lombardi. Who do you have?"

"Someone named Ms. Flits," she replied.

"What kind of a name is Flits?" Jonathan asked.

"I haven't got a clue. I just hope they're all good teachers."

"We were lucky in San Francisco. The only teacher I ever wished I hadn't had was Mr. Knocks," Jonathan said. "He was kind of weird. He'd say one thing, then do something else. Like he'd say we were going to have an important quiz the next day so we all better study, then he'd show a video. We'd ask about the quiz and he'd look at us like we didn't know what we were talking about. You never knew what to do!"

"I'm sure these teachers will all be good," Mikaia said as she finished reading the letter signed by the Principal, Mr. Edwards.

"Have you guys decided if you're going out for football?" asked Mikaia.

"I'll try out for lineman or defensive back, like Brad Owens recommended. I think I'll like knocking guys down," Jonathan said.

"I could see how you'd like doing that," Mikaia replied. "How about you, Nicholas?"

"I'll probably try out too. For some reason Calvin thinks I'd make a good running back. The fun there is trying not to get knocked down by guys like Jonathan. I should be pretty good at it by now since I've been trying not to get knocked down by him for years," Nicholas replied.

"You do have a good point. Besides you are a fast runner and have some good moves," said Mikaia. "The information calendar that Mr. Edwards sent says that the try-outs for cheer leaders start on the same day as football practice. I think I'll try out for that, then in the spring play soccer."

"You should make a great cheer leader. You've got to be the jumpiest and most bendable girl I know!" Jonathan said.

"I guess that was a compliment, right, Jonathan?" Mikaia asked.

"Yep, the bendiest!" Jonathan said as he finished

reading his letter.

"I wonder if any of our friends are in our classes," Nicholas said. "I know there are at least seven different sixth grade teachers in our school."

"We can ask around at Marie's birthday party tomorrow and find out," suggested Jonathan.

"Good idea, Jonathan. You can ask around if you're not too busy dancing with Marie," Nicholas replied.

"Yeah, and you with Ashlee, but you'll probably find me standing next to the pizza."

"I don't know about you two, but I want to check through the new antique dolls catalogue I got in the mail last week," said Mikaia.

"And I want to check my antique bottles catalogue and see what I want to invest in next. Maybe I can talk Bo into hunting down some of the ones I want so he'll put them in his shop," Nicholas replied, "like the whisky bottles from the Civil War."

"Then I'll think I'll go and..." Jonathan started to say.

"Hey, Jonathan!" their dad yelled. "We've gotten a bunch of new spiderwebs up in the garage the last few days. Do you mind getting them down?"

"Yeah...Okay Dad. Darn, not again," Jonathan mumbled as he slowly left Mikaia's bedroom and Nicholas began to sing, "Spiderman, Spiderman, no one can but Spiderman."

The next morning the triplets tried to catch up on their chores. Jonathan finally got a break from cleaning off spiderwebs when his dad assigned him the job of clearing some Manzanita bushes away from the house to gain more defensible space in case of a fire. Jonathan seemed pleased with the new assignment.

"Dad, we'll need a ride to the Mariposa County Regional Park at noon for Marie's Birthday party. Can you drive us?" asked Mikaia.

"Sure, I'll be glad to."

"Mikaia!" Jonathan shouted. "We don't have a birthday present for her! What are we going to do?"

"I'm glad that finally crossed your mind. But don't worry. Mom and I took care of that a couple of days ago," said Mikaia.

"What did we get her?" asked Nicholas rather shyly realizing he had also completely forgotten about a present.

"At first Mom thought it would be a good idea to get her a new jacket for the coming Fall, but I knew she already had a nice one, so Mom picked up a girl thing for her."

"What's a girl thing?" asked Jonathan.

"You know how girls our age like to experiment with make-up?" Mikaia said. "We bought her a cosmetic and make-up kit. I know she'd like that."

"We bought her make-up?" Jonathan yelled. "I'm giving Marie make-up? No way!"

"At first, I thought we'd get her something from Victoria's Secret, so be glad about the make-up!"

"Mom," Nicholas chimed in. "Jonathan and I

can't give her makeup...can we?"

"Man, I'm not going," Jonathan said. "That would be even more embarrassing than having to dance!"

"Boys, just calm down. Even though you two forgot all about a gift, we covered for you," said their mom.

"Then what did we get her?" Nicholas asked.

"You both got her a nice Jansport backpack for her to use at school," Mikaia answered, "with the cosmetic kit wrapped up inside of it."

"Mom!" yelled Jonathan.

"Don't worry, boys. We wrapped the gift from you two separately," Mom said.

All Mikaia could do was shake her head and say, "Boys!"

"Next time you may want to think about a gift for your friend more than an hour or two before the party," their mom suggested.

"I'm not going to forget next time. That's for sure," Jonathan said and he left the kitchen.

When Dad dropped the triplets off at the park for Marie's birthday, they saw a large gathering of festively dressed people under a sun shelter that covered several picnic tables. They could hear loud rhythmic music with trumpets, violins and guitars. Not until they saw Marie approaching their car were they sure they were in the right place.

"Hey, are you three in for a treat! Looks like Marie Jimenez is having a traditional Mexican birthday party with a Mariachi band and the whole thing," their dad said as he peered out the window.

"A Mariachi band?" Jonathan asked.

"It's a traditional musical group from Mexico made up of guitars, violins, trumpets and sometimes other instruments. The musicians often wear silver studded outfits with wide-brimmed hats. They play at all kinds of celebrations."

"How do you know all that, Dad?" asked Nicholas.

"Well, Spain and then Mexico once owned California. Mom and I have been to Mexico before and have always enjoyed Mexican food and restaurants where they frequently have a Mariachi band."

"Do you dance to that kind of music?" asked Jonathan.

"You sure do, but probably not the kind of dancing that Mikaia taught you."

"Darn, just my luck," said Jonathan. "Then I'd better find the pizza real quick."

"I would say you better find the tacos real quick," laughed their dad as the triplets got out of the car to greet Marie.

"I'm so glad you could come! My whole family's here and so are Ashlee, Calvin, Brad, Larry, Will and Tamara," Marie said excitedly. "This is almost like the Quinceanera birthday party I'll have when I turn fifteen and am considered a woman."

"This is great Marie, especially all the decorations and the Mariachi band," Mikaia said.

"Oh, you know about Mariachis?" she asked.

"I'm learning," said Mikaia.

"The Mariachis are all family friends that came with my uncles from Guadalajara to help me celebrate. That's where my family originally came from too," Marie said. Then she started introducing the triplets to her mom and dad, and uncles and aunts and cousins as the music got even louder.

"Wow, look at all the food!" Nicholas exclaimed, noticing that one table was covered with all kinds of interesting dishes.

"Do you have any pizza?" Jonathan asked.

"Oh no. My aunts cooked all the traditional foods we eat in Mexico. See, there are tacos, tamales, enchiladas, burritos, everything!"

Jonathan could see the excitement in Marie's eyes that made them sparkle all the more. He'd had Mexican food before, but pizza was still his favorite. The tacos did look pretty good and he didn't want to make Marie feel badly, so he reached for one.

"Hey Jonathan," Will Lopez shouted above the music. "Grab Marie and come over here. Mr. Jimenez says we're all going to do the traditional Mexican Hat Dance. I have hats for all of you." He handed each of them a large wide brimmed hat.

"But I was just going to have a couple of tacos," Jonathan replied as Marie grabbed his hand and pulled him towards the Mariachis.

Within a moment everyone was partnered up. Ashlee moved quietly over to Nicholas, and Pedro, one of Marie's cousins, quickly approached Mikaia after she had placed their two presents on the gift table.

"Throw the hat on the ground, Jonathan," said Marie.

"But I kind of like the hat. Can't I wear it?"

"No, it's part of the dance. You throw it on the ground and we dance around it. That's why it's called 'The Hat Dance,'" Marie explained. "Just do it and then follow me."

Jonathan reluctantly threw the hat on the ground as the music started again.

Before they knew it, the triplets were dancing around as though they'd learned The Hat Dance years ago. Jonathan was just thinking how much fun it was when Nicholas circled by and said, *Yes, this is a lot of fun.* Then he clapped his hands above his head and went around again as Jonathan looked over at him with a strange smile.

After several rounds of The Hat Dance, Marie and her friends gathered some food and sat together at one of the large picnic tables, eating, talking, and laughing.

The triplets learned that most of the people they knew were also in Mr. George's and Ms. Trudeau's classes. They enjoyed Larry's funny stories and Calvin's antics. He kept yelling, "go long," then would throw someone a churro.

Nicholas sat next to Ashlee, and Marie sat next to Jonathan. Pedro squeezed in next to Mikaia, but since he spoke little English all he did was stare at her and smile.

Soon Marie opened all the gifts she had received and was particularly pleased with the makeup kit and the backpack from the triplets. Her birthday cake followed and everyone sang "Happy birthday" in their native language. It sounded a bit confusing to the triplets, but Marie smiled broadly and that was what was most important.

"It's about time for the piñata!" signaled Mr. Jimenez.

He walked over to a nearby oak tree and tossed a rope over a high branch. Marie squealed with excitement.

"This is always my favorite time at a party, when we try to break open the piñata and watch all the goodies inside fall out!" Marie exclaimed.

She began running towards the tree with everyone else close behind.

Mr. Jimenez took a large colorfully painted donkey shaped piñata made of thin cardboard, construction paper, and glue, tied it to the rope which he had hung over the branch, and pulled it up into the air. Then he handed Marie a long broom handle and Ashlee tied a blindfold around her head.

"Since it's your birthday, Marie, you get the first few hits to try and break it," Mr. Jimenez said. Ashlee spun her around a couple times and pointed her towards the piñata.

Mr. Jimenez manned the rope as Marie tried to figure out where the piñata was. Each time she took a swing Mr. Jimenez would pull on the rope to make her miss while everyone applauded and laughed. After several tries she finally hit it but not hard enough to break it open.

When Marie took off her blindfold, she handed the broom handle to Jonathan and told him she'd like to see if he could do any better. Rather embarrassed, Jonathan took the handle and Marie tied the blindfold around his head. She spun him around several times and pointed him towards the piñata.

Jonathan concentrated very hard and somehow knew exactly where the donkey was hanging. He took a hard, fast swing only to have Mr. Jimenez tug it away quickly as everyone laughed. He heard Calvin yell, "Air stick" when he missed.

Marie yelled, "Do it again, Jonathan! You have to be quicker than my Dad!"

Jonathan concentrated again, this time focusing on the thoughts of Mr. Jimenez as he approached the piñata. He faked a swing at the piñata just as Mr. Jimenez pulled it up a foot. Jonathan immediately followed through with a sharp swing hitting the donkey's upper back and tail area, knocking them off. Everyone applauded and yelled but his swing hadn't brought the goodies down.

"Great hit!" said Marie, "Now Mikaia gets to try." Everyone yelled and clapped.

"I'll be a little easier on you than I was on Jonathan, since you're a girl," he said laughing and everyone booed and clapped at the same time.

Marie spun Mikaia around and pointed her towards the piñata. She concentrated. Then she felt Nicholas thinking, *to your left and up a foot higher*. She turned left and quickly swung, smashing the donkey right through its center.

Small packages of gum, lifesavers, jaw breakers and candy bars fell as everyone yelled and dove to the ground. Brad grabbed Calvin's legs and pulled him back from the pile as Nicholas jumped in only to find that Ashlee had fallen in right next to him. Within seconds the goodies had all been picked up and everyone's pockets were bulging.

"Nice swing Mikaia!" said Marie. "Now you see why I like the piñatas."

As Mikaia turned and looked at Nicholas, she replied, "Yes, I think it's my favorite too." Nicholas shrugged his shoulders and smiled back.

After the piñata, the Mariachis played more songs and everyone danced. Jonathan and Nicholas, who had figured out that they could get away with just jumping around like everyone else, danced until they got tired and had to sit down. Soon their dad arrived.

Just before they left, Larry ran out to their car and invited them to the river for a swim the next day. He said that on Sunday afternoons a lot of their schoolmates would be there. Mikaia thanked him and said that they'd like to if they could.

After a series of thank yous and goodbyes the triplets were on their way home.

"That was a great party! I wouldn't mind doing

that again," Jonathan said.

"So the dancing part turned out okay and you didn't have to grab a couple of tacos?" their dad asked with a slight laugh.

"No, none of us did," replied Nicholas. "We had a lot of fun dancing the Hat Dance, eating great food, and visiting with our friends. Thanks to Jonathan and Mikaia I've got my pockets full of gum, jaw breakers and all kinds of stuff that fell from the piñata!"

"I've been meaning to ask you about that Nicholas. The reason I was able to break the piñata was because I heard you telling me where to find it," Mikaia said.

"I was just thinking what you needed to do to hit it, that's all," replied Nicholas.

"And while we were doing The Hat Dance," Jonathan said, "you circled by me, Nicholas, as I was thinking how much fun I was having and you said, 'Yes, this is a lot of fun,' and danced away. Now that's kind of weird."

"Even stranger than that was when I got back first from San Francisco and I heard you yelling, 'Where's Jonathan' before you and Mikaia appeared. But you told me that you'd only thought that and hadn't yelled it," Jonathan said. "What's going on anyway?"

"It seems that the Master Inventor has given you three another gift with which to battle Cryptic that will make it easier for you to communicate with each other," their dad said.

"What's that?" asked Jonathan.

"Telepathy!" Nicholas said.

"That must be it. We're telepathic," stated Mikaia.

"What?" Jonathan asked.

"That means you three can now communicate from your minds to each other without actually speaking," said Dad.

"We can do that?" Jonathan asked.

"You just gave us some examples of us doing it," said Nicholas.

"We'll probably have to practice using it until we can depend upon that power, like the rest of the gifts we've been given," Mikaia said.

"Then no one will know we're talking to each other or what we're saying?" Jonathan asked.

"That's right," their dad said as he turned up the road to their house.

"And that's another power we're going to have to use carefully," Nicholas said.

"And not abuse," added Mikaia.

"This is still unbelievable to me," Nicholas said.

"Hey, I was just thinking that!" Jonathan replied when they got out of the Odyssey and headed into the house.

Chapter Four

The Rescue

Just south of town, in a storage shed next to a trucking company, a small group of people were gathered.

"Quiet down now. I know no one wants to have to meet like this, but Cryptic wants us to reorganize and get our act together. I know you're all upset about Terry's accident at the old school when we had trapped those triplets, but they got away thanks to Halo. Terry did her best and sacrificed herself for Cryptic, like we are all expected to do, if necessary," Sam Hawkins explained. "Cryptic is aah... grand and powerful and surely would have destroyed all of them if the Master Inventor hadn't butted in.

"Now, I'm sure you all know Frank. What you didn't know was that he's been a major Follower for years. Cryptic's made him our leader, replacing Terry, so listen to what he has to say!"

Frank stood and glared at the group.

"Cryptic expects action from us. Action that will stop these children who think they can challenge his powers, action that will gain him more Followers in our area. We are lucky though. Cryptic has taken an on-going personal interest in these triplets. He said something about returning the pain. So he's going to play with these three a bit himself, before he destroys them. We just simply have to help wherever we can. We can slow them down, trip them up, and eventually help him get rid of them. That's our task! I expect you all to do your part when you're called upon, or beware! There are still a couple of you who may pay the ultimate price for failing!"

"How did Ashlee's party go?" Mom asked when the Triplets entered the house.

"Great! We had a lot of fun," said Jonathan.

"It was a traditional Mexican birthday party. Oh, and Ashlee really liked the make-up and backpack," Mikaia added.

"I'm glad. By the way, Larry Vidali just called for you on his cell phone. He said it was important and you should call him back. I left his number by the phone."

"Thanks Mom, I'll get it," Nicholas said.

He walked to the phone and picked it up.

"Hey Larry, what's up? You got the call just after you invited us tomorrow to the river...yeah, may cancel...Your dad is what?...fighting a forest fire north east of town near Deer Creek that started yesterday...The base command lost contact with him and another firefighter and don't know where exactly they are...I understand your family's worried...You and your mom are heading up to the base camp this afternoon...I hope all is okay,...Call us and let us know what's happening and if there is anything we can do," Nicholas said as he hung up

"Wow! Looks like Larry's dad, Tom, who we met by the ice cream shop, is possibly trapped in a forest fire. He's been fighting it since yesterday up near Deer Creek, you know, where we took that short hike a couple of weeks ago," Nicholas explained.

"We heard that," said Mikaia. "Is there anything we can do?"

"They don't know what to do besides drive up there and check," replied Nicholas.

"I wonder if we should pop up and see what we can do. I really like his dad," Jonathan said.

"We'll have to be careful and not be seen," said Mikaia.

"I think we should try," Nicholas replied. "Mikaia, you met Larry's dad as well as hiked in that area. Can you focus on that and see if anything appears?"

"I can try," Mikaia said as she went up to her room with her brothers following.

Mikaia laid back on her bed and closed her eyes. Nicholas and Jonathan sat quietly next to her. Her eyes began to flutter lightly as they opened and she stared up at the ceiling. She'd had visions before but not quite like this.

"I can barely make out Deer Creek, near that wooden bridge we hiked over. The smoke is thick and

I see flames all around...now I see them! Two men! Yes one is Tom Vidali. They've taken cover under the bridge, and they're keeping themselves mostly covered with water...There is no way out. The open space around them is being overcome with flames. I see the base camp just east of Bagby Recreation Area...men, equipment...a lot of activity...Wow, that's it...It's gone," Mikaia said, slowly sitting up.

"I think we should use the time-slide sign and get to the base camp at Bagby right away and see what we can do," suggested Jonathan.

"We'll need to reappear in some bushes nearby so we won't be seen," Nicholas said

"Okay," said Mikaia. "Let's all touch elbows as we sign and think Bagby and bushes. Are you ready?...Now!"

They all put their hands together making the time-slide sign. After three 'pops', they were on the ground laying on some sticks and leaves. As they sat up, they could smell smoke and hear voices and engine noises not far away. They carefully stood up behind some small bushes and looked at the scene in front of them.

"There must be a hundred people moving around out there. Looks like some are trying to eat and rest while others are loading up their trucks to head back out," Jonathan said.

"What can we do?" Mikaia asked.

"Let's get a little closer," suggested Nicholas.

They worked their way around so a line of parked

fire trucks blocked them from view.

"Look at that pile of equipment," Jonathan said.

"Yeah, and I see some things that might help," Nicholas replied as he ran out, grabbed a canvas bag, and returned.

"What is that?" Mikaia asked when Nicholas showed her a shiny small tent.

"This is one of those fire-resistant tents that firefighters use to cover themselves as last line of defense. They're made of aluminum and fiberglass. I read that firefighters call them 'shake and bakes'. They can save your life if the fire doesn't burn right on you," replied Nicholas.

"Did Tom Vidali have one of these bags with him Mikaia?" Jonathan asked.

"I didn't see anything like this," she replied.

"Then they didn't expect to get this close to the fire. I think we should take a couple of these up to them," Jonathan said and added emphatically, "quickly!"

"I agree but not before I grab a couple more things," Nicholas said as he ran back out and pulled back two oxygen backpack tanks. "These tanks should give them some air as the fire goes over and sucks all the oxygen out of the area."

"Good idea," Mikaia said.

Jonathan ran out and returned with another fire-resistant tent and several bottles of water.

The triplets pulled what they found back into the bushes where Nicholas and Jonathan each put on an oxygen pack and picked up a tent. Mikaia grabbed the water bottles.

"What's our plan?" Jonathan asked.

"I thought we'd reappear on the wooden bridge above them, toss this stuff down into the river next to them, and get out before they can see us," Nicholas replied.

"Great, let's do it!" Mikaia said.

Nicholas paused for a moment.

"What's the matter?" asked Mikaia.

"I have this strange feeling. Something tells me that if we all go, things won't turn out right. Mikaia, I think you should stay. If we don't reappear in two minutes then come check on us. If the fire and smoke are that bad we wouldn't last much longer than that."

"I don't know why, but I'll stay if you think I should," Mikaia replied.

She handed the water to her brothers and looked at her watch. "Okay then, two minutes. Now both of you focus on the bridge!"

"The boys touched elbows and brought their hands up and together made the time-slide sign and 'popped' away.

They quickly reappeared on a hard, wooden surface that they could barely make out. The smoke was so dense Nicholas could hardly see Jonathan next to him.

The flames were everywhere but had not reached the creek. They both broke into instant sweats from the heat as they took off the oxygen back packs. The noise around them was deafening.

Do you hear me, Jonathan? Nicholas thought as he focused on Jonathan.

Yes, I do. We'd better drop this equipment down to them fast, Jonathan transferred back.

On three, then let's sign out of here! Nicholas replied as they hung the equipment over the side. Jonathan felt Nicholas counting and on three they both let the equipment fall the twelve feet and splash into the waters of Deer Creek.

They both started to raise their arms to sign when they felt something tighten their arms to their sides. They struggled for a moment. Then they heard, "He borrowed some fire from San Francisco to start this one. He knew you'd be here. We saw you coming."

"Who are you? What do you think you're doing?" Jonathan yelled while they both twisted around.

Standing behind them on the bridge was a tall man wearing a red suit and tie with a pearl white long-sleeved shirt. He was smiling.

"You're one of Cryptic's Apprentices!" yelled Nicholas. "We saw several men dressed like you in the cavern!"

"At your service Messieurs Jonathan and Nicholas, or should I say my Master's service," he said with a slight bow. Somehow, they could hear him through all the noise.

"What are you doing?" Jonathan yelled again.

"Oh yes, your second question. My Master thought you'd like to feel the flames as they quickly burn into your flesh. Because of the pain he was forced to feel in the cavern he thought you should taste some also...It's only fair. But in your case your departure, well let's say, will be of a permanent nature. It's quite hot you know. I have to leave. Have a nice day!" the Apprentice said as he disappeared into the smoke.

I still can't bring my arms up! Nicholas conveyed beginning to cough and choke.

Neither can I! Jonathan thought back.

Quick, let's move back to back and see if we can untie each other so we can sign out of here...I'm having trouble breathing! Nicholas returned.

The knot's too tight for me to loosen this way! Jonathan thought. Then they saw a figure approaching them.

Nicholas, Jonathan, hold still. I'll see what I can do! transmitted Mikaia.

Please hurry! I don't think I'll be able to stand up much longer! Nicholas expressed back.

Mikaia worked quickly, mostly by feel through the smoke. She was able to undo Nicholas and began working on Jonathan as he began to cough and gag.

Meet us back in my room, Nicholas, Mikaia conveyed. *You can't help here anymore.*

In a moment Nicholas was gone. When Jonathan's arms were freed he and Mikaia made the time-slide sign and disappeared.

They all found themselves on the floor of Mikaia's room coughing and then gasping for fresh air. The smell of burned hair filled the room. They began to notice small spots where their hair and eyebrows were singed. Lying still for several minutes, they continued to breathe in the fresh air more slowly.

"Are you guys all right?" asked Mikaia, who was the first to sit up.

"I don't know if I want to be a custodian of the old school anymore. Too many people are getting hurt, including us!" Jonathan said as he rolled up to a sitting position. "I feel like I have a big red bull's-eye on my chest, but I can't see who's shooting the arrows."

"I knew something wasn't going to turn out the way we planned, but I sure didn't see this coming," replied Nicholas.

"Yes, but your premonition did make you have me stay, and that turned out to be the key that saved you," Mikaia said. "What happened anyway?"

"One of Cryptic's Apprentices appeared behind us just after we dropped the equipment down. He got those bindings around us before we saw him," replied Nicholas.

"Did the two men get the equipment?" asked Mikaia.

"We don't know. We couldn't let them see us. Even if they had been able to hear any noise above them on the bridge, they couldn't have seen us anyway because of all the smoke," Jonathan replied.

"I sure hope they're okay," Nicholas said.

"Me too," Mikaia added. She looked into her

vanity mirror and began to trim off some singed hair around her ear with a pair of scissors.

"I for one am glad you only waited two minutes, Mikaia. Any longer and the fire fighters would have found two burned skeletons on the bridge in the morning! Thanks!" Nicholas said as he gave her a hug.

"What did the Apprentice say?" asked Mikaia.

"He said that his Master had taken some fire from San Francisco to start this one because he knew we'd come. Cryptic wanted us to feel pain just like he had in the cavern, except we weren't supposed to survive!" answered Jonathan.

"It was just like he said in my vision. I wasn't able to move my arms to sign away from the flames. 'Fire and Ice', Cryptic said, and we almost did disappear in the smoke and fire," Nicholas replied, sitting down on the bed.

"It sounds like anything goes now," said Jonathan.

"The good news is that our powers to fight him are growing too, like your premonitions, Nicholas, and Jonathan's mind reading, and my visions. Hopefully, we were able to save Tom and his partner and still get out of the middle of a forest fire thanks to all the powers the Master Inventor has given us. Now we've even put the telepathy he's given us to good use," Mikaia pointed out.

"That is all true, but do we have to always cut it so close? Sometimes I feel like I'm in a movie left hanging on a cliff," Jonathan said.

"Just remember, Jonathan, in the movies the hero seldom dies," Mikaia said with a smile.

"For some reason the word 'seldom' isn't very comforting," replied Jonathan. "However, I do like the word 'Hero', but we'll never hear that used since no one can know of our powers or what we've done besides Mom and Dad."

"We do it for the Master Inventor and Halo. Doing what's right and good is what we're being trained for. Knowing it pleases the Master Inventor and helps others should be enough," Nicholas added.

"You're right, Nicholas, but at least a free ice cream once in a while would be a nice thank you and an excellent reward," Jonathan said with a smile.

"I'd go for that!" agreed Nicholas.

"Boys!" Mikaia said as she trimmed a little more singed hair.

"Hi kids. Is everything all right? I was working in my office just down the hall and smelled something like singed hair. Wow! Now I can see it is singed hair," their dad confirmed as their mom appeared.

"What in the world?" said Mom going over to the mirror to help Mikaia trim off some more hair.

The triplets explained what they had done and what had happened when the Apprentice had appeared.

"You need to be more careful and you were very fortunate to get out of there alive!" said their very stressed out mom.

"We know, but we did get out and we were prepared, thanks to our powers. And we do know that Halo and the Inventor are looking out for us," Mikaia stressed.

"I know, but it still worries us a lot," their mom emphasized as she began to trim Nicholas' hair.

"After all that I sure hope Tom Lopez and his partner survived. It looks like you did everything you possibly could have done to save them. Whether you did or didn't, you three were very courageous!" Dad said.

Jonathan sat there thinking for a moment before he said, "Then you'll treat us to some ice cream?"

"We sure will and as much as you like at the Ultimate Ice Cream Store. You three deserve it!" their dad said.

"Now there's a reward!" Jonathan enthused as Mikaia began to work on his hair with a second pair of scissors that she had pulled from her drawer.

About two hours after dinner the phone rang. Nicholas ran to answer it as everyone followed him.

"Hi Larry, any word...He is, and so is the other firefighter...Fantastic! This is great news, Larry!...They saw them waving to the helicopter that was looking for them after the fire blew by...They took them to the hospital for the night because of smoke inhalation along with some minor burns...Everyone's calling it a mysterious miracle...Somehow someone dropped some fire tents and oxygen right next to them...The equipment disappeared from home base and ended up right next to them...Your dad said something about making out some voices on the bridge above them but he wasn't sure exactly what he heard...So the river is back on for tomorrow afternoon...great!...We'll see you there..."

"I take it you heard that?" Nicholas said as he turned around.

"We sure did and that's excellent news," their dad said.

"Not a bad exchange, some singed hair for their survival!" said Nicholas.

"I still don't like it...but I do understand it," their mother sighed.

"I am glad Tom Lopez couldn't make out the voices he heard on the bridge. If he had, we'd be doing some fast talking right about now," Mikaia added.

"I'm surprised he could hear anything," added Jonathan. "That fire was roaring!"

"Well, I've got work to do," Mikaia said as she started up the stairs towards her room.

"What do you have to do?" asked Jonathan.

"We're going to the river tomorrow aren't we, that is if Dad will drive us over," Mikaia said.

"I'd be glad to," Dad replied.

"Then I've got to go up and check through my swim suits to see which one looks best, do my hair and nails, especially after the fire, and fix my face so I look presentable."

"But you're just going to jump in the river, aren't you?" asked Nicholas.

"Probably," Mikaia answered as she turned at the top of the stairs.

"Girls! I'll never figure them out! Give me a pair of cut offs and an old towel and I'm on my way," Jonathan exclaimed as he climbed the stairs to his room.

Nicholas stood there for a moment looking back and forth at his parents.

"Then it must be time for me to catch up on my reading. However tomorrow, unlike Jonathan, I plan to wear a nice swimsuit and take a new towel," he added and started towards his room mumbling something about image being important.

Chapter Five

Heroes

Late the next morning the triplets gathered the things they thought they'd need for their trip to the North Fork of the Merced River. They had been there briefly before when Ashlee, Marie, and Larry had shown them all the hangout spots around Opportunity a week or two earlier. The river's slow flow and sandy beach made it Larry's favorite spot, especially on warm late summer days like this Sunday afternoon. The triplets had packed up an ice chest with some soft drinks and snacks along with some sandwiches that Mikaia and their mom had made.

"Are you three about ready?" asked Dad.

"Just a second," Mikaia yelled from the kitchen.

Five minutes later their dad was driving them to the north-west side of town where the river slowly looped around Opportunity before heading several more miles into Lake McClure.

"I'll return about five to pick you up," their dad said as Nicholas and Jonathan lifted the ice chest from the Odyssey. Mikaia grabbed their backpacks and started towards the beach. They could see a few families scattered around. However, the beach closest to the two trees that over hung the river with three rope swings, was covered with kids their age. As they got closer they heard Larry and Ashlee calling to them.

"Glad you guys could make it," Larry said as the triplets spread out a large beach blanket on the sand next to theirs. "Marie and Tamara are swimming and Will, Brad, and Calvin are trying out the rope swings along with Arnold."

"Oh, Arnold came?" asked Jonathan.

"Yeah, he and North like to hang out here too. North's in the shade by the second tree having a soda. He can't swim so he just helps catch people when they don't want to get wet and swing back," replied Larry.

"I'm glad he's being useful," Nicholas said.

"How's your Dad doing?" asked Mikaia.

"He's doing much better. He's home resting for a few days before he goes back to work. They still can't figure out what happened. When my Dad and Mike, the other firefighter, went to check out the north-east side of the fire line, the fire was still a couple of miles up the hill from them and Deer Creek. They hadn't taken any equipment because they weren't planning on fighting it, just check on its movement. All of a sudden blazes broke out behind them blocking their way back to their truck."

"What did they do then?" asked Ashlee.

"They quickly radioed back their general position

then took shelter in the creek water under a bridge. They thought that was pretty much it for them since there was no way anybody could walk or fly in to help them."

"How'd they get out if they were trapped?" Ashlee asked as she listened intensely.

"That's just it. All of a sudden two oxygen tank back packs along with two fire tents and some bottled water fell from the bridge into the water next to them. They quickly put the tents over them in the river and breathed in the oxygen as the fire luckily burned through the tree tops just above them. It was like a miracle! Dad said he thought he heard some noise on the bridge above them. He said he thought he heard a male voice yelling, 'Who are you? What do you think you're doing?' but the roar from the fire was so loud he's not sure."

"That's hard to believe!" Ashlee said as she looked over at Mikaia. "That's kind of like me finding a coat with matches and a flashlight in its pockets when I got lost near Mt. Hoffmann."

"But the strangest thing was he thought he heard someone use the names Jonathan and Nicholas," Larry said. "Go figure."

"Our names?" asked Nicholas.

"Yeah, but Dad also said that by then they were so hot and burned and dehydrated that he could have been hallucinating," replied Larry.

"Wow, that is amazing," said Jonathan while Larry looked inquisitively over at him.

"I think it's about time to cool off in the river," Nicholas said, changing the subject.

He jumped up, took off his shirt, kicked off his flip flops and headed for the water with Jonathan following close behind.

"Glad you guys made it," Marie said.

Both boys decided to test the water before jumping in. It was cold but refreshing and after a couple of minutes they were swimming around trying to grab hold of Marie and Tamara as they floated by on their air mattresses.

Mikaia decide she'd test the water too, not sure if she was ready to jump in and mess up her hair quite yet.

"You know, Mikaia, it's seems strange to me that every time a miracle happens you and your brothers are involved or at least your names pop up," Ashlee pondered when Mikaia started walking toward the river.

"Yeah, it does. What's up with that?" added Larry.

"I guess we're lucky to be in the right place at the right time or get credit for something we haven't done," Mikaia replied and kept on walking. "Aren't you going to join us?"

With that invitation both Ashlee and Larry got up and followed her down to the river.

Mikaia stood ankle deep in the water where she soon fell victim to Jonathan and Larry who seemed to feel that the best way to cool her off was to splash her with as much water as possible.

Ashlee laughingly watched their attack until Nicholas snuck up behind her and pulled her in. They all swam around and then grabbed hold of Marie and Tamara's air mattresses and slowly floated down the river towards the tree swings.

"Hey, Nicholas, Jonathan, you've got to try the swings!" yelled Calvin as they floated by.

Arnold just missed bombing them as he dropped off the rope next to their group float.

"Sounds good to me," Nicholas said.

He and Jonathan swam for shore while the rest of the group started paddling the mattresses back up the river.

"If you take the longest rope and walk way back up the riverbank, and swing out as high and as far as you can get, you can drop right into the middle of the river," Will advised. "But you need to swim back fast since the river current is a bit stronger out there."

"Here, I'll show you," Brad said grabbing the rope and climbing up the bank.

"You've got to watch Brad. He really gets out there in style!" Calvin said as Brad sailed by them and out over the river.

Instantly, Brad arched high into the air, let go of the rope and did two somersaults before diving into the water. Everyone applauded when he surfaced.

"See what I mean!" said Calvin. "He owns that rope. He plans on going out for the diving team when he gets to high school."

"I can see why," Nicholas said just as Arnold

climbed up the bank.

"I'll have a go at it," said Jonathan.

Calvin handed him the rope he had caught when it swung back.

Jonathan climbed up the bank, grabbed hold and swung out above the river letting go just as he started to swing back. The rope spun him around, causing him to twist and fall onto his stomach as he hit the water. As he surfaced everyone was laughing and yelling, "belly flop!" Jonathan regained his composure, waved, and swam back in.

"Actually, not bad for your first try, Jonathan," Brad said.

"I guess I'm next," Nicholas declared as the rope was passed to him.

He quickly thought back to when he had practiced flips on his neighbor's trampoline back in San Francisco. He concentrated as he climbed the bank and started his swing over the river. At the highest point he let go of the rope, spread his arms and legs out and floated through the air before piking into a dive just as he entered the water.

"Fantastic!" yelled Calvin.

When Nicholas surfaced and swam towards shore, everyone was applauding.

"Hey, you're not bad!" Brad said as he patted him on the back.

"I'm just glad I got lucky and didn't mess that up!" Nicholas said with a big smile.

Everyone was applauding as Arnold approached.

"I'd say you got lucky. Bet you can't do it again," Arnold said.

"No thanks, I'd probably mess it up," replied Nicholas.

"Bet even North could do better than that and he's never tried! Hey North, come down here and try!" yelled Arnold.

North stepped back a couple of feet and shook his head no.

"You're such a chicken. How do you know you can't do better than this guy unless you try?" Arnold called back.

North looked a little embarrassed and confused. He wasn't sure what to do now that he'd been challenged and called a chicken.

"Hey man, he can't swim," said Calvin.

"If he wasn't a chicken he could at least see how far out he could swing on the rope. We'd catch him when he came back!" continued Arnold.

North slowly came down the bank and grabbed hold of the longest rope.

"I'll show you I ain't afraid to swing way out. You just catch me when I swing back," he said.

Nicholas and Jonathan were surprised by the fact that North could talk since he always let Arnold do the talking for him. They also felt badly that his supposed "'friend" was making him do something he didn't want to do for Arnold's own amusement.

By now North had pulled the rope up the bank to its highest point. They watched as he stood there for a moment. "Now catch me on the way back," he said.

"Don't be such a baby. I got you covered," Arnold called back.

North took a deep breath and jumped out. The rope arched way out over the river and swung about as high as it possibly could. Everyone began to clap as the rope carried him back. As he approached the bank and Arnold, Arnold jumped aside and yelled, "surprise" and laughed as North swung back out over the river. Nicholas noticed that Norths hands had already begun to slip from his weight and the force of the rope swing. Just as he was at the height of his arch over the river his grip gave way and with a terrified expression he splashed down into the river.

Everyone stood still for a moment waiting for him to surface, but he didn't.

Nicholas caught the rope that had swung back and raced up the bank. In a flash he was swinging out over the river dropping near the spot where North had gone under. At the same moment Jonathan dove into the water and was swimming out towards Nicholas.

A minute or two later Brad and Calvin followed.

North had still not surfaced. Nicholas knew that the stronger current in the middle of the river was probably carrying him down stream so he began to swim in that direction. He dove down a couple of times opening his eyes in the murky water trying to catch sight of him but to no avail.

Just then he heard Jonathan, using telepathy,

calling to him. *Nicholas, I'm right behind you. Can you see him?*

No, it's too murky, Nicholas replied.

Can you see him with your mind? Jonathan asked.

I'll try, Nicholas replied.

He dove again, trying to locate North in his mind. Suddenly a different voice startled him.

"Fire and ice, Nicholas. Don't swallow too much water. The fire didn't get you, but we will."

Then there was silence.

Somehow, in his mind, Nicholas saw a shadow below him about ten feet away. He quickly piked back down and swam towards it. As he reached out he felt a hand grab onto his arm. He turned and swam for the surface with North holding on.

Jonathan, who had heard Nicholas convey to him that he'd found North, was there to help him. As the boys pulled North towards shore about a hundred feet from the rope swings, Calvin and Brad were there to help pull him up onto the bank.

North was gasping for air and spitting out water. Mikaia had run along the bank, when she'd heard Nicholas message her while he was swimming North in. She arrived and quickly wrapped a beach towel over North as he sat up still gasping.

"How are you doing?" Nicholas asked North.

He looked up and gasped a few more times and nodded that he was all right.

Then Arnold arrived.

"Hey man, all you had to do was hold on!"

With that North looked up at him with the most threatening expression possible and slowly said between gasps, "And all you had to do was catch me, like you said you would."

Everyone had gathered along the bank to check on North. Several kids started patting Nicholas and Jonathan on their backs saying, "Good job, you guys sure saved him!"

After a couple of minutes North was able to stand up. The first thing he did was to reach out his hand and shake Nicholas's and Jonathan's saying, "Thanks guys, without you two I'd still be down there. I owe you!"

"Looks like you just saved this young man's life!" a lady stated who had just appeared next to them.

"We were lucky to find him in the river. I'm glad he's okay," said Nicholas.

"Yes, I watched from the shore when I heard all the kids yelling," she replied. "My name is Deena French. I was here with my family enjoying the river. I'm also a reporter with the Opportunity Journal. You two did a brave thing. Not a lot of young people your age would have acted so fast and risked their lives for another. I was told that the two of you are Nicholas and Jonathan Frazier. Is that correct?"

"Yes, ma'am," replied Jonathan.

"And I'm the one they saved," they heard North say over a few more coughs.

"I'm North. I was at the bottom of the river and

71

couldn't swim. If they hadn't found me I would have drowned! It's good to know who your real friends are," North continued looking over at Arnold who was hiding in the crowd. "I owe them!"

"I'm really glad you're all right. Are you sure you shouldn't be checked by a doctor?" Deena asked.

"No, I'll be okay, although a minute longer and you would have been calling the County Coroner."

"And your last name is?" Deena asked.

"West," replied North.

"Just a moment, your name is North West? I just want to get it right," Deena asked.

"It's a long story lady, but yes."

Nicholas and Jonathan looked at each other, smiled, and shrugged their shoulders.

"Well good job. Thanks for talking to me," Deena said as she headed back to her family.

"See Mikaia," said Ashlee, who along with most of their friends was standing nearby. "I was right. Whenever you and your brothers are around either a miracle or something special happens!"

"That's for sure," Larry added, as they walked back to their beach blankets.

The rest of the afternoon the triplets continued to have a great time with their friends. Other kids came over and congratulated them or stared at them from a distance.

When they got home they changed, then met in Mikaia's room.

"That was quite an afternoon," said Mikaia. "I'm

really proud of both of you. Looks like your surfing and swimming experience near San Francisco really helped."

"At least it was fresh water when I opened my eyes and not salt water. It didn't sting nearly as much," replied Nicholas, "but we weren't alone."

"What do you mean?" asked Mikaia.

"When I was diving down I heard another voice besides Jonathan's. It said 'fire and ice, Nicholas, don't swallow too much water. The fire didn't get you but we will'."

"Wow, they've gotten into your head!" said Jonathan.

"That means that no matter what we do, Cryptic and his Apprentices will know and probably tell his Followers," Mikaia said.

Then they heard a soft 'popping' noise.

"Not necessarily," Halo said.

"Halo, are we glad to see you!" Jonathan said.

"First, I'd like to applaud both of you for saving North's life. That was quick thinking. You didn't worry about your own safety, but rather put North's first. That is showing the kind of love that makes the Master Inventor very pleased. Secondly, it is true, Cryptic and his Apprentices can get into your minds, if you let them."

"That's terrible. What should we do?" Mikaia asked.

"Whenever you use telepathy or have deep thoughts when you're fighting Cryptic or his

Followers, you must always block your mind to them."

"Block our minds?" asked Nicholas.

"Yes, it's kind of like a computer security check. You have to pause for a moment and concentrate on shutting off your thoughts to everyone except the ones you want to share them with. After you do it a few times it becomes automatic."

"This keeps getting more complicated," Jonathan said.

"All this will become second nature to you as you use it, just like using the time-slide signal has become for you," replied Halo.

"I'm still concerned how close Cryptic and his Apprentices are to us. It seems like they can attack us whenever they choose, like today in the river," said Nicholas.

"Yes, they are keeping a close watch on the three of you. Jonathan. Do you still have the little brass Golden Rule bell?" Halo asked.

"Yeah! When we ring it, it does to others what they intend to do to us. Like if they want to hurt us, it will hurt them instead," Jonathan replied.

"That's the bell I gave you."

"Yes, I carry it most of the time."

"Good! Keep it near especially when you're away from home, school, or on a field trip. All of you have the telepathic power to help you know when someone wants to harm you. Jonathan can also read minds, while Mikaia can see visions, and Nicholas has premonitions and can foresee the future. But you all are able to feel the thoughts of someone who intends to harm you. With that power you will always be alerted and can take the necessary precautions. I know you'll continue to use these powers for good the way the Inventor intended," Halo said as he popped away.

"There he goes again!" Jonathan said. "Just pops away without warning us. What if we had more questions?"

"I guess he figures we'd asked enough for what we need to know," Nicholas said as Jonathan started to chuckle.

"What's that all about?" asked Mikaia.

"I was just thinking...North West? What kind of name is that?"

"Yeah, I had to keep myself from laughing too. I guess he had trouble finding his way west too," Nicholas noted.

"I have a feeling that North won't be hanging around with Arnold anymore. I think he finally saw him for the selfish and careless person he is," said Mikaia.

"I'm glad he's okay and was so grateful to us. It made me feel better about him. Maybe he isn't going to become a full-fledged Follower," added Nicholas.

"Are you guys ready to start football practice tomorrow morning? I'm going to cheerleading."

"I plan to go," said Jonathan.

"Me too! We'll get to meet more kids and feel a

part of the school if we participate," Nicholas added.

"Dad said he'd drive us to school at eight, so, set your alarms!" Mikaia said as the boys left for their rooms.

"Good morning!" Mom said as they came down the stairs.

"Hi Mom, Dad," replied Mikaia.

"I've fixed the three of you a hero's breakfast this morning," their mom said with a big smile.

"What do you mean?" Nicholas asked.

"You're in the morning Journal," Dad said when they sat down at the breakfast table. "Why didn't you tell us you rescued someone?"

"In the Opportunity Journal?" asked Jonathan.

"Yep, on the front page," replied their dad.

"Amazing," Nicholas said.

"We just felt we did what we needed to do and that it was something most people would have done had they been there," Jonathan said.

"Well, you're wrong. According to Deena French, you two 'acted like an adult rescue team and pulled North up from sure death at the bottom on the river!'" Dad quoted from the paper.

"He wasn't quite on the bottom," Nicholas said.

"Wherever North was, we're very proud of you. You never cease to amaze us," Mom said.

"I think we never cease to amaze ourselves either," replied Nicholas.

"Now for the important part, Mom, what's a

hero's breakfast?" Jonathan, who never missed a meal, quickly asked.

"For you three anything you'd like. But I've already prepared some ham and eggs, pancakes, orange juice and for your sweet tooth I made fresh cinnamon rolls."

"This is great! In just two days we get to be treated at the Ultimate Ice Cream Shop and we get a hero's breakfast," Jonathan exclaimed. "It looks like there are some rewards for all we go through...besides knowing we've done the right thing! Thanks, Mom, I'll have a bit of everything."

"Thanks, that sounds good to me too," Nicholas added.

"I'll just have some eggs and orange juice," replied Mikaia. "Nicholas and Jonathan need to bulk up for football while I need to keep my svelte figure for cheerleading."

Chapter Six

Old Friends

After breakfast Dad dropped the triplets off at Lowe Middle School for the morning practice, saying he'd be back to pick them up at noon.

The boys' P.E. teacher, Mr. Lombardi, was also the head football coach. He immediately started them on conditioning. Nicholas, Jonathan, Calvin, Brad, Larry and even the big guy Chuck, along with the others, began running around the track and jumping over everything Mr. Lombardi put in their way. Fortunately, it wasn't a very hot day. Between some shade and a large cooler of cold water they all managed to survive.

Mikaia met with twenty-five girls who were trying out for the ten cheerleader spots. Ashlee and Marie had decided to try out when they heard Mikaia was going to. A young woman named Candy L'Heur was their coach and trainer. Candy started right off teaching them some basic cheering moves and routines. At the end of the week there would be a competition to determine who would be on the team.

The girls all worked hard and even seemed to get along.

At noon Dad pulled up and the tired triplets climbed into the car.

"I've got a stop or two to make in town. Then I thought we'd have lunch at Wong's for some of this fantastic pizza you three keep talking about. How does that sound?" asked their dad.

"I thought you'd never ask!" Jonathan said.

"Good idea, Dad," added Mikaia.

Dad pulled into the grocery store parking lot. "I'll be a few minutes if you want to wait. Or you can look around and meet me back here in ten," he said as he headed into the store.

The triplets got out and walked up the street to see if any of their friends were in the ice cream and candy shop or the café. They almost walked into a tall man coming out of the pharmacy.

"Hi, you three," greeted a familiar voice.

"Henry Lowe! What are you doing here? We thought you were back in Florida," said Mikaia.

"I told you I might move back to Opportunity from Orlando, and here I am. I even brought my family with me."

"That's great news. We could use another friend of the Master Inventor in town." Nicholas said quietly.

"That's one of the reasons I came back," replied Henry.

"What are you going to do here? And where are

you going to live?" Jonathan asked.

"Actually, I've partnered up with a man named Jud Day who has a surveying business in town."

"Jud Day? He's a friend of ours," replied Jonathan.

"That's good to know. I plan to do the engineering work while Jud does the surveying. It should be a successful business combination. As to where we're living, I rented a small ranch just north of town. It's near the Wilson's place."

"Ashlee Wilson's place?" asked Nicholas.

"Oh, are you a friend of hers too?"

"Oh, yeah, you could say that," Nicholas said shyly.

"Yep, just down the block from them."

"I'm glad you decided to come back to Opportunity," said Mikaia.

"So am I. I needed to get my priorities straight and now I think I have."

Just then they saw their dad waving for them to come.

"Hope to see you soon," Nicholas said and they ran towards the parking lot.

"By the way," Henry called out, "That was a nice article about you in the Journal this morning!"

The triplets looked back and smiled and Mikaia waved.

They drove along the street to the post office where their dad said he needed to run in for a moment. While they were sitting in the Odyssey,

Jonathan suddenly yelled out, pointing down the street, "Hey, look! Halo or Harold is over there!"

Nicholas and Mikaia looked down the sidewalk about fifty feet and saw a man turn into a small bakery.

"I don't think so, Jonathan," Mikaia said, but Jonathan was out the door and hurrying towards the bakery.

"I guess we should follow," Nicholas suggested as he opened the door.

When they approached the bakery, they could see Jonathan standing in the doorway staring at something. "I can't believe it. It is him!"

A man who looked just like Harold Lowe was standing at the counter. When he turned they recognized him immediately. When he saw the triplets, he walked towards them with a big smile.

"It is you!" Nicholas said. "What are you doing here?"

"You don't think I'd stay in Florida when my son Henry and his family moved back here. Besides, this is my home."

"Yes, but..." Jonathan started to say.

"It's also a good place to be if I'm trying to make sure the old school custodians are getting along all right."

"Does that mean you're going to live here?" asked Mikaia.

"I already have a place to stay and a job."

"A job?" Jonathan replied.

"Are you going back to work with the school district?" Nicholas asked.

"Oh no, I retired from the school district as the head custodian. I don't intend to do that job again."

"Then what..." Jonathan started to say, but he was cut off.

"We'll spend more time talking later. For now, I'll just tell you that I have a job at the bank with Mr. Peters and I'm renting a room just down the street at the old hotel."

"Hi, Harold, welcome back," the triplet's father said as he entered the bakery.

"Thanks, Nathan. It's good to be back home."

"Dad, did you know that the Lowes were back?" asked Mikaia.

"No, but I'm not surprised since I knew that Henry might be moving back. I just wasn't sure when. Aren't you glad to see them?"

"We're very glad. We can use all the help we can get!" Nicholas replied.

"I hoped you'd feel that way!" Harold said with a big smile.

"Okay kids, it's off to Wong's for a pizza lunch. Would you care to join us, Harold?"

"Thanks, but I'm still getting settled. Perhaps some other time would work out."

At Wong's the triplets ordered a large pepperoni pizza while their dad ordered a small sausage with anchovy.

"Are your sure you're glad Harold moved back?"

Dad asked.

"I sure am!" Jonathan exclaimed.

"Me too," Mikaia added as Nicholas sat quietly.

"What about you, Nicholas?" his dad asked.

"Of course. I'm glad he's back. But it also worries me."

"How's that?" Jonathan questioned.

"Well, if he found it necessary to come back along with Henry, we could be a big part of their decision."

"Okay, Nicholas, just say it," an impatient Jonathan replied.

"He might be concerned about us because Cryptic and his Apprentices are so close. That could be the real reason he came back."

"I never looked at it that way," said their dad. "It's kind of like circling the wagons and joining forces for the fight."

"Fight?" said Jonathan.

"The fight against evil seldom ends for long. You always have to be prepared," Dad said as he looked off across the room. "But I don't mean to scare you. Perhaps his main reason was to just bring all of his family back home. After all, if it were that dangerous, would he have allowed his grandchildren to return to Opportunity?"

"You're right, Dad," Jonathan said and finished off his third slice of pizza.

"How are the Fraziers today?" a voice said, "and great job at the river, Jonathan and Nicholas. You two are real heroes."

"Good to see you, Bill," Nathan replied. "Yes, we're very proud of them."

"Hi, Mr. Peters," added Mikaia.

"You know that you three always surprise me with what you've been able to do, with or without any help from the Inventor," Bill replied.

"We understand we should congratulate you, too, on your new hire at the Bank," said Nathan.

"Yes, I'm pleased Harold took the job. He'll be handling all our real estate sales and loans. He knows just about everyone and every piece of property for a hundred miles. Besides, he has other special abilities too," he smiled and winked at the triplets.

"We're happy that he and Henry both moved back to Opportunity!" Mikaia added. "It makes us feel more comfortable knowing they're both around."

"I understand," Bill said. "By the way, did you hear about the sheriff's case against Sam Hawkins and Phil Steward? They've been charged with storing explosives within the city limits."

"No, we haven't," replied Nicholas as he looked up curiously from his pizza.

"Apparently Sam is trying to set Phil up to take the fall. He's told the sheriff that Phil's the one who bought the dynamite and brought it that night to his hardware store. He's also saying that when the sheriff arrived, he was just trying to get rid of it since he knew he shouldn't have dynamite stored in town."

"That's not the way it happened," Jonathan said. "Sam said he was going to get the dynamite and Phil didn't even arrive until after Sam had loaded the truck. That was when Sam ordered Phil to help move the dynamite into the old school."

"Now Sam's saying that since Phil is a mining engineer from Mariposa, he knew people he could buy explosives from without any written sales slips."

"Boy, Sam Hawkins lies all the time, even to set up another Follower," said Jonathan.

"Well that's just it. I heard from my sources that both Phil and Pete Rider don't want to be Followers any more, but Cryptic and the rest of them won't let them leave," Bill added.

"It sounds like they're trying to get rid of Phil by sending him to jail," Nicholas stated.

"That seems to be the plan," replied Bill.

"I think I need to have a little talk with Sam and convince him that's not a good idea," Jonathan said. "I could always go to the sheriff and tell him what I saw and heard."

"What if they ask how you happened to be behind the hardware store just at that moment?" Bill asked and he sat down in a chair next to them.

"Simple, I just tell them that the three of us had come into town to get an ice cream and pick up some groceries. We'd split up and I saw a pickup truck drive down the ally and thought I'd check it out," Jonathan replied. "That's sort of true. I was there to check things out."

"That will probably work," Bill said.

"I am glad to hear that some of Cryptic's

Followers are trying to break away and live good lives," added Mikaia.

"I think we need to do all we can to help them," added Nicholas. "If they can get away from Cryptic and survive, then others who finally see his evil may also try to leave."

"Good point, Nicholas," said their dad.

"Yes, Mr. Peters would you please let us know of anything else you hear?" Mikaia asked.

"I'd be glad to, Mikaia." Mr. Peters stood up, waved, and left.

"Dad, would you drive us back downtown so we can have a little talk with Sam Hawkins?" Jonathan asked.

"We're on our way," their dad said just as Jonathan pushed his last piece of pizza into his mouth.

Dad dropped the triplets off a couple of buildings short of the hardware store and told them he'd meet them at the café. The triplets walked to the hardware store and saw through the window that Mr. Hawkins was talking to some customers. They kept watch until the customers had left, then walked in.

"Not you three again, now you're even playing up to the press to get your names in the paper. Is one of you getting ready to run for Mayor?" Sam asked sneering.

"Not yet, Mr. Hawkins, but we'll think about it since you brought it up," Jonathan replied as Sam snarled again. "Actually, we came to talk to you about your charges against Mr. Steward."

"What do you mean?"

"We understand you're trying to set him up by saying he bought the dynamite and placed it in your storeroom without your permission. Then, when the sheriff showed up, you told him you had just discovered it and were trying to remove it from town. Isn't this true?"

"Where'd you hear something like that, boy?"

"As you know, we hear a lot of things," replied Jonathan.

"Well just the same it ain't none of your business."

"Actually, it is. Since we saw and heard you and reported it to the sheriff, it's as much our business as yours," Jonathan quickly replied.

"Who do you children think you are?"

"You know who we are and you know a little about our powers. I'm surprised you have forgotten so soon. But just in case the sheriff's memory needs jogging, or the courts need an eye witness, I just wanted you to know that since I heard everything and my brother and sister saw some of it, we would make it three against one in court. Not very good odds for you I'd say if you intend to lie," Jonathan stated matter-of-factly.

Nicholas and Mikaia were quite impressed.

"Why do you care what I say or do to Phil after what he did?"

"We don't like liars and we believe in justice," replied Jonathan.

"I'll do what I want to do," Sam answered. He turned and spat onto the wooden floor.

"May I suggest you talk with your attorney, Mr. Steffini. If he hasn't lost a case in five years, he's not going to like the contempt of court charges filed against you after we have our say about who really did what. Besides, three witnesses against one in court, especially since we are heroes now, probably won't go well for you," Jonathan stated.

"Why you little…"

"You're the one who wants to harm us and this community," Mikaia cut in. "All you have to do is mind your own business and be a good neighbor."

After they left the store and started towards the café, Nicholas patted Jonathan on the back. "Man, you were great. I've never heard you as eloquent as that. You reminded me of Mikaia. Every time he said something you changed it around and placed him on the spot. Maybe you should be a lawyer too," said Nicholas.

"Nicholas is right! You were fantastic! I don't think you left him with any choices but to tell the truth. And the part about being heroes to further our credibility as witnesses was genius," Mikaia added as they turned into the café.

"Actually, I am rather proud of myself. I am pretty good when I apply myself and I think it worked."

"Could you tell what he was thinking?" asked Nicholas.

"Yes. At first, he was confused and uncertain.

Then I could tell he was thinking about telling the truth and throwing himself on the mercy of the court by emphasizing his many years as a successful businessman in the community and his clean record. Boy, little do the courts know," Jonathan said.

"Let's hope that's what he decides to do," Mikaia added as they walked into the café and took seats next to their dad who was just finishing up a coffee.

"Did everything go as you planned?" asked Dad.

"It sure did and Jonathan was great. He talked Mr. Hawkins right out of lying," replied Mikaia.

"I'm glad to hear it. Now, are you three ready to go home?"

"I'm ready," Jonathan answered and Nicholas and Mikaia nodded.

Just as they left the café they saw North approaching.

"Hey, look there's North. Do you see Arnold yet?" Jonathan asked.

"Oh! Hi North," Mikaia said. "How are you feeling?"

"I'm feeling fine, thanks to Nicholas and Jonathan,"

"Where's Arnold?" Jonathan asked, looking around.

"I'm not hanging out with him anymore. I finally saw what kind of friend he is. I decided I needed to be me and not what Arnold tried to make me into."

"We're glad to hear that, North," Nicholas said. "Have you ever thought about playing football? With your size and strength, you'd make a great lineman."

"Hey, great idea!" Jonathan added. "From what I saw of our line earlier today at practice, we could use a strong guy like you in the center."

"I don't know. I've never thought about it before," replied North.

"We're both going out for the team and practices are in the morning at the school. We'd sure like your help," stated Nicholas.

"You're both going to be there?"

"Yep, and Mikaia's practicing cheerleading near us." Nicholas added.

"Well, maybe I'll give it a try."

"Great, North! By the way, this is our Dad. Dad, this is North," Nicholas said.

"Nice to meet you North and I'm happy to see you're all right after the river incident." Dad shook North's hand."

"Yeah, thanks, I am too," North replied.

"Then we'll be looking for you tomorrow morning about eight, okay?" Nicholas asked,

"Uh, yes, at eight."

"Good, see you then," Nicholas said and they followed their dad over to the car.

"That was quick thinking, Nicholas," complimented Mikaia as they started back home. "You provided North with a way to make some real friends and really break away from the hold Arnold has over him."

"I really don't want to see him ending up a

Follower. Besides I'm getting to like the guy. I didn't think I'd ever be saying that," Nicholas said smiling.

"And we really could use his size and strength on the team," affirmed Jonathan.

"I've got to admit we may have won a couple of rounds for the good guys today," added Mikaia.

"Once again you three never stop amazing me," Dad said as he drove up towards their house.

.

Chapter Seven

The Fort

At practice the next morning Coach Lombardi had the team running again and had added more obstacles for them to maneuver under, over, and around. North showed up right at eight much to the surprise of the other team members. After a couple of hours of sweat, he became just another part of the group. Nicholas and Jonathan gave North a couple of pats on the back after which Nicholas noticed a slight smile appear on North's face. Even Brad began to think that North, with his size and power, could really help the team.

The coach told them that tomorrow they'd keep doing conditioning but he'd also break them into offensive and defensive teams and begin to evaluate them for positions.

Mikaia continued to work on various cheerleading skills as Candy L'Heur taught them more about the routines they'd be evaluated on at the end of the week. Mikaia caught on very quickly and executed the skills extremely well. Mikaia, Ashlee, and Marie hung out together whenever they received a few moments of rest time.

Nicholas and Jonathan saw their dad drive up at the end of practice and passed by North on their way to the car.

"Good job today, North, and welcome to the team," Jonathan said. North nodded back.

"We'll see you tomorrow, won't we?" asked Nicholas.

"You bet. I really like this stuff," North replied as he downed a quart of water and wiped sweat off his face.

"How'd things go today?" Dad asked.

"Great," Jonathan replied.

"I see North showed up."

"He sure did. He worked hard, fit in with the guys, and even seemed to enjoy all of this abuse," replied Nicholas.

"I'm glad to hear that. By the way, when I stopped in town before I picked you up, I bumped into a deputy sheriff named Stan who said he knew you, Mikaia. He thought you'd be interested in knowing what happened in court this morning with Sam and Phil."

"Yes, I do know him and we're all interested!"

"Apparently Sam's lawyer, Mitch Seffini, made a plea deal with the District Attorney and got Sam's charges reduced to a misdemeanor for a guilty plea from Sam. Due to his standing in the community and his clean record he was given one hundred hours of community service at the hospital and put on probation for six months."

"So he didn't dump on Phil then?" asked Jonathan.

"Apparently not. Your little talk yesterday must have worked."

"Then what happened to Phil?" Mikaia asked.

"Since Sam received such a light sentence, when Phil pleaded guilty, the court had to give him the same deal. Both of them dodged any jail time."

"I'm glad to hear about Phil, but I would like to have seen Sam locked up for a while where he couldn't cause any more trouble," said Mikaia.

When they started to turn off the main street and head up the hill, their dad was cut off by a long silver big rig that rolled through the stop sign.

"Boy, he sure must be in a hurry," explained their dad as he applied the brakes.

Having the best view of the truck, Nicholas replied, "I can't see the driver's face, but it looks like the same silver truck with red lines down the side that tailgated Mom up the hill a couple of days ago."

"What gives with that?" Jonathan asked as he turned to take a look.

"Just some local driver throwing his weight around," said Dad.

"Are you two about ready for another field trip somewhere?" Jonathan asked. "I sure am."

"Aren't you worn out from practice?" asked Mikaia.

"That just warmed me up!" Jonathan replied.

"Did you drink one of those energy drinks the coach had by the water cooler today?" Nicholas asked and then added, "Because I'm beat!"

"Nope, not when I found out he wanted three dollars a can for them to cover costs!"

"I suspect that would be one of the few things that could curb your thirst," Dad added with a laugh.

"Really, Jonathan, that is a good idea," Mikaia said. "When we get busy with all of our school activities, we'll have less time to take field trips. Let's take one."

"Good! Then how do we travel and where do you want to go?" asked Jonathan.

"Let's go into the future! We haven't traveled through time much in that direction," suggested Nicholas.

"I don't know," Mikaia replied. "Knowing too much about the future, unless we travel there for a certain reason, scares me a bit. Besides I always like to learn more about our past and how we got here, especially things about California."

"Okay, that's fine with me." Nicholas said as began to perk up. "Let's grab something from one of the trunks in the attic that Harold's dad saved from the the old school. We can follow its Essence and see where it leads us,"

When they arrived home, the triplets went to their rooms, cleaned up and changed their clothes. Jonathan was first to finish and quickly headed up into the attic. He reached deep into the second trunk and felt along the bottom. His hand touched something metallic. He grabbed hold and pulled it out.

"What'd you find?' a voice behind him asked.

"Man, Nicholas, don't sneak up on a guy. You startled me!"

"Sorry, I thought you heard me climbing up the stairs."

"It's a small pocket knife," Jonathan said as he handed it to Nicholas.

"I didn't see this before when we searched through these old trunks. It must have fallen out of a pocket from a piece of clothing that's in there," Nicholas said as he examined it.

"Does that have a strong enough Essence to follow?" Jonathan asked.

"It sure should," Mikaia said from behind them as she bent over to look at it.

"Everyone's sneaking around today!" complained Jonathan.

"Are you both ready?" asked Mikaia.

"We sure are!" replied Nicholas. "But we won't be able to use the time-slide sign to travel with the knife since it's a lot older than fifty years. So, let's hit the school's slide and go to Midst to follow this Essence."

"We'll have to walk over to the old school then," Jonathan said as he turned towards the stairs.

"I'll grab the list of students who attended the old school," Mikaia added. She disappeared into her room then quickly reappeared and followed the boys out the front door.

"We're going to the old school, Mom," Nicholas called into the kitchen where their mother, Cathy, nodded as she worked at the sink.

When they approached the old school they checked to be sure no one was around.

"Darn," said Nicholas. "We still need to bring some gardening tools and clear off the weeds that are coming up."

"Let's do that after practice tomorrow," Jonathan said as they climbed the ladder leading to the top of the slide.

"Fine with me," said Mikaia.

Jonathan sat down first, followed by Mikaia, then Nicholas.

"Do you have the knife, Jonathan?" asked Nicholas.

"Yep, let's go!"

"Okay," Mikaia said. "Ready. Set. go!"

They all pushed off as she yelled, "Think Midst!"

They hit the bottom of the slide and floated out into the swirling white cotton candy like fibers and felt themselves softly land on the clouds of Midst.

"Buenos dias, amigos," Yon said.

"Oh man, I forgot that they only have a western and a Spanish channel on their television," Nicholas said.

"No problem, partner!" they heard Hither reply. "Are you three passing through on another cattle drive?"

"Yes, we are, Hither. Back in Abilene again and we're in a hurry," replied Mikaia, trying to avoid spending too much time discussing things with Hither and Yon, especially in Spanish.

"Well ma'am, Halo said to be sure to tell you 'Howdy' for him the next time we saw you. That's right after he told us that we both needed to send you on your next trip. He wants to be sure no cattle rustlers get ya," Hither said.

"We really appreciate that and would like to get on with the..." Mikaia tried to finish.

"Do you want to vamoose quickly, senorita?" asked Yon.

"Well we're anxious to keep the herd together and find them fresh grass," said Mikaia hoping she could speed things up if she played along.

"There is some mighty sweet grass just down the road," Hither said.

He turned and spit something onto the cloud next to his foot.

"I thought that spitting onto clouds wasn't allowed in Midst," Jonathan stated.

"Creo que si, hombre," replied Yon as he looked down at the brown spot where Hither had spit. "Amigo, you need to clean that up, por favor... pronto!"

"Darn, you're right, partner. I forgot I'd left my spittoon in the ranch house. I'll just grab that there shovel and clean it up," Hither replied.

He picked up a shovel from out of the clouds, carefully scooped up the brown mark, walked over to the edge of the cloud and tossed it off. Nicholas moved over to the edge just in time to see it falling towards the earth.

"I sure hope that doesn't hit our house," he said as he continued to watch it fall.

"That's the best thing about homesteading this high up. You never know where stuff like that is going to end up," Hither returned as he also looked down.

"Hither, Yon, are you about ready to send us?" asked Jonathan.

"Anxious little feller ain't ya," Hither replied.

"Si, he is," Yon returned with a big smile.

"Then grab your partners' hands, close your eyes and..." Hither said as the triplets heard a loud "hasta luego!" They felt a strong wind blowing across them and heard the sparking and hissing of the time machine...

"Dirt, again. We're lying in dirt," Nicholas said as he stood up.

"Yeah, but I smell something baking. It could be bread!" replied Jonathan.

"Hey, it's a walled city. Look at the people, we're in the old west again!" said Mikaia.

"I see some Native Americans!" replied Jonathan.

"This looks like some kind of fort," Nicholas said as he looked around. "Man, there sure is a lot of activity going on in here. We always seem to land in the middle of things.

An old cannon sits in front of it.

"I see what you smelled," Mikaia said pointing at a small black sign on a shop next to them.

"Bakery, now we're talking," Jonathan started walking towards it.

"Look to your left. There's an old clay beehive shaped oven," Nicholas said.

"How'd you know that?" asked Jonathan.

"Because I can see some heat coming off of it and that's where the bread you smelled is baking."

"Hey, and a large cannon sits just in front of it. This must be a fort," Jonathan added.

"Of course it's a fort. How did you get in if you didn't know where you were headed?" a man asked.

Quickly they turned around and saw a man in his late teens standing next to them.

"Oh, excuse us sir, but we are a bit confused and have traveled quite a spell," said Mikaia.

"I can understand that. I just arrived at Sutter's a few months ago. Came from Illinois with a group by wagon," the young man replied.

"Sutter's you said?" Nicholas asked.

"Yeah, Sutter's Fort, or New Helvetia as John Sutter calls it. Most of us just call this place Sacramento."

"Then we're in Sutter's Fort!" said Nicholas. "It must be around the 1840's?"

"Boy, you are confused! It's 1847, in September. Are your parents around here somewhere?" he asked.

"Oh, they're still outside the fort. We're the Fraziers, I'm Nicholas and they're Mikaia and

Jonathan."

"Nice to meet you. Captain Sutter likes to see new settlers arriving. My name it James Noah. Have you seen much of the fort yet?"

"No, we just arrived," replied Mikaia.

"I'll be glad to point a few things out to you. Oh, good morning Captain!" James said as he turned and smiled."

"Same to you, James. It looks like you've got yourself some young immigrants."

"These are the Frazier's. They've just arrived and seem a bit confused."

"I can understand that. It's a long, hard journey for those who make it. But I think you'll find out it's well worth it! Do you folks need anything? Some supplies? Some feed for your stock, some food?"

"Food, I could sure use some of that!" said Jonathan as he lit up.

"Then James, tell Carlos I said to give them some of that bread he's been baking in the oven. You kids can also tell your folks that if they plan on settling around here I have a small parcel of land they can have, if they plan on farming," Captain Sutter said as he walked away.

"He sure is a nice man," Mikaia said. "He has a strange accent, though."

"That's because Captain Sutter was born in Germany, but he says he's Swiss. He sailed to New York, and then traveled to Fort Vancouver, then to Hawaii and Alaska before landing in Yerba Buena in

1839."

"He's sure traveled a lot," said Jonathan.

"He sure has, but then a lot of us immigrants have. When he got here he became a Mexican citizen so Governor Alvarado would give him this land grant. That's when he built this fort."

"You sure know a lot about him," Mikaia said.

"You're always wise to know as much as you can about your host and employer, especially when he's such a generous man," replied James.

"Do you want to see more of the fort? It's very large, over three hundred and twenty feet long with walls two and a half feet thick and almost eighteen feet high. This fort is very secure."

"Sure," said Jonathan, "but didn't he say something about fresh bread?"

"That's right!" James said as he walked over to the bakery and came out with a small loaf for each of them. "Carlos had just finished these before he put the new batch in."

"This is very good," Mikaia said as she broke off a piece.

"It's an old Indian recipe Carlos uses."

Jonathan pulled out his pocket knife, and using a small work bench, cut a piece off his loaf.

"That's a nice-looking pocket knife you have there," said James. "Could I see it for a moment?"

"Sure," Jonathan said as he filled his mouth with bread.

"I lost one just like this up by a lake on the

mountain pass a few months ago. Except mine had my initials cut into the bottom of the small blade." He pulled the small blade open. "I can't believe it! Look!" he yelled.

The triplets gathered round James so they could see. There at the base of the small blade were the initials, J.N.

"Did you find this on the trail?" he asked a surprised Jonathan.

"Yeah, ah, that's what I did. I found it on the trail...in the mountains. Since it's yours you're welcome to have it back," Jonathan added.

"That's very kind of you. My father gave this to me when I was a young boy. I used it a lot along the trail. I even trimmed my boss George Donner's hair with it once."

Nicholas quickly came to life as the others looked at James.

"You we're part of the Donner party?" Nicholas asked.

"Yes, I was one of the teamsters for the Donners. I drove a wagon for them until we got stuck in the snow on the Sierra pass. Then things really got bad. Almost half of the party died. I don't like to talk about it, although everyone around here has heard of it. Some of the men volunteered to come up and save us. Captain Sutter sent supplies and a rescue party too. They brought us back here. He even sent Salvador and Lewis, two of his best vaqueros to help, although they never made it back. I've been at the fort for the last five months working for him."

"What happened to the other party survivors?" Nicholas asked.

"Most of them are scattered at various ranches and small towns around the valley, but a couple, like me, have stayed near the fort to work for Captain Sutter. Do you still want to see more of the fort?" James asked trying to change the subject.

"Yes, but if you don't mind I'd like to know how Leanna and Elitha Donner are doing?" asked Nicholas.

James looked at him rather strangely before saying, "Then you do know some things about our tragedy?"

"Yes, a little," replied Nicholas.

"Both girls are doing well, but of course none of the Donner adults survived."

"And Virginia and Patty Reed?" continued Nicholas.

"They are also well."

"I'm glad to hear that," Nicholas replied. James looked at him not sure how he knew the four girls' names and why he had asked specifically about them.

"That large three-story building is the center building and holds Sutter's quarters and dining area. His office along with some staff offices and quarters are also in that building. Along the west wall are some guest quarters, a trade store and carpenter's shop. We also have a blacksmith, a room for weaving, a kitchen, a work area for the cooper, a candle making area, and various storage and stable areas."

"This is quite a place," Jonathan said leaning against a large cannon.

"Oh, and the cannons he bought from the Russians who sold him Fort Ross up north along the coast when they left a few years ago."

"Russians lived near here too?" asked Jonathan.

"Yes, it was a supply fort for the Russian fur trade and fishing ships."

"Man, there sure are a lot of things I need to learn," said Jonathan.

"Just a few months ago some settlers around here revolted against Mexico's authority and declared California independent. They took down the flag of Mexico and put up one with a bear and a single star on it. Now the United States is claiming it, so Captain Sutter has just started flying the American flag. It all gets confusing sometimes," James said.

"Are you planning on settling down nearby?" Nicholas asked.

"I'd like to if I can get enough money to buy some property further south. The Captain has already told me he'd give me some farmland around here."

"We'd better see if we can find our parents. They'll be looking for us by now," Mikaia said.

"You're right, they probably are," replied James.

"Thanks for showing us around. And be sure to thank Captain Sutter for the bread," Mikaia said.

They all headed for the gate and passed the blacksmith who was leading a horse towards his shop.

"It would take a large army to break into this fort," Jonathan observed when he saw the gun platforms and protective bastion towers at the ends of the fort.

There were many people, along with their wagons and livestock, camped around the fort's exterior. The triplets hurried over to a small grove of trees that didn't seem to be occupied.

"It's probably time to get back, although we don't seem to be in any danger around here," Nicholas said.

"There's danger everywhere, son!" a deep voice said and they all jumped at the same time.

Two men wearing mostly leather clothing and carrying rifles suddenly appeared from the small grove of trees. The triplets quickly moved back a few feet.

"Don't worry. We probably ain't going to hurt you none. At least not with all these settlers so close by," the taller one with a short beard and a wide hat said.

"Why would you want to hurt us at all?" Nicholas asked.

"No offense to you three, well maybe a little. We just like to have some fun every now and then. We like to see how many problems we can cause. It makes us feel good inside, don't it Jorge?" the taller one said.

"It sure does, Dingo. Makes us feel real good," the shorter one said as he lowered his rifle towards the triplets. "Besides, everyone's got a job to do," Jorge said as he started to laugh.

"And your job is to threaten and scare people?" Mikaia found herself saying.

"Often more than that," said Jorge pointing his rifle at Mikaia.

"Who do you think helped get things all riled up around here between the Mexicans and the new settlers?" replied Dingo. "And who's going to be helping to make this whole place explode with chaos in a few months when James Marshall finds gold up at Captain Sutter's mill in the foothills?"

"How do you know about that?" an astonished Nicholas gasped.

"Let's just say we have a mutual acquaintance who also told us that you'd probably head for these trees after you left the fort," said Dingo, smiling with pleasure.

"You can't be Followers too, can you?" Jonathan asked. With that both of the men broke out laughing, a laugh that seemed both joyful and evil at the same time.

"Si!" replied Jorge, "you catch on pretty fast!"

"What do you plan to do with us?" Mikaia anxiously asked.

"That's just it! We ain't going to do nothing! Well, not much, at least. Not that we wouldn't like to, little girl," Dingo said as he also started waving his rifle near the triplet's heads.

"Let's just say this is a little exercise in humility...for the three of you so you can go back and tell your friends who really has the power around this world," Jorge said.

"Although we're pleased to say we are allowed to leave you with a little pain...It's only fair!" He pulled out a knife and started laughing again as he moved closer.

Nicholas looked over at Mikaia and thought, *Quick, back to the fort!*

Jonathan caught Nicholas's message as he sent it to Mikaia and quickly nodded back. Within a flash the triplets each made the time-slide sign and instantly reappeared in the fort.

"What was that all about?" asked Jonathan.

"Looks like Cryptic's still one step ahead of us," replied Nicholas.

"Or just one step behind," Mikaia said.

"Could you tell if they really meant to hurt us, Jonathan?" Nicholas asked.

"As Jorge moved towards us with his knife he was reminding himself to just leave a little cut on each of us. He was having a hard time holding back and not cutting deeper, because he was thinking that if he disobeyed Cryptic he'd not see the sunrise. Yeah, he was going to hurt us."

"That's what I felt too. Where does Cryptic get these guys?" Nicholas asked.

"I don't know. I'm just glad we got away from them. A cut is not the kind of beauty mark I prefer. Let's get out of here," Mikaia added.

"I'd heard you'd left. How did you like Carlos's

bread?" a voice nearby called out.

They turned towards the voice in time to see Captain Sutter heading towards the large center building.

"Very much, thank you," Mikaia yelled back as all three of them waved.

"Quick, let's try that storage room," Nicholas said. He headed a few feet to his left and Mikaia and Jonathan followed. The dark room was filled with boxes and bags of supplies that they could barely make out thanks to the light that came through several cracks in the door.

"I say we get out of here now!" Mikaia exclaimed. "Quick, join hands and think back to what we were doing and what you were thinking at the very moment we slid off the slide!" At that moment they saw the swirling cotton candy like fibers and felt themselves floating down and landing on something hard.

"Ah," Jonathan sighed, "my desk."

"And welcome back," Tique said.

"Hi, Tique!" responded Nicholas. "We keep bumping into more of Cryptic's Followers no matter where we go! He wants some kind of revenge for what happened to him at the old school!"

"That seems to be what is happening," replied Tique.

"It certainly takes a lot of the enjoyment away from our field trips to other places," Jonathan stated, "when we know that someone could be waiting to harm us."

"That's exactly what he's trying to do. He wants us to become scared so we won't use our powers and increase our knowledge by taking trips," replied Mikaia.

"At least we were able to meet Captain Sutter and learn what things were like in early California just before the 1849 gold rush," added Nicholas.

"And meet the guy who owned the knife I found in one of the trunks, James Noah," Jonathan noted.

"That was strange. Imagine the odds of that!" said Nicholas.

"Well, we were following the knife's Essence, and the knife did belong to James Noah," Mikaia said.

"Yeah, but how did it end up in one of our trunks?" asked Jonathan.

"Let's see," Mikaia said as she pulled out the list of names of the students who attended the old school.

"Here it is. There was a Rebecca and David Noah who attended the old school from 1858 through 1860," Mikaia said. "Apparently James did settle down and lived for a while near Opportunity. I suspect that James gave the knife to his son, David."

"You three did learn a lot, and Mikaia, you're right. Rebecca and David were James Noah's daughter and son. If you remember, I was their teacher at the old school back then," Tique said.

"Then were they in the same class as Ronnie and Donnie Smith when they disappeared?" Nicholas asked.

"Yes, they were."

"Man, this sure is a small world for being so big!" Jonathan said shaking his head.

"It seems that everything is somehow connected to everything else. Everything has an effect on what follows it in history," Nicholas said.

"You have learned a lot," said Tique. "Even though the Master Inventor sees everything happening at the same time, and we can slide through time at the same moment everything else is happening, from the world's perspective, time is important. Earlier events affect later events."

"You know, I'm tempted to go ahead in time just to see how we can get Cryptic off our backs!" Jonathan suggested as he opened and closed the lid on his desk.

"I still feel we should only travel into the future to see a particular person or event. We need a real strong reason to change the future," Mikaia said.

"I agree with Mikaia," Nicholas chimed in. "We may find out some things that will really upset us, or we may go to a point in the future where we find we're not there. I for one don't want to spend all my time trying to figure that one out."

"I see what you mean. Okay, you've convinced me, only when necessary then," Jonathan said as he stood up.

"Why don't we clean up a few weeds before we go? We left some gardening supplies in the closet."

He turned to look at Tique.

"Don't let me slow you down." She said with her usual smile. "You've obviously learned a lot on your field trip, so...class dismissed.".

Chapter Eight

Custodial Duties

The triplets grabbed the shovel, rake, and bucket they'd left in the old school's closet and walked outside.

"We're still left with the problem of how to get Cryptic and his Followers off our backs," Jonathan said sliding the shovel under a tall weed.

"And how to stop his Followers from growing in numbers and doing more harm to the community," added Nicholas.

"It looks like we have a lot of thinking to do," Jonathan replied.

He chopped at two more weeds. Mikaia reached down, picked them up, and tossed them into the bucket while Nicholas stood very still.

"Aren't you going to help, Nicholas?" asked Mikaia.

"Do you feel anything strange?" he asked back.

"What do you mean?" replied Jonathan, who had paused for a moment.

"Am I just dizzy from our trip, or do you feel the

ground vibrating?"

"Yes, I feel it too," Mikaia said.

"Maybe it's the beginning of an earthquake. We do live in California," replied Jonathan.

"No, it's something I felt when we came out of the school and the vibrations have remained constant," Nicholas said. He laid down and placed his ear to the ground.

"Could it be a cave in?" Jonathan asked.

"No! Something's going on in the mine tunnel below us," Nicholas reported.

"Let's pop on down and take a peek!" Jonathan enthused, bored with chopping weeds.

"Then let's go about a couple hundred feet down the mine from this point below us," Nicholas suggested.

"I'm ready!" replied Jonathan.

"We might as well check it out," said Mikaia.

The triplets looked around to make sure no one was watching, then made the time-slide sign, and popped into the mine tunnel below.

Nicholas pulled out the small pen size flashlight he carried with him on field trips. They could hear the sound of an engine coming from up the tunnel. As they got closer they heard loud pounding and cracking, almost like a gun was going off.

"Quick, stick something in your ears. That sound is almost deafening," Nicholas said.

Mikaia quickly pulled out a couple pieces of tissue she carried and gave them each a piece to stuff in their ears. As they got closer they could see a gas driven generator with a cord going up the tunnel. Dust was flying everywhere.

"Do either of you see anything?" Mikaia thought.

"It looks like two men working with a pneumatic jack hammer are breaking up some of the larger stones that are blocking the cavern entrance," Nicholas conveyed back.

"I can't believe it!" Mikaia sent back. "They're trying to get through to destroy the time machine."

"It's going to take them several days, even if they do use the jack," Jonathan added.

"Do either of you recognize them?" asked Mikaia.

"The older one is Sam Hawkins. I don't know who the other one is," Nicholas conveyed.

"The sound and dust are terrible! Let's meet back in my room," Mikaia said.

They all made the sign and popped into Mikaia's room.

"They must really want to destroy the time machine to go to all that trouble," said Jonathan.

"My head's still throbbing from all the noise," Nicholas replied as he pulled the tissue out of his ears. "We knew Cryptic's Followers might try to dig their way in. If they succeed they know they can stop us as well as past students like our dad and Henry Lowe from taking some field trips."

"It would also make Cryptic think more highly of his Followers in the area," Jonathan noted. "You know, score some points with the big guy."

116

"I wonder who the second man was?" asked Mikaia.

"He must be a new Follower since we didn't recognize him," replied Jonathan.

"Of course we have to stop them!" exclaimed Mikaia. "Any suggestions?"

"If we were evil like the Followers, we'd simply put some of the old charges in the mine where they're digging and blow them up along with more of the tunnel," Jonathan said.

"That's a good idea," Nicholas replied.

"What do you mean? We're not going to blow two people up! That would make us as bad as they are!" exclaimed Mikaia.

"Of course not, what I meant was that Jonathan's plan to use the charges to bring down more of the mine tunnel to seal the entrance was a good idea. We just do it when Sam and his friend are gone," replied Nicholas.

"Oh, okay, that's a good idea," agreed Mikaia.

"It would take weeks of work for them and they'd realize they shouldn't bother to keep digging if we were only going to keep blowing it up," Nicholas replied.

"Do you want to do it tonight?" asked Jonathan.

"I doubt that they'll be working much more today. Between the hard work, noise, and dust, they really can't work for a very long time," replied Nicholas.

"Early tonight sounds good to me," said Mikaia.

At dinner the triplets explained to their parents

what they planned to do that evening.

"So, you plan to stop the Followers by blowing up more of the mine tunnel near the cavern entrance?" their dad asked.

"Yes, we felt that would discourage them so they'd leave the time machine alone," replied Jonathan.

"What about the entrance through the cupboard in the old school?" Mom asked.

"That whole section leading to the cavern and time machine was entirely blown in by Cryptic. It would take them months to clear that away," Mikaia answered.

"You know the one thing we haven't thought about is if they try to dig down to the cavern from above," Nicholas added.

"That would be highly unlikely since anyone going up the road to the old school would see their diggings and report it," replied Dad.

"That would be a hard thing for them to explain. People aren't allowed to dig tunnels on school property without permission," Nicholas added.

"Then it sounds to me like you have no choice but to seal the cavern entrance to protect the time machine," Dad agreed.

Their mom looked down for a moment and said, "All I ask is that you be very careful."

"Mom, you know we will be and you also know we have some unusual responsibilities," answered Mikaia.

"Yes, I know," she replied.

The triplets decided they would travel by way of the time-slide sign since they needed to go into the cavern and retrieve the radio transmitter that Nicholas had left next to the time machine. Besides jamming incoming signals, it also sent them. They could use it to set off the explosives they would retrieve from the bag they had buried at the end of the tunnel.

From Mikaia's room they popped into the cavern.

"I'm sure glad the cavern with all the wiring and crystals still glows. It makes it a lot easier to find things," Jonathan said. They pulled back part of the invisibility shield that covered the time machine.

"I agree," said Nicholas. He reached down and grabbed the radio. "I don't feel any vibrations so they've probably stopped digging for the evening. Let's pop to the tunnel's end and dig up some explosives."

They all made the sign and reappeared up the tunnel.

"Time for the flashlights!" Jonathan said. "If you two point them down, I'll use the small shovel I brought."

"Just be careful, Jonathan. A blunt force could set them off," Nicholas reminded him.

"No problem! I'll be as careful as an anthropologist digging up valuable fossils!" he replied as he carefully started moving the dirt away.

Leaving the bag in its uncovered hole, Nicholas untied it and pulled out three explosive devices.

Jonathan tied the bag back up and refilled the hole.

"These should do it. They have the longest antennas left of the ones we clipped. Now let's go back down the tunnel a-ways, just below where we saw them digging earlier," Nicholas directed a they made the sign and reappeared near the gas generator.

"No one's around. Let's get to work," Jonathan said and they moved up the tunnel to where the jack hammer lay on a pile of rocks.

"We'll add some extra wire to the antennas to make sure they'll receive the signal. Nicholas, you decide the best place to put them so we can cause a cave-in at the cavern entrance."

Mikaia and Jonathan added wire to the antennas as Nicholas searched around the tunnel for the best three locations.

"Are you about ready?" asked Nicholas. "I want to place one behind this large rock along the tunnel wall, but I'll need you two to help me move it out a bit."

"We're done. Now which rock?" asked Jonathan and Nicholas while aimed his flashlight at it.

They all took hold and pulled. The rock reluctantly rolled a couple of feet away from the wall. Nicholas shined his flashlight behind it as he bent down to place an explosive.

"What in the world!" Nicholas said.

He pulled a small rock back out.

"Do you see what I see?"

"That's white quartz with wide golden veins of...gold!" yelled Jonathan.

"That's what it looks like to me," said Mikaia. Nicholas handed it to her and knelt back down.

"Behind the rock we just moved there's a large vein of this leading down and into the ground. This must have been uncovered by the explosion and Sam didn't see it behind this large rock," Nicholas reported while he stood up holding several more loose quartz rocks.

Both Jonathan and Mikaia looked at the gold veins that led down into the ground.

They all looked at the gold vein.

"It looks like the mother lode to me!" said Jonathan. "There's no telling how much more is in there or how far that vein goes. This certainly creates a bit of a problem."

"Everyone knows that there is still plenty of gold

left around these foothills. They just don't know where," said Nicholas.

"It looks like we know where at least some of it is," replied Mikaia.

"Do you feel like becoming gold miners?" Jonathan asked enthusiastically.

"That would be fun for three kids from San Francisco. We could have our own claim!" Nicholas replied.

"There's only one problem," cautioned Mikaia.

"Yeah, I know," Jonathan said sadly. "Sam and his friend are coming back tomorrow. If we start digging and picking they'll see it and figure out that they might as well grab it before we do."

"Then we'd have them mining and digging into the cavern. They'd end up with a lot of gold and destroy the time machine. What a bummer!" Nicholas said.

"It looks like we have only one choice and that's to do exactly what we planned on doing," replied Mikaia.

"For some reason I don't like that choice so much anymore" Jonathan said. He reached down and placed a couple of gold quartz rocks into his pockets.

"I hate to say this but I agree with Mikaia," Nicholas replied. "We'll keep the Followers from getting the gold and stop them from destroying the time machine. That's the most important thing. Besides, what would you do with a lot of gold?"

"Have you ever thought I just might like to collect

gold instead of historical documents?" Jonathan exclaimed.

"Yeah, you and the rest of the world!" Mikaia replied.

"You're right though. As the custodians of the old school our first priority is to protect it, even if we can't become millionaires!" Jonathan added.

"Then it's agreed that I place the charges?" asked Nicholas.

"Fine with me," said Mikaia.

"Me too," Jonathan answered, picking up as many loose gold quartz rocks as he could.

Nicholas placed the other two explosive charges about fifteen feet apart further down the tunnel. They then made the time-slide sign and popped into the old school.

"The charges should receive the signal from here and we won't be anywhere in the mine tunnel in case the explosions trigger other cave ins," Nicholas said. "I've turned the radio transmitter to channel five which is the one Sam used when he set the charges."

"We might as well blow it," said Mikaia.

"There goes my new hobby," Jonathan said as Nicholas sent the signal. They felt several strong vibrations.

"I bet the earthquake center in Sacramento picked up on those. They'll probably record it as a small quake. But no problem, they get a couple hundred tremors each year so I don't think they'll come out to investigate," Nicholas said as he put the radio in his pocket.

"Are you ready to go back to my room?" Mikaia asked. Her brothers nodded.

When they got home their parents were anxious to find out how things had gone.

The triplets explained what had happened.

"And you say you actually found a vein of gold behind the rock you moved?" their father questioned.

"We sure did," said Jonathan. He emptied his pockets and put the gold quartz rocks onto the kitchen table.

"Wow, you're right. That is gold and there is quite a bit in those rocks," their dad said. He carefully examined them as Nicholas pulled out the rocks he'd picked up and laid them down next to Jonathan's.

"It looks like you three have a new collection," said their mom.

"It sounds to me like you did exactly what you had to do given the circumstances," their dad said. "The gold will always be there, but if someone ever mined it he would be sure to find the cavern and the machine. You protected the time machine which is much more valuable than gold. We're proud of the choices you three make again."

"Thanks, Mom and Dad. It will take forever to clear away the rock piles which block the entrance to the cavern," Mikaia said with a big smile.

"Hello! Sam? Why are you calling me? We were going to meet in the tunnel in an hour...What do you mean don't bother to come?...The tunnel caved in?...How did that...the part we were digging in is the only part of the whole tunnel that caved in?...You think the triplets blew it up?...The generator and jack hammer are gone?...You can say that again!...Yeah, you told me how they threatened you when you were trying to set Phil up for the dynamite...I agree. Something more drastic has to happen to them, kids or no kids. We can't carry on our business with them around...I'll contact Cryptic...He's not going to like this...He has to let us use all our 'resources' to stop them...I know he wants to enjoy his revenge, but we can't do anything with them still around. He'll have to listen...Yeah, I'll let you know."

Chapter Nine

Football and History

"Aren't you going to finish your breakfast?" Mom asked.

"Sorry Mom. We've got to get to the school for practice and Dad already has the car running," answered Mikaia as the triplets ran out to the Odyssey.

"Let's go Dad. The coach gets upset when we're late," Nicholas said and he jumped in.

"You boys are really starting to like football," their dad replied.

"Actually, we mostly don't like being yelled at," said Jonathan. "At least today we're being put into teams and not just doing conditioning."

"Do you know what positions you're going to play?" Dad asked.

"Hopefully we find out today. The coach already knows the positions we want, but he says he'll put us where we can do the team the most good. Jonathan still has a chance as water boy!" Nicholas said with a laugh.

"And if I'm lucky enough to make water boy,

you'd better check every bottle I toss your way or you may be running other places besides on the field!" replied Jonathan laughing.

"Then I've changed my mind," said Nicholas. "Now I'm rooting for you to make bench warmer, just to keep you away from my water!"

"Boys!" yelled Mikaia.

When they approached the middle school, they could see the football players gathering at one end and the cheer leaders on the track near the bleachers.

"Shall I pick you up at noon again?" their dad asked.

"Fine, Dad, thanks," said Mikaia as they hurried out of the van.

"Hi, Mikaia!" Marie called.

"Hi Marie!"

"Do you think you're going to make the team?"

"I hope so. I do like the routines and cheerleading is a great way to stay in shape for soccer. Besides, I'll be able to keep an eye on Nicholas and Jonathan while they play football," Mikaia replied.

"Yeah, I plan on doing that too," said Marie as she looked out onto the field.

"I'd say you're doing great, Marie, and have a good chance of making the team on Friday."

"I hope so. Candy has to cut fifteen girls to get to the ten team members and most of the girls look very strong."

"If we keep working hard, hopefully Ashlee, you, and I will all be on the team together," replied Mikaia walking with her to the bleachers.

"Okay now, everyone listen up!" Coach Lombardi yelled as the boys stopped their activities and hurried over.

"Today I'm setting the offensive and defensive teams. I may want to have some of you play both ways later on. I've watched you practice and noted your strengths. I know what positions you want to play, but I'll be placing you in positions that will help the team most. We have enough players to field a full team so a few of you will be asked to leave. If I don't call out your name you can still help the team, but you won't be playing. Any questions?...Okay. Pay attention! As your name is called get behind your team captain, Calvin Hill for the offense and Brad Owens for defense.

The coach started reading through his list of names as various boys took their places behind their captain. "Frazier, Nicholas, offense, for now a running back... Vidali, offense, receiver...North, offense, tackle...Lopez, defense, defensive back...Frazier, Jonathan, defense, also a defensive back...The coach kept reading until only a few boys were left standing.

The boys followed their captains over to one of the assistant coaches who broke them into various positions for more specific conditioning and practice.

"Congratulations, North! You made the team and get to play offensive tackle," Nicholas said as he patted him on the shoulder.

"I didn't think I would," he replied.

"Naw, you're good, and if the coach keeps me as a running back, I want to follow you through the line. You will open up a big hole for me, won't you?"

"I can't think of much I'd rather do!" replied North as Larry came over.

"Hey, we're all playing offense and I get to receive the ball!" Larry said with a smile.

"Yeah, and then get creamed by a defensive back like Jonathan," Nicholas replied with a laugh.

"I hadn't thought much about that," Larry said as his smile disappeared.

Across the field Jonathan, along with Will, was being taught some of the basics of tackling while Brad helped the defensive coach learn some of the players' names.

Near the end of practice Nicholas found himself at the water cooler with North.

"I owe you and Jonathan a lot," North said as he put a cup under the cooler. "I just want you to know that Arnold's Dad and Grandfather, Sam Hawkins, don't like you or your sister. I think they'd even harm you if they could. I'm not sure why, but I know that Arnold doesn't plan on being friends with you either. He says it's a family matter."

"Thanks for warning us. We knew that Sam Hawkins and Arnold don't want us around but we don't even know his dad," replied Nicholas.

"He's not around much. He has a small trucking company near Mariposa and is on the road a lot."

"What's his name?" asked Nicholas.

"Oh, he's Frank, Frank Hawkins."

"He doesn't drive a large silver sixteen-wheeler with two red strips down each side, does he?"

"Yeah, that's the rig he usually drives, why?"

"Let's just say we've seen that rig in town a couple of times."

"I just wanted you to know," North said as he tossed his water cup into the waste container.

"Are you still hanging around with Arnold?"

"No way, not after what he did to me. Besides I was getting tired of being bossed around by him. I've got better things to do now," North said and he ran back onto the field.

"Hi kids!" Dad said as he pulled up. "How'd it go?"

"It looks like I get to tackle everyone, Dad," Jonathan answered.

"Then I take it you're going to be a defensive back?"

"Yep, I get to knock everyone down!"

"You're really into that knocking down stuff aren't you Jonathan?" Mikaia asked.

"It's a tough job, but somebody has to do it!"

"How about you, Nicholas?" his dad asked.

"It looks like the coach is going to try me as a running back."

"Hey, I'll get to knock you down at practices!" Jonathan exclaimed.

"That's where Mikaia's dancing lessons will come

130

in handy. I'll just two-step around you," replied Nicholas with a smug look on his face.

"How about you, Mikaia?"

"Well, Dad, I've got the routines down and seem to be getting Candy's attention, so I think I've got a chance. I just hope that Ashlee and Marie will make it too."

"Yeah, it would be nice to have the three of you cheer us on to victory," Nicholas added.

"And Marie can watch me smack them down!" Jonathan said with a smile.

"By the way, I've got to drop something off at the bank for Mr. Peters. Hope you don't mind."

"Not at all Dad," replied Jonathan. "That's just a stone's throw from the ice cream shop!"

"I think I follow you, Jonathan. Here's a ten, the ice cream is on me," Dad said. He pulled up in front of the Bank of Opportunity and the triplets jumped out.

"This will taste good after the warm practice today," Mikaia commented as they hurried down the street.

"At least it's been cooler than the ninety-degree weather they usually have around here in the late summer," Nicholas replied.

Just as they were passing the Café, Phil Steward walked out. They paused for a moment and he took a couple of steps towards them.

"I just want to thank you kids for what you did. I never thought I'd be saying that but now I can see that you've been right about a lot of things," Phil said.

"Thanks, Mr. Steward. We appreciate hearing that," said Mikaia.

"If Bill Peters hadn't told me what Jonathan said to Sam Hawkins, I never would have known about Sam's attempt to stick me with everything he'd done. Enough of friends like him! Mabel and I plan to mind our own business from now on...if we're allowed to."

"We're pleased to hear that, Mr. Steward," Nicholas replied.

"If there is anything we can do to help, we'd be glad to," added Jonathan.

"Thanks! It's amazing how the three of you are more mature and caring than many of the adults around here," Mr. Steward said and he walked off.

The triplets looked at each other for a moment, then hurried into the ice cream store. Willow was at the counter when they lined up.

"What if I serve Mikaia and Nicholas first, then you Jonathan, since I know you like to read through all the flavors before you order a double chocolate chip," Willow said.

"How'd you know our names and remember what ice cream I order?" a surprised Jonathan asked.

"Everyone in town knows who the Frazier triplets are, Jonathan, and it's part of my job to remember what people order. People like to feel remembered," she said.

"Then bring it on!" Jonathan exclaimed. Willow handed Mikaia a rocky road, then Nicholas a mint chip, and finally Jonathan his double chocolate chip.

When Jonathan pulled out the ten dollars their dad had given them for the ice cream, Willow said, "Thanks, Jonathan, but it's on the house this time."

"That's nice of you," said Mikaia.

"You can thank my boss for that. He read about the near drowning rescue in the Journal and told me that the next time you came in, the ice cream was on the house!"

"Well, be sure to thank him for us, Willow," Jonathan replied. He put the ten back into his pocket, took a lick of his double chocolate chip, and headed out the door followed by Mikaia and Nicholas.

On the way home Nicholas told them about his conversation with North by the water cooler.

"So Frank Hawkins owns that truck," said their dad.

"Yeah, and he's obviously a Follower just like his father, Sam," Nicholas said.

"And Arnold's probably a Follower wannabe," added Jonathan.

"I sure hope he doesn't become a full-fledged member," said Mikaia. "That kind of sickness has to stop somewhere in a family."

"We'll need to watch for Frank. We don't know what he's capable of doing yet," advised Nicholas.

"But we do know that North doesn't want to have anything to do with Arnold," Nicholas shared.

"That's the good news," commented Dad.

"Actually, there's more," Nicholas said.

"More good news? I like that," he replied.

"We just saw Phil Steward leaving the Café and he thanked us for what we did to convince Sam not to set him up," Jonathan summarized. "He basically told us he wanted nothing to do with the Followers anymore. But I could read in his mind that he was still scared about what Cryptic might do to him."

"I would be too," Dad said. "If Cryptic and his Followers are able to hurt him or Pete Rider, they'll certainly stop others from ever thinking about getting out of their grasp."

"We'll need to keep our eyes open for anything they may do to harm them," added Mikaia.

When they got home, Mom had some sandwiches waiting. While they all sat at the kitchen table eating, the triplets told their mother what had happened.

"Most of that is good news. I'm glad to hear you two boys made the team and you received more free ice cream for your rescue. That was a nice gesture. By the way, you received another letter from Lowe Middle School. This one is from a Mr. George and it's addressed to all three of you," said Mom.

"Mr. George?" asked Jonathan.

"He's going to be our Social Science and English teacher," replied Mikaia.

"Oh yeah, that Mr. George, "Jonathan said.

"I left it by the hall phone," said their mother as Mikaia retrieved it.

"What does it say, Mikaia?" Nicholas asked.

"It welcomes us to Lowe Middle School and to his

Social Science and English classes. It says that since we will be studying about ancient world history and geography this year as a class project, we're required to write a paper on our family history. We're supposed to follow it back as far as we can and research the lives, problems, and accomplishments of our family members and the people around them. It says that because we're all from the same family we can turn in a group research paper. Since there are three of us, he expects an exceptionally well written and researched paper," Mikaia explained as she read.

"Man, that sounds like a lot of work!" Jonathan exclaimed.

"Mr. George does say that he's giving us a head start since he knows we'll want to do a good job on the paper," Mikaia added.

"That's sure nice of him to help end our summer like that," said Nicholas sarcastically.

"Actually, we could use the time," Mikaia replied.

"What do you mean?" asked Jonathan. "We're already doing all kinds of stuff like football and field trips!"

"I think that's what Mikaia's talking about," replied Nicholas.

"More time for football?" Jonathan asked.

"No, for field trips," replied Nicholas.

"I've got it. We can simply take a field trip and visit our Fraser ancestors and interview them," Jonathan exclaimed.

"Something like that," replied Mikaia.

"Then I'm ready! Let's go!"

"Hold on, Jonathan. We need to do some research to determine where we should go and in what year. We need to find our earliest recorded ancestors," Nicholas explained.

"We all know that from our Dad's side we're from the Fraser Clan of Scotland!" Jonathan replied.

"Yeah, but how far back can we trace our Fraser heritage?" Mikaia asked.

"Legend traces our name back to Jules de Berry, a tenth century French gentleman who was kind to King Charles the Simple serving him a plate of strawberries. The king knighted him with the name 'Fraser' which is French for 'strawberry'. Since then the Fraser coat of arms has always had strawberry flowers on it," their dad explained.

"We're related to strawberries?" Jonathan asked.

"That's the primary legend," their dad replied.

"What else do you remember, Dad?" asked Nicholas.

"Well, the earliest named Scottish Fraser was Gilbert de Fraser around 1109 A.D. He lived in Scotland along the border with England," Dad explained. "You have to remember that since most people couldn't read or write, the Fraser name took on various spellings over the years. Like we spell our name with a "z", but no matter how it's spelled, we're all still related."

"How do you remember all this, Dad?" Jonathan asked.

"Where you come from has a lot to do with who you are today, so it's important to know your family history. You've probably forgotten, but over the years both your mother and I have told you about your paternal and maternal family backgrounds. It's just that now, with this assignment, you've become interested and ready to learn more about it."

"We have learned how important history is. We've seen for ourselves how family characteristics and personalities can be passed down and how one set of events causes later events," Nicholas shared.

"In a way, Mr. George is doing us a favor, isn't he?" stated Jonathan.

"That's a good way to look at this assignment," Mom. "It will let you discover more about yourself and give you a greater appreciation for your heritage."

"What else do you remember, Dad?" Mikaia asked.

"Over the years the Frasers had several strongholds in the southern part of Scotland. They even had some nice castles."

"Now we're talking!" Jonathan exclaimed.

"Probably the best example of one of our castles that's left today is Castle Fraser near Aberdeen and Kenmay. That one was built in the late 1500's by Thomas Fraser and added onto later by Michael then Andrew Fraser in the 1600's"

"That's where I want to take a field trip!" exclaimed Jonathan, "back to our own castle!"

"That's probably a good time to get a feel of what was going on and what the people were like," their dad replied.

"Okay then, it's Castle Fraser," Nicholas said. "But we'd better hit the internet and library to dig up a little more information before we travel there."

"I'll check the internet tonight," said Mikaia.

"And I'll pull out some books and material I have on our family and let Jonathan and Nicholas read through them," Dad added.

"Hello Sam? This is Frank...Yes, I did contact Cryptic...He is getting bored with the triplets and told me we can do whatever we want...Yeah...He just doesn't want too big a problem in the community and nothing that can be traced back to him or us...He also wants us to deal with Phil and Pete once and for all...He gave me a little present he says we can use. With that, I've got a plan that will get rid of all of them at the same time...It will cause a stir in the community for a while, then become a passing mystery...I'll come by the store tomorrow to fill you in..."

"This stuff is even more interesting than reading historical documents!" Jonathan said as he lay across Mikaia's bed and read one of the books their dad had given them.

"Mine gives us more information on the Frasers in recent history," Nicholas added, sitting on the

138

floor.

"I'm getting a lot of good stuff off of my computer," Mikaia replied as she read through an article she'd called up.

"I was just thinking about Cryptic's Followers as I read through some of the conflicts in English/Scottish history. It's always an advantage to know exactly who and where your enemies are. Tomorrow I want to go to the antique store and size up Bo Flanders."

"What do you mean, size up, Nicholas?" asked Jonathan.

"I want to see if we can find out whether he's a Follower or not. Maybe you can try to read his mind again, while we're asking questions, Jonathan," Nicholas explained.

"I could try," Jonathan replied.

"That's a good idea," added Mikaia. "We know about Sam, Evelyn and Frank Hawkins. We also know that Phil and Pete want out and that Sam's attorney friend, Mitch Steffini, is probably a Follower. But we're not sure about Bo or anyone else in town."

"Fine with me," Jonathan said. "Then after practice we'll stop by the store. Besides I want to buy a little something I saw in there a few days ago."

"An original copy of the U.S. Constitution?" a grinning Nicholas asked.

"I don't think Bo could find me one of those," Jonathan replied. "No, just a little something."

That night Nicholas had trouble falling asleep. He found his heart was racing but he couldn't figure out why. He was a bit worried about their role as the custodians of the old school and the responsibilities it entailed. He also knew that Cryptic would be much happier if something happened to the three of them. He was used to being concerned about that. No, it was something else.

It was completely dark. Nicholas was being bounced around like he was in a large box. He sensed that others were with him, but he didn't know who. Suddenly there was bright light and he found himself falling and spinning. He could hear loud noises and then a terrible scream. Then there was complete silence, almost like he was in a complete vacuum.

Nicholas finally heard a faint and distant voice whisper, "It's only fair".

With that he found himself sitting up in bed, his heart still racing. Apparently, he had fallen asleep, at least for a moment.

Chapter Ten

Bo Flanders and North

The next morning their mom had breakfast ready for them. Their dad and Jonathan were already eating and even Mikaia had beaten Nicholas to the table.

"Hey, Sleeping Beauty, why are you looking like you fell out of the castle window?" Jonathan asked.

"I had another dream or premonition last night. It was hard to sleep before and after that," Nicholas said as he thumped down in a chair. "I might need a cup of Dad's coffee this morning, Mom."

"How about a half, that's all that's left."

"I'll take it," Nicholas replied.

"Well?" said Mikaia.

"Well what?" replied Nicholas.

"What was your premonition?"

"Oh, okay. First, I was in something dark, like a box. Then I saw the light as I tumbled and fell and I heard screaming. Then a distant voice whispered, 'It's only fair.' That's about it," replied Nicholas.

"That was it?" Jonathan asked.

"Yeah, I guess you really had to be there to get the full creepy effect," Nicholas added as he ate some scrambled eggs.

"It sounds to me like Cryptic is at it again... Some kind of warning," said Mikaia.

"That's what I figured," Nicholas replied between sips of coffee.

"I sure wish there was a way to keep that guy away from us," said Jonathan.

"To keep him away from everyone around here," Mikaia added.

"I'm taking off in about five minutes if you want a ride. I have a meeting this morning too," their dad advised. "With this last premonition I want you all to be very careful!"

They all grabbed what they needed and hurried out to the Odyssey.

"Dad, on the way home after practice can we stop in town for a few minutes?" Mikaia asked.

"More ice cream, Mikaia?"

"No, just a little business at the antique shop," she replied.

"More custodial work?" asked her dad.

"Yep, we need to clear up a few things."

"Fine with me," he said as he pulled up near the athletic field.

"Look, North is already out there exercising," said Jonathan

"Great, he's really into this and the other players are beginning to like him. Besides, the stronger he gets, the bigger holes he can make for me in the line when I run through," Nicholas pointed out.

"That's one of the holes I plan on filling during practice," Jonathan said.

He and Nicholas ran onto the field as Mikaia joined Marie and Ashlee.

After a couple of hours of practicing in their assigned positions, Coach Lombardi decided to try a couple of plays against the defense to see what they had learned.

Calvin was going to play quarterback. Nicholas took a position next to him with Larry to the far right side. North was playing right guard and Jonathan defensive back. Calvin had called a passing play to Larry. The ball was hiked as Larry shot out then crossed back across the field. Calvin threw a nice pass to him at the very moment Jonathan hit him. Both the ball and Larry went tumbling.

"Nice hit, Frazier," the coach yelled. "And there was good timing on that pass between Hill and Vidali. But take it easy. We're not in helmets and pads yet so go light on the contact."

"Man, Jonathan can hit," Larry said in the huddle as Calvin called a running play over North's position. North considered this a real honor. The ball was hiked as Calvin faked left then handed the ball to Nicholas. Nicholas shot through a nice hole in the line made by North only to be greeted by Jonathan who grabbed him as they both fell.

"Nice hole, West, and that's the way to hit it

143

Frazier. Jonathan, again a great play, you really have a knack for figuring out where the ball is going," the coach said. They ran a few more plays before stopping for the day.

"Good going, Jonathan," Larry said.

"And thanks for those big holes, North," said Nicholas. "Now if we can only stop Jonathan from filling them so quickly, maybe I'll get my hundred yards," he continued with a smile.

"Man, Jonathan, you're dynamite!" said Nicholas as their dad drove up. "But I've got a sneaking suspicion I know why."

"Well, if a man can't read minds when he needs to, what good is it?" Jonathan replied.

"You've got a point but you have to be careful how you use it," said Nicholas.

"That's just it. I try not to, but it happens automatically most of the time. I usually just ignore it, but when I'm concentrating on something, it just happens."

Mikaia arrived and they all got into the car.

"Did everything go well today?"

"Great Dad," Mikaia said gleefully. "I think I made the team."

"Isn't the final selection tomorrow?" Dad asked.

"It is, but Candy had me lead the group for a couple of the routines, so I could show the others the proper way to do them. I felt good about that!"

"I can see why. Good job. I think you've got a shot at a position."

"How about you guys?"

"The coach had us run a few plays just to see how fast we caught on," Jonathan replied.

"I hit some nice holes in the line made by North, but Jonathan always seemed to be wherever the ball was," Nicholas added.

"I guess I was just lucky," said Jonathan.

"It sounds like more than luck to me," Mikaia shot back, giving him a sharp look.

"I've got to pick up a couple of items from the grocery store. Why don't we meet back at the car in fifteen minutes?" said their dad.

"Fifteen it is!" Nicholas said as the three of them bounded out the sliding door and headed towards the antique shop.

"Before we talk much to Bo, I want to see if he has any new merchandise," said Nicholas.

"You mean bottles, don't you?" asked Mikaia.

"Yep! But I bet you'll take that time to check out the antique dolls." Nicholas returned.

"And I'll see if he has gotten an original copy of the Constitution," Jonathan said as he followed them with a smile.

When they entered the store, they saw Miss Ivy talking to Bo. Bo looked over at them and said, "The Fraziers, glad you came back. I'll be with you in a moment."

Miss Ivy turned around and smiled as she looked back at Bo.

"Then Bo, as a businessman in town you do plan

to contribute to our annual Gold Festival coming up next month?" they heard Miss Ivy ask.

"Of course, you told me that my sister, Terry, promised you a couple of weeks ago before she died that she would contribute. So, if she was going to, I'll definitely honor her decision. You can count on the antique shop for a donation. Besides, it sounds like an exciting way to raise money for our city schools and parks."

"Then speaking for the committee, I thank you and also welcome you to our beautiful and historic town," Miss Ivy replied, turning to leave.

"It's nice seeing the three of you again," she said as she walked out the door.

The triplets noticed that there were more bottles and dolls to look through, but decided since they were the only ones in the shop it was a good time to talk to Bo.

"Hi Bo," Mikaia said. "We're glad you have new things for us to check out."

"Yes, I want my customers to see that I'm trying my best to have available the items they want. By the way, you're welcome to buy as much as you like!" he said with a laugh and a smile. Mikaia smiled back.

"It's nice that you're going to donate to the town fundraiser," Mikaia said. "I couldn't help but overhear your conversation with Miss Ivy."

"Yes, she's a nice lady and I know Terry would want me to donate."

"I hope you don't mind my asking if Terry ever

said anything to you about the 'Followers'?" Mikaia asked as Jonathan carefully concentrated on Bo.

"The Followers? What kind of Followers?" he asked with a confused look on his face. "Is it like a Masonic or Rotary group?"

Mikaia surprised by his response, managed to answer. "It's more like a secret society we've heard of since we moved here. We were just wondering, since you were also new to Opportunity, if anyone had said anything to you about it?"

"I can't say that they have, that I remember. I suppose if it's a secret organization, newcomers wouldn't be told much about it. Why are you so interested?"

"We just heard from someone that if anything goes wrong around here, then often the Followers know about it," Mikaia replied.

"Then that certainly is a strange group and a group that would probably want to remain secretive," Bo said.

"Yeah, I guess you're right. We're just curious."

"It's good to be curious and learn new things," Bo replied.

"Bo," Jonathan said. "I'd like to buy this pocket knife."

"That's a nice little one. It's actually quite old."

"I know. I once had one like it for a short time," Jonathan replied as he handed the knife to Bo.

"It's good and sharp and I can let you have it for twelve dollars."

"That's a fair price," Jonathan said and handed him the money.

"We're kind of in a hurry right now or we'll miss our ride," Nicholas said. "We'll come back soon and take a closer look at your new items."

"I'll look forward to that," Bo replied as the triplets left the shop.

"You sure threw the Followers right at him, Mikaia," said Nicholas. "Jonathan, could you read anything?"

"You won't believe this, but when Mikaia asked him about the Followers he wasn't really sure what she was talking about. He was searching his mind, like he had heard something a long time ago, but he really couldn't remember. I don't think he's a Follower," concluded Jonathan.

"I was hoping that was the case," said Mikaia.

"You kind of like that guy," Jonathan said.

"I was hoping he wasn't a Follower since he seemed so nice. But I was also hoping he wasn't so there'd be one less Follower to worry about."

"We still need to be cautious, but I feel Jonathan is right," Nicholas added. "Also, I don't feel we need to worry about Miss Ivy being a Follower."

"Yeah, I felt that too," Jonathan replied.

"Even though Terry wanted us to believe that Miss Ivy was trying to stop us from getting the Creekside Mining claim in order to save Jonathan, it seems that was a lie," Mikaia added. "From what I heard her just say to Bo, she was just trying to get a donation for the Gold Festival."

"That's the way it sounded to me," Jonathan agreed.

"Then that's good news. Probably two people we can cross off our list," said Nicholas.

"What's this with the pocket knife, Jonathan?" Mikaia asked.

"That's the other reason why I wanted to come here today. I remembered seeing this knife here a couple of weeks ago. It looked almost like the one I found in the trunk, the one that belonged to James Noah. After I gave it to him I wanted to replace it and I remembered seeing this one. Now it's mine!"

"So now you're carrying both the pocket knife and the brass bell?" Nicholas asked.

"Most of the time, but not when I go to school. Wow! We still haven't asked if it's all right to bring cell phones to school. If we could get Dad to let us have them, it would save us some time," Jonathan added.

"Yeah, we need it to call our parents and friends. Between each other we have telepathic phones!" Nicholas said as they all laughed.

They met Dad at the Odyssey. On the drive home, he reminded them of the chores they needed to do before they could do more research on their relatives at Fraser Castle. After all, they needed to earn their allowances and there was always more to do around a ranch.

The next morning they were all up earlier than

usual. Mikaia was excited because she had to perform a cheering routine in front of Candy and two other cheerleading coaches who'd make the final team selections. The boys were excited because they'd get their uniforms, helmets and pads and be able to run some real plays later in the morning.

"The first guy I want to tackle is Josh," Jonathan exclaimed. "He tripped me up a couple of times in practice. Now that he's an offensive end, I can't wait till he gets the ball. I'll make him wish he was playing water boy."

"I'm sure glad to hear you don't hold any grudges, Jonathan," Mikaia said, eating some cereal.

"Yeah, that does sound kind of childish," Nicholas added.

"Did it sound that bad?" Jonathan asked as he buttered some toast that had just popped up out of the toaster.

"Yeah, you tripped me so I'll bang into you," Mikaia answered.

"Oh, well let me rephrase it then," Jonathan replied. "I can't wait until I can use the skills the coach taught me in order to help the team."

"That does sound a lot better, Jonathan," said Nicholas.

"I'm glad to hear it. But I still plan on knocking his lights out!"

"Boys!" Mikaia exclaimed as she shook her head.

"Are you about ready to go?" Mom asked. "Your dad's on his way to the car."

"I'll take this last piece of toast with me then," Jonathan replied. He got up and hurried out with Mikaia and Nicholas close behind him.

"Good luck, Mikaia!" Nicholas yelled as she headed towards the bleachers.

"She'll be selected," Jonathan said. "Like I said before, she's not only good, but she's the bendiest girl I know. She can work her through any routine."

"I think you're right. I'd like to have her at our games cheering us on," Nicholas said as he slapped North's hand when he passed by.

Coach Lombardi led them into the team room near the gym. He explained to them how to put on their new equipment and how it would help and protect them. One of the assistant coaches clarified how it would affect their ability to see and move and how to adjust to its limitations.

"Now put on your equipment and meet me on the field in twenty!" Coach Lombardi yelled out.

Meanwhile Mikaia, Ashlee and Marie were anxiously waiting for their turn in front of the judging panel.

"Are you nervous, Marie?" Ashlee asked.

"Yes, I can't wait to get it over with!"

"Me too," added Mikaia. "I think I'm next."

Mikaia's name was called and she stepped out onto the track in front of the panel and other girls. The music started and she energetically did her routine. There was applause when she walked back to Ashlee and Marie.

"You nailed that, Mikaia!" enthused Ashlee.

"I hope I can do half that well," Marie said as her named was called.

Marie received a nice applause as did Ashlee who performed after her.

"Now for the wait," Ashlee sighed as the last few girls finished their routines.

Candy, along with the other two judges, walked over to the far side of the bleachers to compare notes for their final selections.

Meanwhile, out on the field, Coach Lombardi was shouting instructions.

"I hope you all study the play books you've been given. If you don't I'll know right away when you mess up your assignment and that won't make your teammates very happy either. Now let's run through what we practiced yesterday!"

The boys worked on a few plays a got used to their equipment. Jonathan found that with his new shoulder pads he could tackle even harder without bruising his shoulders. This seemed to make him quite happy as he moved around the field making most of the tackles for the defense.

Likewise, Nicholas and Larry found that being tackled wasn't as bad as they'd expected, now that they had on some protective gear. Nicholas discovered that he could anticipate where the best hole would be to run through. He figured that like Jonathan with his mind reading, it was probably due to his ability to foresee the future.

Back at the cheerleader tryouts, the girls listened anxiously as the chosen names were announced.

"Edger's, Mello, Rivers, Frazier, Wilson..." Candy L'Heur continued reading as Mikaia and Ashlee hugged, then waited anxiously to hear if Marie's name would be called.

"Smith, Von, Roddy, and Edwards," Candy read out as Mikaia and Ashlee looked over to Marie who looked like she was about to cry.

"But you were so good," Mikaia said. "I just knew you'd be selected!"

"I guess I wasn't," Marie sadly replied.

"Sorry girls! I just read out nine names. The tenth member of the team is...Jimenez. Congratulations to all of you. See you all at practice!" Candy added.

With that the girls hugged each other as they giggled and jumped around.

"This is exactly as I hoped it would turn out!" Ashlee said, "the three of us cheering together!"

Coach Lombardi had just released the team for the day. The boys were making their way to the locker room to change when North walked up to Nicholas.

"Nice plays today," he said.

"That's because you made some pretty good holes for me to run through," Nicholas replied.

"I just wanted to tell you that I'm glad you and Jonathan talked me into going out for football. I really never thought that I'd be on the football team."

"I think if you keep working like you have in football, you will be able to do anything you want to do," Nicholas replied.

"Thanks!"

"How's Arnold doing?" asked Nicholas.

"I try to stay away from him. A couple days ago he came to me trying to buddy up again, but I know what he's really like. I don't think he's hanging around with anybody right now. Most people will talk to him but they don't really trust him."

"That's too bad. I know he's not the easiest guy to like," Nicholas said.

"I did hear something that bothered me," said North.

"What's that?"

"When we were talking, he got a call on his cell phone from his Dad. I heard him saying something about Mr. Stewart and Mr. Rider. When he finished the call he was laughing," North said.

"I know Arnold knows those men," said Nicholas.

"Yeah, so do I. He kept saying something about his Dad having a real surprise for them at four tomorrow afternoon that would solve a problem for him. I don't know what it was about, but knowing a little about his Dad, Frank, it got me wondering."

"It could be anything. I know that all of them used to hang out together," added Nicholas.

"Yeah, it's probably just Arnold trying to act big again," North said as he started to walk away.

"I'm just curious. Did Arnold say anything about where they were supposed to surprise Mr. Steward and Mr. Rider?"

"They did say something about the old school, but I'm not exactly sure."

"Thanks, North. We'll see you Monday morning at school for orientation, and then back on the field for practice."

By the time the boys got back to the car, Mikaia had already told their Dad and Mom about making the cheerleading team.

"Good going, Mikaia," Nicholas said as he gave her a little hug.

"I knew you were the best!" Jonathan said and he patted her on the back. "Now you can cheer me on as I knock them all down. By the way, did Marie make the team?"

"And Ashlee?" Nicholas asked.

"They both did. That's why I'm so excited,"

"Great, the more fans the better," Jonathan said.

"Jonathan, you sound to me like you have already been invited to the Pro Bowl?" his dad said.

"I guess I am a little psyched, but...the Pro Bowl huh? Yeah, some day that would be fun," replied Jonathan.

"With your gifts from the Master Inventor you'd probably make it," Mikaia said. "But I don't think that is what he had in mind when he gave us our powers."

"I know you're right. I need to be careful, but it sure is fun knocking everyone down," he replied with a big smile.

"I hate to stop the party, but I had a talk with North just now. He overheard a phone call between

155

Arnold and Frank, Arnold's father, about having a surprise for Phil Steward and Pete Rider tomorrow. He told me because he seemed to be worried," Nicholas shared.

"What kind of surprise did he think they were planning?" Dad asked.

"He wasn't sure. It's supposed to happen tomorrow afternoon, at the old school. It sounded rather sinister when Frank told Arnold that it would solve a problem for him."

"Maybe they're just getting together to talk,"

"Or maybe they're getting ready to do something to the old school or the cavern," Mikaia suggested.

"It could be anything. I am a bit worried. We know that Frank and Sam Hawkins don't like Phil and Pete because they don't want to be Followers anymore. I think we should be nearby, just to see what's going on," Nicholas suggested.

"Sounds like a plan to me," Jonathan agreed.

"As always, you three be careful," Mom said.

When the triplets got home they decided to take care of their chores before doing more preparation for their field trip to Fraser Castle. Mikaia was concerned that their clothing would look out of place in the 1600's, so she and their mom had been working on an appropriate dress for her and shirts and pants for the boys. They had originally planned to take the field trip in the morning.

"I say we spray for those darn spiders in the garage from now on," Jonathan said as he walked into the kitchen. "They just crawl right back up after I knock their webs down."

"Did your Dad put you on spider patrol again, Jonathan?" his mother asked.

"Yeah, I must be his insect specialist! Nicholas got to clean up stuff in the barn and Mikaia is doing the laundry. I'd give anything to stop chasing spiders."

"We do need about a hundred-foot trench dug from the barn towards the back field with piping dropped in to drain a low spot," his mother replied.

"Man, Mom, that's not much better than chasing spiders. Don't you need a few shelves in the kitchen lined?"

"Sorry, Mikaia and I took care of all that a few weeks ago."

"Who gets to line shelves?" Nicholas asked as he walked in.

"Nobody, now," replied Jonathan.

"How's Mikaia doing on the laundry?" asked Nicholas

"She's folding it up in her room," Mom replied.

Nicholas and Jonathan started for the stairs.

"Nice pile of laundry you got there, Mikaia," Jonathan observed.

"It should be. I washed four loads."

"I bet you didn't come across even one nasty spider with that job," noted Jonathan.

"No. I think they all realize by now they need to wait for you in the garage."

"Not to change the subject, Mikaia, but do you

157

and Mom have the clothes fixed up that we'll need to wear on our trip to Scotland?" Nicholas asked.

"Just about. We still need to take the zippers out of your loose cotton pants so we can sew the front up."

"Don't sew my front up. It just may come in handy," Jonathan said.

"You worry too much, Jonathan. They're going to put in a draw string," Nicholas replied.

"Then I've got to pull the whole thing down!" Jonathan said.

"Welcome to the world of girls!" Mikaia said. "Don't worry, you'll figure it out."

"Do you think we should still take the field trip tomorrow if we're going to check on Frank and Sam in the afternoon?" asked Mikaia.

"Time wise it should be fine, since we won't lose any earth time when we slide through to the 1600's. But we may be tired, depending upon how long we stay at Fraser Castle," Nicholas replied.

"I say we go for it!" Jonathan exclaimed.

"Then I need to finish our clothes," Mikaia said, carrying a stack of laundry down the hall to their parents' room.

"And I need to do some last-minute research," said Nicholas as he left for his room.

"Me too," Jonathan said and he followed Nicholas down the hall.

Chapter Eleven

Castle Fraser

The next morning when they awoke the boys each found some clothes folded on the end of their beds. Jonathan quickly pulled on his baggy pants and tightened the draw string just to be sure he'd know how it would work. He then slipped the long sleeved baggy cotton shirt over his head and let it drop down to his upper hips. Walking over to the mirror, Jonathan stood there for a moment looking at himself as Nicholas walked in wearing his outfit.

"Not too bad. All I need now is a broad sword," Jonathan said, using both hands to pretend he was swinging a heavy sword.

"Actually, the way we look we'd better be carrying a shovel or walking behind an old horse and plow," Nicholas replied.

"Yeah, I think you're right. We don't look like we belong in a castle, do we."

"Remember, we're only visiting. I don't think they're going to ask us to stay for dinner," said Nicholas.

"Actually, I was hoping they would. A boy can get

real hungry plowing behind a horse."

"Just remember, in those days, that old horse you were plowing behind could be part of the evening meal. You never know," Nicholas replied.

"In that case maybe we should bring a pizza," said Jonathan.

Mikaia walked in wearing a fluffy white blouse with a long brown and blue skirt that hung down to the floor and a white cap tied over her head.

"All you'd need is a couple of beer mugs in your hands and you'd look like a serving wench in one of those grog shops," Jonathan said, looking over at her.

"At least I wouldn't look like I'd been at the back end of a horse all day," she replied slightly offended.

"Well you made these! What ever happened to shining armor and stuff like that? Maybe you could fix something that would make me look like a knight?"

"First of all, we're only twelve! Secondly, as a knight, if the castle men don't know you, they could feel threatened and charge you!" Nicholas replied. "But as a simple farm boy, they may let you look around."

"You're right. Okay, I'll be a simple farm boy."

"You look like you didn't get much sleep again," Mikaia said as she looked at Nicholas.

"I did have another premonition last night, but nothing that I need to share right now. I'm fine."

"So, what's the Essence going to be that we'll be following?" Jonathan asked.

"I think the best essence would be the big picture of Fraser Castle and the chapter from that old book about when it was built," Mikaia suggested.

"I agree. That should leave a time-slide trail that Hither and Yon can send us on. But they will have to work harder, since it's not a personal Essence from the 1600's," replied Nicholas.

"Then let's eat a big breakfast, just in case the castle chef is planning horse for tonight's dinner. Then we'll go over to the old school and slide," Jonathan suggested.

Mikaia and Jonathan waited on the front porch while Nicholas ran up to his room to get his leather sandals and a couple of other items for the trip.

"All ready finally?" Jonathan asked.

"Let's go!" replied Nicholas.

"I'll just pop over to the school," Jonathan suggested. "I don't want anyone to see me looking like...an ancient farm boy."

"Didn't we agree that we'd only use our powers when we had too?" reminded Mikaia. "Besides, who's going to see us hike to the old school from here?"

"You're right, let's hike," Jonathan replied.

As they approached the old school they paused in the apple orchard to be sure no one was around. Then they ran out onto the playground and climbed up onto the slide, Jonathan first, followed by Mikaia and Nicholas.

"This is the furthest we've ever gone on a field trip before. This should be fun!" Nicholas exclaimed.

"On ready, set, go, think Midst!" Mikaia yelled, as they started down the slide. Like so many times before, they found themselves floating into the swirling, white, cotton candy fibers, then landing softly on the clouds of Midst.

"I'd like to be the first to welcome the three of you back to Midst," Yon said as he approached.

"Thank you, Yon," said Mikaia. "It's good to see you again."

"I hope you all have a nice field trip today. We can't wait to be of service to you," Hither added.

The triplets looked at each other for a moment wondering what happened to Yon's Spanish and Hither's western speech. Jonathan spoke up, "Hey, what happened to the western and Spanish stuff you learned from your television?"

"Oh sir, we couldn't be that common. We are very refined and proper gentlemen," said Yon as he gave them a slight bow.

"Did you find a new channel on your television?" Jonathan asked.

"Maybe something from 18th century England?" Nicholas added.

"Oh no, young man, we just wish to leave a worthy impression of ourselves. We want you to see how capable and responsible the two of us truly are," Yon replied.

Nicholas looked around very quickly then asked, "Your television seems to be gone. Did Halo make you give it away?"

"You got it! He took that puppy right out of here when he saw it!" Yon replied, his proper speech slipping.

"Yon!" Hither called out.

"Oh, I'm terribly sorry for my unfortunate comment. I meant to say that our esteemed friend and guide nicely suggested that we not participate in that particular media for the present. He kindly disposed of the distractive item for us," Yon replied.

"So, he didn't like your Spanish or western speech?" Jonathan asked.

"He said we sounded like channel surfers, whatever that means, and that he hardly understood what we were saying."

"That's exactly it, my fine young friends, and I for one have to admit that I find our present conversation much more appealing, especially for such an important place like Midst," Hither added.

"Actually, Hither didn't like my Spanish anymore," said Yon. "I was getting so good at it that he couldn't understand anything I was saying! Isn't that right Hither?"

"That is true. I was getting tired of being called 'hombre' and being told to come 'pronto'. Besides, Halo did suggest that we needed to be more dignified and create a more professional environment. I have to say that I thoroughly agree with him."

"He basically said to do it now!" Yon added.

"That was a prime motivator," Hither had to agree.

163

"I'm glad you two are getting this worked out, but we are on the longest field trip we've ever been on," Mikaia reminded them.

"That is true. We humbly ask for forgiveness and are immediately at your service," Hither replied. "As before, we are both pleased to be able to work together to make sure you arrive at your appointed destination."

"Then can we leave now?" an impatient Jonathan asked.

"At this very moment," Hither replied with Yon beside him. "Now hold hands, close your eyes, and we'll do the rest."

In an instant the triplets could feel a strong wind blowing across them. They heard electrical sparking and hissing as everything turned white and they found themselves sitting in some dirt.

Mikaia and Nicholas were startled by a loud yell followed by, "What in the world is that?" When they turned in the direction of the voice, they saw an alarmed Jonathan face to face with a large goat. The goat's green eyes and runny nose were almost against Jonathan's forehead. The goat didn't seem alarmed at all by Jonathan's sudden appearance but kept right on chewing whatever he had in his mouth.

"Jonathan, it's only a goat," Mikaia said standing up.

"It might be only a goat to you, but from my perspective it's not the first thing I expected to see. Besides, its nose is running and slimy. Do you want to come over and take a look?"

"Where do you think we are, Nicholas?" asked Mikaia.

"If you ask me I'd say we were in a goat pen," Jonathan interjected.

"Seeing those small stone houses over there, with thatched roofs, I'd say we're definitely not in Opportunity anymore," They all continued to look around.

"I think I see the castle," Mikaia said pointing to a tall cone shaped tower protruding above some trees about a mile away.

"I hope it's our castle," Jonathan said. "I mean Fraser Castle."

As they started walking towards the castle they saw a woman raking in a large vegetable garden next to one of the stone houses. Another woman was carrying a bundle of large sticks through the doorway of second house. More goats appeared among them as did a few sheep and chickens as they continued.

"Don't they keep their animals penned up?" Jonathan asked as he side stepped a slow chicken.

"They probably know who owns each animal and this way they can find food for themselves," Nicholas replied.

"I'd have a hard time knowing which chicken was mine and which chicken was somebody else's. They all look the same to me," said Jonathan.

"I guess you get used to them. You would recognize that goat again if you saw it wouldn't you,

Jonathan?" asked Nicholas with a laugh.

"I sure would, but I'd have to get closer to it than I'd ever want to again to see if it's that same one!" Jonathan replied.

"I hope it's our castle, Fraser Castle."

"Look over there?" Mikaia said as she turned to her left. "That boy looks a lot like you, Jonathan.

"No, he doesn't," replied Jonathan, "although we are kind of dressed alike. He's used to not having a zipper."

"I meant because he is plowing behind a mule," Mikaia said and she was the next to laugh.

"Wow, no dignity for that poor guy. At least I'd be plowing behind a jet-black stallion. I'd look good!" Jonathan said.

A boy approached them with an empty water

bucket in each hand. The triplets stopped him as he started to walk by.

"Excuse me, could you please tell us where we are?" Mikaia asked as sweetly as she could.

The boy paused for a moment looking like he wanted to move away as soon as he could.

"You are in the Grampian Hills near Aberdeen," he replied with a strong Scottish accent and started to leave.

"Is that Castle Fraser?" Mikaia said pointing.

"Aye" he replied.

"Where are you going?" Mikaia asked.

"I'm walking down to the River Don to fill these buckets. I have to put the water out for the livestock."

"Do you mind if we walk with you for a moment. We're new in Aberdeen and are trying to learn more about the area," continued Mikaia.

"You are strangers, and I don't know who you are."

"In that case, I'm Mikaia, and these are my brothers Nicholas and Jonathan Frazier."

"Then you're part of Clan Fraser?" he asked, looking a bit more comfortable.

"I guess you could say we are distant relatives from the border country," Mikaia replied.

"Then my name is Alex. My father is named Alex too. I'm named after him. We are tenant farmers."

"What's a tenant farmer?" asked Jonathan.

Alex looked curiously at him, and then said, "My dad rents farmland from the Frasers. We grow crops and pay them money from our sales in town and give them food."

"Oh, so you're in business together with them," Jonathan said.

"Aye, but we do all the work," replied Alex walking towards the river. "It can be a very hard life. We don't know if we will grow enough food to feed the family and pay the rent. Then if there is a war or a feud, we have to hide or be killed."

"It does sound like a hard life," Jonathan stated.

"We're a bit disoriented because we have come a long way. Do you know what day and year it is?" Nicholas asked as they walked along beside him.

"It is Thursday and the year is 1640," Alex replied. He looked back at Nicholas and asked, "Do you not keep track of the years in the border areas?"

"We do. It's just that I had forgotten," Nicholas answered and Alex nodded.

"Have you lived here all your life?" Nicholas continued.

"Aye, my father feels it is wise to stay near the Castle for protection. As you know between the feuds and the English troops in the area, it is not safe to wander too far."

"Are the Frasers feuding?" Nicholas asked.

"It seems they are always feuding," Alex replied as another boy walked over.

"Who is always feuding?" he asked as Alex looked rather uncomfortable for a moment.

"They are just asking me how safe it is around

here and I was telling them my family stays near the castle for protection." Alex tried to change the subject a bit.

"It is good for us to stay together, just in case the English or their mercenaries come by and want something," the boy said.

"This is Simon, my friend. He lives in the castle. We meet by the river sometimes and do things together. Our parents don't really want us playing together. You won't tell them, will you?" Alex asked.

"Of course not," Mikaia asked. "But why can't you play together?"

"It can just be awkward," replied Simon, "because my father is Andrew Fraser, the Lord of Castle Fraser. I am not supposed to spend time with the tenants. But since there are not many boys my age around the castle, Alex and I have become friends."

"Your father won't mind if you spend time with these three," said Alex.

"Why? They look like farmers to me," Simon replied.

"It is because they are Mikaia, Jonathan and Nicholas...Frazier...from the border area."

"Then you are relatives!" Simon said with delight.

"Probably, but distant," replied Mikaia as Alex splashed a bucket into the River Don.

"What are you doing in Aberdeen?" Simon asked.

"We're on a quest," said Nicholas.

"What kind of a quest?" asked Simon.

"We're trying to learn more about our ancestors,

our heritage."

"Does not your family teach you these things?" asked Simon who seemed a bit confused.

"Of course," responded Nicholas, "but we're trying to learn more about the rest of the Fraser Clan."

"That does sound like an adventurous quest, especially when you're so young."

"Our family felt that we were strong enough to take this journey and to do it before we had greater responsibilities," continued Nicholas.

"Aye, I wish I could pursue such a quest! It would be exciting to travel the countryside and learn about the rest of my Clan. You should come to the castle with me. My father would be pleased to greet you."

"We'd like to meet him," Mikaia replied.

Simon's eyes grew large as he yelled, "Quick everyone, duck down below the riverbank!"

Everyone ducked down and they all heard several men gallop by on their horses.

"Who were they?" Jonathan asked as the horses disappeared up the road towards the castle.

"They were several of my father's men just returning from scouting our land and collecting tenant rents. They must not see me with Alex or they'd have to inform my father about where I was and who I was with. If they had seen the three of you alone, they would have immediately taken you to the castle. If you walk in with me, you won't be bothered,"

Simon replied.

"You go ahead, Simon," Alex said. "We can meet again tomorrow and maybe you could bring your three relatives."

"If that's possible I will do so," Simon said as he walked up the river bank followed by the triplets.

"Are there a lot of Frasers around Aberdeen?" asked Jonathan.

"Our Clan is growing, but many Fraser Lords were killed at a battle in 1544 at Clanranald on the shores of Loch Locky."

"What kind of battle was that?" asked Nicholas.

"The Frasers had been feuding for many years with the Mac Donald Clan over land, water rights, and clan leadership. They finally decided to settle it. Over two hundred clan leaders fought along the banks of Loch Locky until only five Frasers and eight MacDonalds were left standing. Since then both clans have been rebuilding."

"That's a rather drastic way of solving problems," Mikaia said.

"That is true. But often for us Scots, loyalty and honor are more important than life. You should know that," replied Simon.

"Yes, we understand," agreed Nicholas.

"Hey, look at that man wearing a dress!" Jonathan exclaimed.

Nicholas quickly added, "You mean that man wearing a kilt?"

Jonathan paused for a moment looked over at

Nicholas and then continued, "Aye, that man in the kilt. I was just wondering who he was."

"Simon looked over at Jonathan for a moment then said, "That is Lord Fraser, my father. He is just back from a hunt. He is wearing the Fraser hunting tartan and kilt. He likes to dress formally when he hunts deer. Besides, the dark green tartan makes it harder for the deer to see him when he sneaks up with his bow."

"Simon, come here lad. And who do you have with you?" Lord Fraser asked.

As the triplets approached they observed a tall, strong looking man with the air of nobility and the confidence that went with it. He had a curious smile on his face as he handed the reins of his horse to a stable boy. He was dressed in his hunting tartan kilt, a waist high buttoned jacket and had a shawl like blanket, with the same tartan, wrapped around his shoulder and arm. He wore dark green and blue socks, with a diamond pattern pulled up almost to his knees.

"Father," said Simon, "I would like to introduce some Frasers from the border country. They are Nicholas, Jonathan, and Mikaia."

Not knowing exactly what to do, the triplets all stood still and slightly lowered then raised their heads.

"It's a pleasure to meet you, Lord Fraser," Nicholas said.

"And a pleasure to meet Clan relatives from the

borders," he replied.

"The three of them are on a quest to learn more about our Clan and to meet northern clan members," Simon shared.

"Ah, that is a worthy quest. You are welcome to sit at my table and enjoy our hospitality."

"We'd be honored," replied Nicholas.

"You have a most beautiful castle," Mikaia stated as she looked up at the four-story tower with a conical top that added another story to the impressive stone cut building.

"Aye, that it is. My grandfather, Thomas Fraser, built the first part in 1575, which was a rectangular tower house. Then my father, Michael, added the four story tower. By the new stone, you can see I just completed the last addition. It has a large Z-plan four story building and additional tower. It was very costly and a lot of work, but well worth it."

"It does our Clan proud," commented Nicholas.

"Join with Simon and me in the grand hall for a bit of refreshments. You certainly must be hungry and thirsty from your trip."

"We would appreciate that," Mikaia replied.

They followed Lord Fraser through a large, high and very heavy wooden door into a big open room. The ceiling was close to three stories high. At one end was a fireplace in which they all could have stood, with an arched rock front and an inviting fire that crackled when they approached. There were several large wooden chairs, each with several pillows on them lined up near the fire. A rectangular table with more chairs sat at the center of the hall. A young woman in a long brown dress with a white linen apron approached.

"Would you care to have some fine apple cider that we make ourselves from a grove near the river?" Lord Fraser asked.

"That sounds great to me," Jonathan answered.

"Then, Kaylee, bring a mug for each of us along with that delicious shortbread I hear you have been making."

Kaylee, curtseyed and left as they took seats by the fire.

"So, you're seeking answers about your relatives?" he asked.

"Yes, about our relatives and ancestors," replied Nicholas.

"Well, as you know we Scots are a mixture of 6th century Celtic settlers from Ireland, 8th century Normans or Norsemen, Angles from England, and a variety of other adventurers. We seldom get along but we are unified in keeping Scotland free from English rule. Clan Fraser is of Norman origin with one of the bloodlines brought by a knight named Frezel from the Anjou region which is now France."

"Wasn't there also a Frenchman named Jules de Berry who was knighted by King Charles with the name 'Fraiser' after strawberries?" Nicholas asked.

"You have done some studying. That is probably why we have strawberry flowers on our clan coat of arms, but many suspect that is a legend. The earliest Scottish Fraser was Gilbert de Fraser who in 1109 lived near you in the Borders."

"So Clan Fraser goes back to the 12th century?" Mikaia asked.

"That is where we trace it. But our proudest moment was when our Clan, under Simon Fraser in the late 1200's, supported Sir William Wallace in the first years of our fight to free ourselves from English tyranny. Then we fought with Robert the Bruce until we had him crowned as the first Scottish king in 1306. Those were difficult, but proud times!"

"You sure know a lot about our history," Jonathan said as he was handed a mug of cider and some Scottish shortbread.

"It is the duty and privilege of every Scotsman to know our heritage. That is probably why your family let you travel on this quest. They know how important it is."

"My Lord, my Lord!" came a voice from the front door.

"Yes Barth, you may enter," Lord Fraser replied.

Several men, who looked like the ones they had hidden from earlier, walked in.

"When we were collecting rents from some tenants in the south near Gyllerock, they complained of a band of poachers stealing their livestock. They said they last saw them heading north. We searched but couldn't find them. However, we just got word from a local tenant that he had seen them east of the castle."

"Then have my horse readied and procure some provisions for we ride to protect what is rightfully ours! Have my sword and light armor brought up," Lord Fraser ordered as he turned to the triplets.

"You must forgive my quick departure. As you heard, duty calls. I'm sure my son, Simon, will extend to you further hospitality. It was a pleasure meeting you. Please send my salutations to your parents and our Clan along the border," Lord Fraser said as he hurried from the hall.

"Is your father often called away on such matters?" Mikaia asked.

"There is always something that needs to be done to protect our lands and tenants," replied Simon. "That is why my father added on to the castle. It is more functional and also offers better protection for more people. The stone walls are three feet thick. It would take a strong army to overpower us."

"As Lord Fraser's son, are you being trained to one day take over all these responsibilities?" asked Nicholas.

"Of course, I have lessons in arms and warfare, castle business, politics, history, literature and many other areas. My mother, who is presently visiting some relatives in East Lothian, even instructs me in music. I remain quite busy. That's why I enjoy sneaking off now and then to do things with Alex."

"We probably need to be on our way," Nicholas said. "We had planned on being a few miles north east of here before sunset."

Simon seemed a bit surprised as he asked, "What is your destination?"

"Our goal is to reach Edinburgh in the next few days," replied Mikaia, "where we're expected to meet our uncle," she added trying to make Simon feel better about their quick departure.

"I was hoping you could spend some time at the castle. I seldom receive guests my age."

"Maybe we could visit again sometime?" Jonathan stated.

"I'd like that," Simon replied. Nicholas stood up and slowly moved toward the door

Mikaia and Jonathan followed him.

"Be sure to thank your father for his hospitality and please tell Alex we enjoyed meeting him," Mikaia said as they turned toward a dirt road that seemed to travel north.

"That I will do," Simon replied and the triplets headed up the road.

"I feel bad about leaving so soon," Nicholas said. "But, we have learned a lot and need to get back home."

"Let's walk through the countryside for a mile or two before we leave. It's so beautiful with the river winding among the rolling green hills and forests," Mikaia said.

"That's fine with me. It's a nice day for a hike anyway," replied Jonathan.

As they walked they watched the sunlight peek

down between the tree branches that overhung the narrow dirt road before them. They could hear a bird and the whispering sound of the river running along beside them.

"This is very pleasant," Mikaia said as she looked around.

"They sure have worked hard piling a lot of stones to make all the stone fences we've seen," Jonathan remarked.

"Wood can be hard to find and cut. Those stone fences mark their property boundaries forever," Nicholas said. "The stones are piled high enough so few animals can get out...except for that doe that's hopping the fence in front of us," he added. He pointed in the direction of the deer.

"That deer is moving! Something must have really scared it," replied Jonathan.

"They look so graceful when they run," noted Mikaia.

"And I see what scared it!" exclaimed Nicholas, looking through some trees that ran along a stone wall where the road made a turn.

The three of them paused for a moment when they saw three men climb out of a wagon pulled by two horses. The men hopped the stone wall and ran out into the pasture and grabbed a startled sheep.

"I think I know where those animal thieves are," stated Jonathan.

"Good guess," Mikaia said.

The men carried the sheep over the wall and

placed it in their cart before starting back for another.

Jonathan got a big smile on his face which meant something devious was about to happen. "No one knows us around here, right?"

"Right, why?" asked Nicholas.

"We can't let them just steal Lord Fraser's sheep, so let's have some fun," he replied He made the time-slide sign and immediately disappeared, then reappeared standing in the back of the men's cart. Nicholas and Mikaia stood there for a moment trying to figure out what he was up to.

"Hey you guys, it's not nice to steal!" he shouted from the back of the cart as the men, who were holding another sheep, turned and looked.

"You there, get out of my cart!" one of the men yelled and all three of them carried the sheep toward Jonathan.

"Then we'll all get out," Jonathan said, dropping the first sheep off of the cart and jumping down.

"You had better be gone by the time I get there," the largest of the three yelled.

With that Jonathan made the sign again and popped to the spot in the pasture where the men had just grabbed the second sheep.

"Hey, you forgot these three! Do you need some help?" he yelled at them as they turned around to find him behind them now.

"How did you get over there?" the shorter of the three yelled.

"You told me to get out. I just thought I'd help!"

Mikaia got only a glimpse of the smile on Nicholas's face before she saw him appear in the back of the cart just as the men were approaching with the second sheep.

"You need a hand getting that one into the cart?" Nicholas asked. "It looks like the first one is headed down the road."

"Where'd you come from?" the largest man said as he dropped his end of the sheep and headed towards Nicholas.

"Looks like we'll have more than mutton tied up in our cart in a minute," he added as his friends laughed.

When he approached, Jonathan suddenly appeared in the cart standing next to Nicholas.

"Then you better have more rope than this to tie us all up with," Jonathan said as he picked up some rope from the cart and tossed it onto the dirt road.

The largest man immediately stopped and rubbed his eyes before taking another look at the cart. "How did you do that?" he asked.

Nicholas smiled, "Simple, we're leprechauns visiting from Ireland. We are just trying to make the world a little better!"

The second two men had dropped the sheep and were starting to back away from the cart. The largest one started moving towards the two boys who were still standing in the wagon. In an instant they both disappeared and reappeared back in the pasture right where the men had just been standing.

All three turned towards the boys and stared. Their mouths dropped open. For a moment none of them seemed to be able to talk.

"It's not nice to steal," Nicholas said. "Strange things can happen to a man who steals, especially from Lord Fraser."

The men weren't sure what to do. They looked both scared and puzzled. The largest man started walking back into the pasture towards them. "You two aren't leprechauns."

Just as he finished that statement, Mikaia suddenly appeared next to her brothers. "Then how about the three of us!" she yelled.

At that point the largest man started backing towards the cart of the other two men.

"We like it here in the Fraser country. We plan to stay for a while and keep an eye out for thieves like you," Mikaia added and the men quickly climbed into their cart.

When they heard the sound of hooves beating down the road, they turned and saw a cloud of dust rising.

"That would be our friend, Lord Fraser," Nicholas yelled.

Then the largest man cried, "Let's get out of here!" The shortest of the three pulled up a whip, snapped it over the horses' heads, and yelled "Gedup".

The cart jumped forward only to be jerked backwards a few feet as the rear wheel broke off. The surprised men fell to the ground. The shortest one looked around and said, "Someone's tied our wheel to that tree!"

The boys both looked at Mikaia who shrugged her shoulders and said," When Jonathan threw the rope from the cart, I got an idea. You didn't expect me to just stand there when you two were having all the fun, did you?"

"Good going, Mikaia," Jonathan said.

Seeing Lord Fraser and his men ride up the road, they all agreed through telepathy that it was time to leave. They waved at the three men, who were just starting to get up. The triplets held hands and thought back to exactly what they were doing and thinking the moment they slid down the slide...then vanished.

When Lord Fraser and his men rode up, they heard the thieves mumble something about the Frasers having Leprechauns as guards.

After a few seconds of swirling cotton candy like fibers, the triplets landed in their seats at the old school.

"Welcome back," Tique said. "You slid way back in time on this field trip."

"Yes, it was exciting," Mikaia replied, "and no Cryptic or his Followers to bother us."

"The thieves could have been Followers," Jonathan added, "but I was having so much fun I forgot to ask them."

"Then as always, let's critique. What did you learn

on this field trip?"

As usual, Jonathan spoke up first. "I learned that life was hard in the sixteen hundreds, especially if you were a tenant farmer just trying to make a living and survive. It was also hard if you were the landowner, because you always had to protect your land and the people who worked for you."

"Very good, Jonathan, everyone has to do his part for man to survive. What did you learn, Nicholas?"

"I learned a lot about our Clan Fraser, which should make for a great early family history report. I also found out that the clans were always feuding and killing each other over land and especially politics. It seems that even when things were going well, somebody would have to find something to be upset about. That's kind of sad. I just wish people would cooperate with each other."

"Thank you, Nicholas. There have been brief periods of time when people have gotten along. I also wish we would all work hard to share and cooperate," Tique replied. "Now how about you, Mikaia?"

Mikaia sat for moment thinking before she said, "I learned that family is very important because we are a big part of each other's history. Our ancestors are part of what we are today. Even more important, the choices we make can affect our future family for generations. It's important to remember that and do what's right and best for everyone."

"You three have all brought some special understanding and knowledge back with you from this field trip. You are learning so many valuable lessons in your travels that will help you be better people and guides for others."

"I wonder what Lord Fraser said to those men when they asked him about his leprechauns?" Jonathan said and laughed.

"I can't help you there," Tique replied, "so class dismissed!"

The triplets waved goodbye to Tique as they left the old school.

"That was the most fun I've had on a trip in a while," Jonathan said. "And these pants turned out okay, zipper or no zipper."

"As long as you're happy," replied Mikaia.

"I do want to get home and change though," Jonathan added.

"We need to get ready to come back to the old school at four and see what Sam and Frank Hawkins are up to," Nicholas reminded the others.

"I hope everything is okay and they're not going to do anything harmful to Mr. Steward and Mr. Rider," replied Mikaia.

"They're probably just going to scare them," Nicholas said. "At least I hope so. But I am concerned about my premonitions. They do seem to fit in somewhere and I really haven't liked what I've seen in most of them."

"Then we need to be careful," Mikaia said as they walked through the apple orchard towards their ranch.

Chapter Twelve

Trapped

When Mikaia, Jonathan, and Nicholas arrived at home they shared with their parents what they had learned on their trip. Their dad was quite interested in Lord Fraser and the Fraser Clan. He knew a lot about their family history but wanted to know more about what the people were actually like. Jonathan especially enjoyed telling them about the sheep thieves and the leprechauns.

"You sure had a valuable field trip. I suspect your report can be written with a lot of insight and understanding for our background and history," Dad said.

"Yeah, we'll have to start working on that when we get back from the old school," Jonathan replied, "won't we Mikaia?"

"What do you mean, 'won't we Mikaia?' You're going to help too!"

"I just thought that..." Jonathan started to say.

"Your part is going to be writing about the common people, the tenant farmers," Mikaia quickly replied, "and even what it's like to be face to face with

185

a goat!"

"And I'll write about Fraser Castle and Lord Fraser," added Nicholas.

"Then I'll write about the rest of our early history and put your parts into the report," Mikaia said.

"That's a great plan," noted their mother.

"Okay, but I really want to add something about the thieves and the leprechauns. The thieves were common people," said Jonathan.

"Jonathan, you can't say anything about leprechauns or how we messed with the thieves. Remember, as far as our teacher, Mr. George, is concerned, we were never there," explained Nicholas.

"I was afraid you'd say that. Can't I just make it a legend we read about with three farmer kids who could do magic?"

"Jonathan! That's a different kind of story. This is family history," replied Mikaia.

"If it's family history, then it's a true story. We're part of our family, aren't we?" Jonathans asked.

"Jonathan!" shouted Nicholas in exasperation.

"Okay, okay, I get the point. I'll just have to write my own version after we finish the report."

"It's getting close to four. Didn't you say yesterday that you needed to go to the old school?" asked their father.

"Oh, yeah, we'd better get moving. We should be hiding nearby before four," Nicholas replied.

The triplets quickly changed and grabbed what they needed before hiking back to the old school.

"Hey, look!" Jonathan said as they started back through the apple orchard. Backed up in front of the old school was a silver big rig with two red lines down its side. One of its back doors was partly open.

"That's Frank Hawkins' truck!" said Nicholas.

"I wonder what they're up to," Jonathan asked.

"Who knows," said Mikaia, "but if we sneak around behind the old school and get a look in the back of the truck, we may find out."

"You think they're stealing things from the school?" asked Jonathan.

"If Sam's involved, it could be anything," Nicholas replied. "Let's sneak around and take a peek."

The triplets carefully worked their way through the orchard to the trees and bushes that grew along the backside of the school. Then they snuck along the side of the school, just short of the front stairs, where they could get a view into the back of the truck.

"It's kind of dark and hazy in there. Can you see anything?" asked Jonathan.

"I think I see a man sitting along the back wall. It looks like he's tied up." whispered Nicholas as Mikaia conveyed they should use telepathy.

Now I see him, Jonathan transferred.

I can't believe it, Mikaia thought. *It's Phil Steward! They have Phil Steward tied up in there.*

What do you think they're up to? asked Jonathan.

I don't know, but it doesn't look good, expressed Nicholas.

I wonder where Frank and Sam are, Mikaia

pondered.

I haven't seen anybody since we came through the orchard, replied Jonathan. *You keep watch and I'll jump into the back and get him out,* he added.

Be careful, Nicholas conveyed. *Something's telling me that we should get out of here.*

And leave Mr. Steward to the Hawkins? asked Jonathan.

No, you're right. Go ahead. We have to try and help him, replied Nicholas.

Jonathan took one last look around before he ran quickly towards the truck and jumped in disappearing through the partly opened right side door.

What's taking him so long?" expressed Mikaia.

Maybe he's having trouble with the knots. It's getting harder for me to see inside, replied Nicholas. *I still don't see anybody. I'm going in to help.*

Hurry back! Mikaia conveyed as Nicholas ran and jumped through the door.

Mikaia waited another couple of minutes but saw no sign from Jonathan or Nicholas. As she got more worried she also ran towards the truck and jumped in the back. It was dark and hazy inside. She could barely make out three forms lying on the floor up near the front. As she moved toward them everything suddenly went dark and she fell to the floor. A moment later the doors shut.

"What did I tell you? I knew that sleeping gas Cryptic gave me would do the trick," Frank said.

"That phone call to Arnold, that he made sure North heard, really did the trick. I knew North was getting soft and would tell his do-gooder new friends."

"Quick, let's get out of here and drive up the canyon along Old Ridge Road before somebody see us," Sam replied.

They both got into the truck and Frank cranked up the engine. "What about Phil's car that's parked just down the road?" he asked.

"That's just where I want it. Are you sure that Pete's going to meet us at the overview pull out up the canyon?" asked Frank.

"Yeah, I told him that Cryptic would let him go if he did one more simple job for him, but he needed to bring his car and meet us at the overview," Sam replied.

"Then it looks like we're about to solve several of our problems all at once," Frank said with an evil smile as he drove east.

After winding up Old Ridge Road a couple of miles, Frank pulled his truck onto the canyon side overview area where they both got out.

"This is perfect, Sam. Since they built the new road up and over the pass, Old Ridge Road is hardly ever used."

He looked down into the deep canyon below them.

"Here comes Pete now, right on time!" Sam said when they saw a car winding up the road.

"Okay, now what do you want me to help with?"

Pete asked as he pulled next to the truck and got out.

"We want to get rid of some stuff for Cryptic that's in the back of my truck. We need your help tossing it into the canyon," replied Frank.

"You know I have a bad back. Besides I'm thirty years older than you. How much help can I be?" Pete angrily asked.

"I told you that this was the last time that we'd ask you to help. You want Cryptic to let you go, don't you?" replied Sam.

"Yeah, I told all of you that," answered Pete.

"Then let's get moving," Frank said and opened the back door of the truck just a crack.

"Jump on in Pete, we're right behind you," Frank said as he put his hands down to help boost Pete up and in.

As Pete crawled in he made out four forms lying on the floor of the truck. He quickly turned towards the door and said," Hey, what's going on here?"

Just then the door slammed shut and within a moment, Pete joined the other four unconscious on the floor.

A few minutes later the truck doors opened and Frank jumped in wearing a gas mask. He quickly moved around the truck tying everyone's hands behind their backs. When the truck started to air out, Nicholas was the first to slowly awaken.

Nicholas squinted as the darkness quickly turned to light. "What's happening?" he groggily asked.

"Just sit still and enjoy the view," Frank replied.

"You'll all know soon enough."

Nicholas, he heard Mikaia think, *what's going on?*

I don't know, but the Phil and truck thing was a trap for us. That haze must have been some kind of knock out gas they'd put in here, Nicholas answered back.

You can say that again, they heard Jonathan express as he wiggled around trying to pull his hands free. *They've got our hands tied tight!*

Sam knows we can't pop away if we can't hold our hands up and make the time-slide sign. He obviously doesn't want that, expressed Nicholas.

"Where am I?" Phil Steward said as he slowly started moving.

"You're in the back of Frank Hawkins' truck with the three of us," Mikaia replied as they heard Pete Rider start to mumble something.

"What are you doing here? Sam told me to meet him and his son, Frank, at the old school so they could tell me the way Cryptic would let me out of being a Follower. Then they had me climb into the truck and that's all I can remember," Phil said.

"We came to help you. We thought that you and Pete Rider could be in danger from Cryptic and his Followers since you two wanted out," answered Nicholas.

"We got in the back of the truck to untie you but they must have had some kind of knock out gas in here," added Jonathan.

191

"You came to try and help me and Pete?" he asked.

"Yes, we knew you both didn't want to be Followers and wanted to live a peaceful life in Opportunity, so we came to see what Sam and Frank were planning. We fell into their trap too,"

"They told me to meet them here at the Old Ridge Road canyon overview," Pete shared slowly. "They said if I helped them one more time they'd let me leave the Followers."

"Looks like we're all in for it then," Phil said. "The fact that we're at the edge of the canyon isn't a good thing."

"Why's that?" asked Jonathan.

"Because it drops off several hundred feet into a deep wooded ravine, if we fall in there, we'll only be found by rattlesnakes!" replied Pete.

The triplets looked at each other for a moment. Their mental messages to each other expressed much concern. They could see Sam standing just outside the door of the truck and heard a car engine start up. They could see Frank driving Pete's car up to the edge of the canyon.

Nicholas, quick, back up next to me, Jonathan conveyed as he twisted different directions.

What are you doing? Mikaia, asked as she read the thought.

I'm trying to get my pocket knife out and I almost have it. I'll see if I can cut our ropes most of the way through. There, I've got it. Now a bit closer,

Nicholas, and Mikaia come closer too.

Jonathan carefully felt for Nicholas's ropes, and then moved up and down working behind his back to slice through them. *It's almost through. Now Mikaia,* Jonathan conveyed as Phil and Pete watched. After a few seconds Jonathan could feel that Mikaia's rope was cut most of the way. *Now take the knife from me and work on mine,* he told Mikaia as his back pushed up against hers.

This is hard, Mikaia said. A minute later the door opened further.

I think it's almost through, Jonathan expressed to Mikaia. *Quick, pass me the knife and move away. I'll try to slip it back into my pocket before they see it.*

"All right, now for the fun!" Frank said as he held up a big hunting knife. "If you don't do exactly as I say, I'll cut whoever's standing closest to me. It's time for the five of you to take a ride in Pete's car. Thanks for bringing it Pete."

"What do you think you're doing?" Phil yelled. "You can't do this. Cryptic won't like the attention and you'll get plenty when they find us at the bottom of the canyon."

"Actually, Cryptic supplied the sleeping gas and he doesn't mind if all of you, let's say, are missing. But don't worry, they'll certainly find you or at least part of the car," Frank said with an evil smile. "We loaded the trunk with a little extra gasoline so when it hits the hot engine and blows up, they're bound to see the smoke! Everyone will simply think you went for a ride together. They know that Pete and Phil are friends and that the Frazier kids are all over the place. It will be a mystery, but they'll never link it to us. We all like a good mystery, don't we?"

"They will get you. Several people know we came to the old school today because we found out you were planning a surprise for Pete and Phil," Nicholas explained.

"I don't think so. We've already covered our tire tracks at the old school, and only Phil's car is parked nearby. Without any evidence or the five of you, who can say for sure we did it?" replied Frank.

"You couldn't have already covered your big rig tire tracks. You didn't have enough time," Mikaia quickly declared.

"Of course we didn't. We told Arnold to arrive there at four thirty and conceal our tracks," replied Sam.

"You mean you'd let your son get caught up in this?" asked Nicholas.

"He doesn't know anything. He thinks that we're just going to scare Phil and Pete. We'll tell him we saw them driving away with the three of you when we showed up. We don't tell him much of anything, just have him do some chores for us once in a while," replied Frank.

"Let's get this thing over with," Sam exclaimed.

"You three kids get into the back seat. Pete, you get behind the wheel and Phil get in front next to him," Frank ordered as he swung the knife at Mikaia.

"Since you're all nice and tied up I'll be glad to open the doors for you...with my gloved hand," Frank said with a laugh.

"I'm warning you, we'll make sure you pay for this," said Nicholas.

"You and what other piece of charcoal?" Frank replied slamming the doors.

"By the way, Cryptic wished he could be here, but since he can't, he asked me to tell you 'fire and ice...it's only fair!'"

Do you think both of you can break your hands free? Nicholas conveyed to Mikaia and Jonathan.

I've already got mine off, Jonathan answered in his thoughts.

I do too, Mikaia added.

We can pop back to the old school, but what about Phil and Pete? conveyed Jonathan.

Remember in the cavern, when Halo, Dad and Henry Lowe, grabbed hold of us and popped us with them into the old school classroom when we were tied up? Nicholas expressed as both Mikaia and Jonathan returned a nod. *When we go over the edge we'll all make the time-slide sign. Jonathan, you lean forward and throw your arms around Phil's shoulders and I'll have mine around Pete's. I hope it works for us!*

"This is going to be quite a ride!" Jonathan yelled out as they felt the car being pushed toward the canyon.

"They are going to do it, Pete. I thought they were just going to scare us!" yelled Phil. When the car started tumbling over the edge and he began to scream.

"Now!" expressed Nicholas. The triplets made the sign as he and Jonathan threw their arms over the shoulders of Pete and Phil.

The car tumbled down into the canyon and exploded into a large ball of flames when it hit the bottom. Frank's big rig slowly wound up and over the Old Ridge Road Pass as the flames grew higher.

"Man, that was close!" Jonathan said as he found himself sitting in his desk at the old school with a scared and heavily breathing, Phil sitting on the floor next to him. Mikaia was in her desk and Nicholas in his with Pete on the floor next to him.

"What happened?" Pete yelled out. "We're not dead?"

"Why, did you want to be?" Jonathan found himself saying. "I hope you're not mad we saved you."

"How in the world did you do that?" a stuttering Phil asked.

"We told you long ago that we had certain powers given to us by the Master Inventor, so in a way, he actually saved you," replied Mikaia.

"Why would he do that after all we've done?" asked Phil.

"Because he cares about everyone and probably feels there is still good left in both of you, like we do," replied Nicholas.

"I can't believe you've been given that kind of power. Even Cryptic would be envious of it," Pete replied.

"That's the very reason he wants to get rid of us," Jonathan said.

"I for one don't," said Phil. "We owe you big!"

"That goes for me too," Pete agreed. "We've got to get to the Sheriff right away and tell them what Sam and Frank did to us!" he added.

"That could be a problem," said Jonathan.

"Why, they tried to kill us!" Pete exclaimed.

"Are you going to tell them that you escaped because a sixth grader threw his arms around you when you were halfway down the canyon and you suddenly appeared safe and sound in the old school?" Jonathan questioned.

Phil and Pete just looked at each other for a moment and shrugged their shoulders.

"I can see that would be a hard story for anyone to swallow," Pete said as he scratched his head.

"We're not going to just let them walk away, are we? Without us saying anything they'd get off Scott-free!" Phil said angrily.

"They may get off totally free from the Sheriff, but we'll have them where we want them for a long time," said Nicholas.

"How are you going to do that when you can't tell the Sheriff what really happened?" Pete asked.

Nicholas reached into his pocket and pulled out a small recorder. "Because of this. I tape recorded all that happened, all that they said. I'll just take out certain parts and the Sheriff will have enough to see they were the ones that pushed that flaming car they stole from Pete, into the canyon! I think the threat of that will keep them wrapped up for some time."

"I still think they ought to pay, somehow. What do we get from this but a near death experience?" Pete asked.

"You can control them too. I'll simply tell them that you and Phil also know about the tape. Besides, didn't they say you'd be out as a Follower after you helped with this one last thing?" Nicholas asked.

"That will probably let us live in peace around here," Phil agreed, "thanks to the three of you."

"I for one will get a real kick out of seeing the expression on their faces when I see them tomorrow in town and say 'howdy' as I walk by," Phil said with a smile.

"Come to think of it, I like that idea too. After all, they'll never know what really happened," said Pete.

"Then we're all agreed that it's our secret?" Nicholas asked.

"You got it, anything you want," replied Phil.

"Then if that's all settled, I've got a stolen car report to file with the Sheriff," Pete said heading towards the door. Then stopped and said, "By the way, thanks again. Anything you ever need, just ask!"

"Hey Pete, do you want a ride to the Sheriff's Office?" asked Phil.

"Oh, yeah, I almost forgot. Sure!" he said as they

both walked out the door.

"I have to admit, I think I liked the trip to Castle Fraser better than an afternoon with Sam and Frank. They don't want to play fair," Jonathan shared.

"We did allow ourselves to get trapped," replied Mikaia.

"Thanks to our powers we escaped without help from anyone. I wonder if Halo and the Inventor knew we'd use our powers and figure things out?" Jonathan asked.

"That's what they've been training us for," replied Nicholas. "Besides, my premonition turned out to be true."

"How's that?" asked Jonathan.

"A dark space, with others, then sudden and bright light, then falling and a terrible scream. That pretty well covers most of it," Nicholas said as he started towards the door.

"Now if you could've only figured out when and where these things were going to happen, we'd never have been trapped," Jonathan replied.

Then he and Mikaia followed Nicholas out the door.

"I do need to work on that," replied Nicholas.

"Speaking of work," added Mikaia, "we have an early family history report to write."

"Darn, I kind of thought we'd done enough work for one day," said Jonathan.

"You're right," Mikaia replied. "Let's take a break for the rest of the day."

Chapter Thirteen

Fewer Followers and A New Plan

When the triplets arrived home, they told their parents about the trap and all that had happened at the old school and canyon.

Their mother was relieved to hear that they were not only able to take care of themselves but to also save Pete Rider and Phil Steward.

Their dad felt that something needed to be done to keep Sam and Frank Hawkins from hurting anyone else, but he also understood why the triplets had agreed not to say anything.

"I just hope the evidence you have on them is enough to keep them in line," Dad said.

"Sam, especially, can't afford to have any trouble. He's still on probation for having explosives in town," Nicholas replied. "Frank has a business to run and a son, Arnold, who if pressured enough in court, would probably tell what he knows and place his father in an awkward situation. I think they'll lay low for a long time."

"The good news is that we're gradually getting rid

of Cryptic's followers," Mikaia said. "Phil and Pete are no longer followers and will do anything for us. Now they just want to live peaceful and productive lives in Opportunity. That's really hard to believe after the evil they and their ancestors have done around Opportunity. Even North no longer wants anything to do with Arnold or Arnold's father and grandfather. The ability of Cryptic and his few Followers to do evil has been weakened and overcome by good."

"I wouldn't be so sure of that," their father said. "You have done a tremendous job of neutralizing the Followers, helping others, and saving the power of the old school, but I'm afraid there is still more for all of us to do."

"What do you mean?" asked Jonathan.

"I was in town this morning and bumped into Bill Peters. He told me that the lawyer friend of Sam Hawkins, Mitch Steffini, had been in the bank asking for old real estate deeds and records. He found that rather strange and wanted to be sure I told the three of you."

"Why would that be something to worry about?" asked Jonathan.

"He seemed to be particularly interested in the old school land and Pete Rider's orchard property next to it."

"That is strange," Nicholas said.

"Then a little later, when I met Henry Lowe for coffee at the café, Henry told me that Mitch had also paid Jud Day a visit and was asking about old surveys of those same properties."

"I wonder what he's up to?" Mikaia asked.

"We know that he's a Follower, so I'd say he's up to no good," answered Jonathan.

"I wonder if he knows how the Rider family ended up with those thirty acres." Nicholas said.

"What do you mean?" his dad asked.

"Remember how Pete's grandfather, Fred Rider, shot Mary Hay's father in 1874 and chased Mary, and her mother Martha, off the land and back up into Yosemite?"

"Yeah, he didn't like Native Americans, so he chased them off, and then supposedly paid Mary's father one dollar for the land," added Jonathan.

"Do you think Pete Rider told Sam Hawkins about the evidence we had on Pete's family when we were trying to stop Pete's land development scheme next to the old school?" Mikaia asked.

"I don't know, but that could have something to do with Mitch Steffini's sudden interest in that land. We'd better ask Pete about it when we see him again" suggested Nicholas.

"You're right, Dad. It seems there is always something else to be concerned about," Jonathan said.

The next morning the triplets slept in and had a late breakfast. Jonathan was the first to wander into the kitchen followed by Nicholas, then Mikaia.

"Did I sleep well last night!" Jonathan exclaimed as he stretched his arms up over his head.

"Me too," added Nicholas. "After all we went through yesterday, I was expecting to have another premonition. Fortunately, I didn't."

"I fell asleep even quicker than that sleeping gas put me out yesterday," Mikaia replied.

"It sounds like you three could use a big breakfast," their mom said as she laid a bowl of scrambled eggs and a large plate of waffles down on the table.

"Thanks, Mom," Jonathan said. He licked his lips and forked the largest waffle.

Nicholas sat for a moment then spooned himself a large helping of eggs and grabbed a waffle. "That does look good, Mom."

"The three of you deserve it. Besides, if you're going to work on that family history report this morning, you'll need a good breakfast."

"I almost forgot about that," replied Jonathan.

"I think we each should work on our part of the report this morning, then go into town at noon and have lunch at the Cafe and Grill!" suggested Mikaia.

"Into town?" said their mom.

"Yes, we still have some business with Sam Hawkins. Not only do I want to see his reaction when he first sees us, but Nicholas has a recording he'd like to share with him," replied Mikaia.

"That will be fun!" Jonathan mumbled having just taken another big bite of waffle.

"I've recorded a few words of his and Frank's conversations yesterday on another tape, which I'll give to him. That way they'll both know we're not kidding," Nicholas added.

"Then we can have dessert at the Ice Cream and Candy Shop!" Jonathan exclaimed. "I wonder if Willow still remembers what kind of ice cream I like?"

"I guess we all have to worry about something," Mikaia.

"Let's get to work so we can go into town," said Nicholas. "Can somebody drive us?"

"I'll drive you," said their mom. "I have some bed comforters to pick up at the dry cleaners. Does noon sound okay?"

"Noon it is!" Mikaia said placing her dishes in the dishwasher and going up to her room.

When Mom drove the triplets into town she reminded them, "Remember that tomorrow you go to Lowe Middle School at eight-thirty for orientation until eleven. I'll be glad to drive you."

"Then I have cheerleading practice until one," said Mikaia.

"And we have football practice until two," added Jonathan.

"What if you pick us up a little after two? I'll spend the last hour watching the boys practice football?" Mikaia suggested.

"Then that's the plan," agreed their mom as she pulled into the grocery store parking lot. "I'll need to get a few things here before I walk down to the dry cleaners. I'll meet you at the café in fifteen minutes."

"The café in fifteen," Nicholas replied as the three of them jumped out of the Odyssey and headed towards Sam's hardware store.

"Who wants to do the talking?" asked Nicholas.

"You were smart enough to bring a tape recorder yesterday. You do it!" suggested Jonathan. "We'll back you up."

As they approached the hardware store they could see Mitch Steffini leaving. He was carrying a briefcase and heading south down the block.

"Looks like Mitch and Sam are up to something," Nicholas noted.

"Yeah, no good!" replied Jonathan.

They looked through the hardware store window and saw only Sam and his wife, Evelyn, working behind the counter. As they walked in they both looked up. Sam froze, he didn't even blink. His wife stood stiff for a moment, then with a slight squeak, ran into the back room. Sam was like a deer in the headlights. He just stood there like he didn't have a clue.

"Good morning," Mikaia said cheerfully as the three of them approached. "We just wanted to make sure you were all right after having such a difficult day yesterday. We know how tiring murder can be."

Sam still didn't move or say a word.

"Apparently Cryptic was right when he said his Followers in Opportunity were incompetent. We're sure he'll be pleased to find out just how incompetent they really are," said Nicholas. "If you're both lucky, he may even reward you...in some manner."

Finally, Sam blinked and opened his mouth at the same time. "How in the name of..."

"We told you we had many powers. We also warned you about toying with us," Nicholas added. "You know we haven't gone to the Sheriff about our little adventure since you're still standing in your store wearing an apron instead of jail house stripes. We just wanted you to know that we don't expect any trouble from you or Frank again, or you both will earn those stripes."

"You can't prove nothin', it's just your word against ours!" were the first predictable words Sam could utter.

"Don't you ever take personal responsibility for anything you do?" Jonathan couldn't help but interject. "You're like a two-year-old, but less mature."

"Well, there are five of us against the two of you...and, I almost forgot, this tape recording I have," Nicholas said as he placed the tape on the counter. "Just a little gift I made for you yesterday during our get together. Fortunately, everything you and Frank said came out quite clear. I've given you a copy of just a few choice comments you two made."

Sam stood there looking furious, then puzzled, then like he'd just been hugged by a bear and all the wind inside had been pushed out.

"Do we make ourselves clear?" Nicholas asked.

Again, Sam just stood still with a look of disbelief.

"You're right," Jonathan said. "There is no way out for you and Frank. You'll have to do as we say and behave, or we'll give that tape to the Sheriff and he'll find out who stole Pete's car and set it ablaze and...much more."

"How'd you know what I was...so you read my mind?"

"Yes, but as usual it wasn't very interesting," Jonathan couldn't help but add.

"Then I have no choice," he said finally.

"You do have a choice. It's just that you've always made bad choices, choices that harm others. You can choose to live peacefully and be helpful, or you can continue your evil ways. But now, if you make the second choice, you'll lose your freedom to choose," Nicholas advised.

"Do we have an understanding?" asked Mikaia.

"Yes, I can speak for myself and probably for Frank, but I can't speak for other Followers," Sam sadly replied.

"Oh, by the way, I'm sure you're concerned about the well-being of Pete and Phil. You'll be glad to know that they are also doing well and know about the tape and will soon know about our little talk," mentioned Nicholas as they turned to leave.

"Have a nice day!" Jonathan found himself saying as he closed the door.

As the triplets walked towards the Café they couldn't stop smiling. They knew that Sam was so frustrated that he'd probably prefer jail instead. In a way, he was in a jail.

"Hey look, there's Pete coming out of the café door.

"Hi Pete," said Mikaia.

"And hi to the three of you," he cheerfully replied. "I see you were in the hardware store?"

"Yes, we just had our little talk with Sam about the tape and his future behavior," Nicholas replied.

"Well, I've got a few words for him too. He doesn't know it yet, but he's going to pay me for any costs my car insurance doesn't cover."

"Sounds like a fair deal to me," said Jonathan.

"And I want to thank you again. I've never had anybody stand up for me before and help me, especially when I was wrong," Pete shared.

"That's one of the things we're being trained to do, Pete," replied Nicholas.

"I can see why Halo and the Master Inventor chose the three of you, and I'm glad they did!"

"Pete, did you ever tell Sam what we told you about how your grandfather, Fred Rider, got the thirty acres by the old school?" Nicholas asked.

"I was so mad at you, and I wanted Sam to know why I couldn't do what the other Followers wanted me to do, that I believe I did tell him. Why?"

"It's just that Mitch Steffini has been researching deeds and survey records about your orchard property and may have something up his sleeve," Nicholas replied.

"That's good to know. I know he's a Follower so

he's probably up to something sneaky. I'll have to do some checking myself," replied Pete.

"If you find anything interesting, would you let us know?" asked Mikaia.

"I'd be glad to. Now, I have a little business with Sam and Frank," Pete said as he headed towards the hardware store.

"I hope we can figure out what Mitch is up to before it hits us in the face," said Jonathan.

As the triplets walked into the café, they saw their mom sitting with Harold having a coffee.

"Hi Harold," Mikaia said. "I'm glad you're here. Will you have lunch with us?"

"Your mom and I were just catching up on things. I can stay for a few minutes but then I have a real estate transaction to make for the bank. By the way, it was a good idea for you to have gone to the source for that family history report. Also, both the Master Inventor and I are very pleased with the way you dealt with Sam and Frank. I know it was quite difficult, but we knew you were capable of doing what was necessary."

"Thanks, Halo, I mean, Harold," said Mikaia.

"Things do get rather confusing sometimes," Harold replied. He looked a little like Santa when he laughed.

"At least we've got Sam and Frank Hawkins out of circulation for a while," said Jonathan.

"That you do. Yet, I wouldn't put it past them to sneak around without your knowing," replied Harold.

"Cryptic will put a lot of pressure on them now that they've failed again."

"That would get them both in jail, if we provide the necessary evidence," Nicholas replied.

"I don't believe Cryptic cares about his Follower's well-being, just that they follow orders and do what he wants," Harold said.

"The good news is that Pete and Phil are no longer Followers and will help us in any way they can," added Nicholas.

"I'm aware of that, and once again thank you for saving their lives and helping them break free from Cryptic's grasp. They can be of great service to us as we try to convince other Followers to break away," Harold stated.

"Harold, did you know that Mitch Steffini was poking around asking questions about the old school and Pete Rider's orchard property?" inquired Nicholas.

"Yes, I was in the bank when he was asking Bill Peters for the information."

"Do you know what he's up to?" Jonathan asked.

"Bill asked Mitch why he wanted the information. He said he was just trying to learn more about Opportunity. He was quite evasive, which makes us believe he has a definite goal in mind. We're just not certain what that goal is. I'm sure we'll find out soon enough."

"I hope we do. It makes me very uncomfortable when we don't know what the Followers are up to,"

Nicholas added.

"I agree, but I must be on my way to that meeting," said Harold as he stood, walked toward the door, then stopped and turned.

"Curious minds, adventurous hearts and caring souls, we knew you were the right three to be the custodians of the old school," he said as he left the café.

The triplets and their mom, ordered lunch. They talked about all kinds of things, especially how glad they were that Mom and Dad had brought them to Opportunity. Because of their curiosity and the desire for adventure, they knew they'd never be happy unless they were able to help others. Being the custodians of the old school allowed them to do this, even though it was a big responsibility.

After the waitress cleared their table Jonathan suggested, "Of course we still have time to visit the Ice Cream and Candy Shop, right Mom?"

"We agreed that dessert was on the menu. I'm ready, are you?" their mom asked as she laid some money on the table and stood up.

"I've been ready all my life!" Jonathan replied jumping up.

"I have to agree, Jonathan, that you've been ready all your life. For exactly what I'm not sure, but you've definitely been ready," Mikaia found herself saying.

"Thanks, I'm glad we agree on that," he said as he held the door open for their mother.

A few doors down the street they turned into the

Ice Cream and Candy Shop. Willow was behind the counter and smiled as she recognized them.

"This is on me too," their mother said as they approached the counter.

"I'll give you a moment to decide what you'd like. I already know that Jonathan likes to look everything over first," Willow said.

"If you look carefully, Jonathan, maybe you can find a little green frog flavored ice cream," Nicholas said as he and Mikaia laughed.

"You mean like the one you put in my sleeping bag on our last trip to Yosemite?" Jonathan asked.

"Yep, that way you can have your lunch and dessert at the same time," Nicholas added.

"Oh, I've found those at Awaanit before," said Willow. "That's one of my favorite places."

"You hunt frogs in Yosemite?" Jonathan asked.

"Why yes, I love the mountains and especially seeking out all the animals that live there."

"If you don't mind my asking," said Nicholas, "why do you call Yosemite by the Miwok name 'Awaanit'?"

"That's the way I learned it as a small girl. My mother is Miwok and I spent many summers there."

"Yosemite is one of our favorite places too," shared Mikaia.

"That's where I got my name," Willow informed them.

"Your name?" asked Jonathan.

"Yes, Willow. Even as a baby I was tall and

slender. My mother said I looked like the willows that grew in Awaanit. That's why I'm called 'Willow'."

"I love that name," said Mikaia.

"And I've liked yours too, Mikaia," Willow answered.

"Doesn't anybody plan on ordering ice cream?" Mom asked. "I do need to get back home soon."

"Then I'll have two scoops of mint chip, since Mom's buying," said Nicholas.

"And I'll have just one scoop of my favorite, rocky road," followed Mikaia.

"You're getting only one scoop when Mom's buying?" asked a puzzled Jonathan.

"Remember, football players need to bulk up. Cheer leaders need to stay sleek and trim," replied Mikaia.

"Gotcha," Jonathan said. "Hey, Willow, who are you scooping that chocolate chip for?"

"Well, if that's not going to be your choice for the first time I'll just put it..."

"No, I'll take it. Make sure you add another scoop though," Jonathan insisted.

"I kind of thought you'd take it. Besides it looks a lot better than our newest flavor," Willow said with a big smile.

"Your newest flavor?" asked Jonathan.

"Yes, double green frog!" she replied as everyone laughed.

Mom ordered a single scoop of vanilla then paid. They kept laughing about the green frog ice cream as they headed back to the car.

"That's pretty neat finding out that Willow is half Miwok and has lived in Yosemite," Jonathan said.

"I know that some Miwoks still live around the area, but they are so much a part of the community I don't always know who they are," replied Nicholas.

"That was interesting," their mom said as she steered the Odyssey up the hill.

"Thanks for the lunch and ice cream, Mom," stated Jonathan.

"You're very welcome," she replied. "That should give you the energy you need when we get home so you can do your chores and work some more on your report."

"I'd much rather be hanging out at Wong's Pizza or the ice cream shop," Jonathan complained.

"Me too," agreed Nicholas. "But with school starting on Tuesday, and orientation and more football practice tomorrow, we need to get that report done as soon as we can."

Late that night Sam and Frank Hawkins met in the storage shed next to Frank's trucking company.

"I'll tell you again, they're alive! They were in my store!" yelled Sam.

"I still don't believe it! We pushed them tied up, over a cliff, in a car that blew up when it hit. There was no chance for them to escape, much less Phil and Pete!" Frank yelled back. "Did they say how they did it?"

"Not a word. Just said they had more powers than we thought. Now they want us to lay low or they'll tell the sheriff," Sam replied.

"It's just their word against ours. We covered our tracks quite well," said Frank.

"There are a couple of problems with that."

"What problems?" asked Frank.

"First, the fact it would be the word of five against two."

"Three are only kids. A jury can easily be convinced that their testimony could be exaggerated."

"But they're the Frazier kids, and that makes a big difference in this community," replied Sam.

"What's the second?"

"This," Sam said as he tossed a tape onto the table.

"What's that?

"It's a little gift from Nicholas Frazier. He had his recorder on throughout the whole thing."

"He what?" Frank shouted.

"I don't believe you searched them when you tied them up, did you Frank?" Sam shouted back.

"I was too busy trying not to breathe the gas! What were you doing?"

"Standing guard as you told me to do!" Sam shouted back.

"Okay, okay, what's on the tape?"

"I guess everything we said. He gave us a sample tape so we'd know he had taped everything."

"Maybe we could say it was a trick, that they put the tape together themselves?" Frank suggested.

"Why would they do that? Sam asked.

"To get us because we're Followers!" Frank said.

"And you plan on telling that story to the same jury?" asked Sam. "Besides, what if they call other witnesses?"

"There aren't any other witnesses," Frank said.

"What about that little phone call to Arnold that his ex-buddy, North, overheard?" Sam mentioned.

"I'm beginning to see your point. Looks like they have us," Frank said as he began to quiet down.

"They and Pete and Phil. Pete even came into my store today and told me that we'd be paying any of his car expenses that his insurance company didn't pay for, or else."

"Cryptic's really going to be mad!" Frank said. Then they both smelled the faint odor of burning sulfur.

"Let's get out of here!" yelled Sam.

"It's way too late for that...my friend," a smooth and pleasant voice said and a tall, dark and handsome man appeared.

Cryptic, as usual, was wearing a designer dark suit and black tie, with a pearl white long-sleeved shirt accented by gold cufflinks. He always said that he gained more Followers by using charm and pleasantries rather than threats and violence...at least usually.

"You've interrupted my visit to Washington D.C.

216

where I have some competent Followers. They at least can talk their way out of anything and put the blame on others.

You two can't even dispose of three children and two useless Followers. Since our numbers are falling, maybe I should bring a few from there to Opportunity. It would be like a vacation for them."

"We, we, can still be of service to you," sputtered Frank.

"I have my doubts," Cryptic replied with a stare that actually singed Frank's hair.

"But the triplets have all kinds of powers," Sam tried to explain. "How many of your other Followers have to put up with that?"

"You dare ask me about my business? It is your incompetence, your failure that brought me here!" Cryptic said, raising his voice.

Sam felt his head turning hot.

"Give us another chance and we'll show you that we can still be trusted," pleaded Frank.

"How are you going to manage that without going to jail?" Cryptic shot back.

"You know about..." Sam started to say.

"Of course I know about that tape you stupidly allowed to be made and the threats those triplets made to you. Who do you think I am?" he said as flames began to appear.

The room lit up as the smell of burning sulfur made them gasp for air.

"But we're planning a way to stop them and

others from using the powers of the old school. They'll have nothing to be the custodians of," Frank yelled out as he put his shirt sleeve over his nose.

The flames lowered and the sulfur smell seemed to dissipate as Cryptic in a calmer tone replied, "At least that would be a start, if you can actually handle it."

"Yes, yes, we're working on it now with Mitch Steffini," Frank replied.

"Steffini, yes, he does show promise. He's gotten several of my Followers out of certain legal situations lately. Is that what he's going to do for you?"

"No, but he'll gather the right information and then take over the land next to the old school and possibly even the old school," Frank stammered back.

"Then what?" Cryptic asked.

"Build a casino!" Sam interjected.

Cryptic stood there in thought for a few seconds before Sam and Frank saw a smile appear on his face.

"From the ashes of the old school and its do-good powers comes forth a gambling mecca? I like that. That would make me take another look at your ability to be productive Followers. Then you build a casino, and I'll personally take care of those pesky triplets. But this is your last chance or you'll be smelling sulfur forever," Cryptic yelled as a bright flash of light appeared and the shed went from extreme heat to icy cold in just a few seconds.

"We better get a hold of Mitch right away and see what progress he's making," Sam said with much urgency in his voice. "I can't stand the smell of burning sulfur."

"I don't think that was all Cryptic had in mind for us, if we fail," Frank replied.

Chapter Fourteen

Orientation

"Boy, I'm sure glad we got that report tied up last night," Jonathan said as he handed Nicholas the salt shaker.

"You and me both! The sixth grade is supposed to have a lot more homework than the fifth. At least we have a major project off our backs. With football and our work for the Master Inventor, we won't have much time left," Nicholas replied and then made a strange face because he realized he'd put too much salt on his eggs.

"The cheerleading team is supposed to practice after school at least three days a week, plus go to all the games. That seems to be overdoing it a bit for me," added Mikaia.

"At least you'll get to be with some of your friends," Mom said as she gave Nicholas some other eggs.

"That's true. Ashlee and Marie are great and most of the other girls are very friendly," agreed Mikaia.

"I can't wait to see what our teachers are like today," said Nicholas, "even if it's only for a half day orientation."

"Yeah, and then we get to scrimmage against each other like it was a real game!" Jonathan added.

"That should be fun," said Nicholas.

Their mother dropped them off at Lowe Middle School around eight fifteen. They all wanted to see their friends before they had the short-day schedule.

When they got out of the car Nicholas saw Larry and Will near the flagpole and Mikaia heard Marie yell and wave at her from the front sidewalk.

"Have fun today. I hope you like your teachers!" their mom said. She started driving and then called back that someone would pick them up at a little after two.

"Welcome to Lowe," Nicholas and Jonathan heard Larry say when they approached him, "our home away from home for three years."

"You've got to be somewhere. It might as well be Lowe," replied Jonathan.

"We're all supposed to go into the gym first for an orientation speech by the principal, Mr. Edwards," Will mentioned. "They've got today's schedule taped all over the school."

"Fine with me. We follow our shortened class schedule for the day and then we scrimmage!" exclaimed Jonathan.

"And I get to run the ball around you!" Larry said with a smile.

"Not if I can help it!" replied Jonathan.

"I saw you guys through the window of the ice

cream store yesterday when I was going by. I wanted to come in but I was late in meeting my Dad at the bank," said Will. "He was doing some things for the Sheriff's Office. Your Mom was with you and you were talking to Willow."

"Do you know, Willow?" Nicholas asked.

"Sure, I buy ice cream from her all the time and my Dad knows her family. She's a senior at the high school and has been in Opportunity for several years. Her mom has lived in the area all her life."

"All her life?" said Nicholas.

"Yeah, she's actually a full blood Miwok Indian."

And Willow is half Miwok," said Jonathan.

"Her Dad is Paul Brown. He manages the grocery store. Her Mom is Ellie, although before she married Paul Brown her maiden name was Hay."

"You sure know a lot about them," said Nicholas.

"Yeah, I have a good memory for things like that, besides, Willow's kind of cute. She's way too old for me, but still cute," Will added.

"Maiden name was Hay, you said?" asked Nicholas.

"Yep, her family here goes back several generations, why?"

"Oh, we're still studying the early history of Opportunity and I think I came across that name before, that's all," Nicholas said.

The bell rang calling them to the gym.

Mikaia and her girlfriends sat next to Jonathan and Nicholas and their friends. Nicholas somehow ended up with Ashlee sitting right next to him.

Mr. Edwards welcomed them and told a little history of the school, mentioning William Lowe several times. He then explained the schedule for the day and some of the school rules. The triplets found out that they could bring cell phones to school, but they could only use them before and after school, or in case of an emergency. Otherwise they'd be taken away for the day and only returned to their parents. Mr. Edwards gave a lot of information, things they all needed to know. After thirty minutes the students were dismissed to go to their first period class.

"That wasn't too bad," said Jonathan. "Now to meet this guy, Mr. George, who gave us that family history report."

"Yeah, that certainly surprised me," said Larry.

"We all have him for the first two periods, Social Science, then English," Mikaia added.

They headed towards his room and Nicholas moved between Mikaia and Marie.

"Before school, while you were with your friends, Will was telling us about Willow," Nicholas said quietly as they were walking.

"So, he probably buys ice cream from her too," replied Mikaia.

"Sure, but to make a long story short, her Mom, Ellie, and her family are full blooded Miwoks and her maiden name was Hay!"

"Hay, like in Mary Hay, who we met on our field trip to Yosemite in 1886? The same Mary Hay whose land was stolen and whose father was shot by Pete Rider's great grandfather in 1874?" asked a curious Mikaia.

"I believe so. I think we need to talk more about this later," Nicholas said as they entered the classroom and took their seats.

"Welcome to Lowe Middle School and to your Social Science and English classes for this year. I'm Mr. George, your teacher. We're going to learn a lot of interesting things this year, as you all know by now, starting with your earliest family histories. By the way, those are due next Monday."

"I can tell already," Larry whispered to Jonathan. "This class is going to have a lot of homework."

After getting their books and another homework assignment in Mr. George's English class, they had a fifteen-minute break before going to the Science and Math classes taught by Ms. Trudeau.

"Mr. George seemed all right to me," Mikaia said as a group of them sat at a cafeteria table sipping juice drinks.

"He should be okay. He's really interested in what he teaches and wants us to learn as much as we can," Larry mentioned. "I hope it's not a lot more than I want to learn!"

"Actually, he just wants us to worry about the amount of work he's going to give us. Then, when we all turn it in, he plans to back off a bit," said Jonathan sipping his apple juice.

"How do you know that?" Calvin asked.

Jonathan swallowed hard and cautiously replied, "Ah, isn't that what a lot of teachers usually do...get us thinking there's going to be a lot of work, then take it easier on us?"

"I had a teacher that did that!" Marie said as Jonathan took a deep breath.

Jonathan heard Mikaia's thought message, *You've got to be more careful in what you say if you're going to read someone's mind, Jonathan.*

Sorry, I sometimes forget that everyone can't hear it. Jonathan returned.

"Before I forget," Ashlee said, "I want to invite the eight of you to Lake McClure next Saturday to go jet skiing with my family. It will be an end of summer, start of school party. We'll bring our three jet skis and all the food. All you have to do is be at the south beach by eleven with your swim suits on."

"Sounds like a deal to me," said Jonathan.

"Your jet skis are a lot of fun. I'm sure I can make it, Ashlee," an enthusiastic Marie replied.

"Thanks! We'll need to check, but I don't see why we can't be there," Mikaia replied.

"You can count me in," said Brad.

"Larry and I will be there, won't we Larry?" said Will.

"After my homework's done I'm all yours," Larry said with a big smile.

"And how about you, Calvin?" asked Ashlee.

"Have you ever known me to pass up free food and jet skis?" he replied.

"Does that mean you're coming?" she asked

"I'll be waiting there for you," Calvin said and they all laughed.

The bell rang giving them five minutes to get down the hall to Ms. Trudeau's class.

"Do you know Ms. Trudeau?" Nicholas asked Ashlee.

"I don't think anyone does. The school district just hired her this summer," Ashlee replied. "I heard from a friend, whose mother is a secretary at district office, that she is an experienced teacher and very nice."

"I guess that's good news," Jonathan mentioned as they went into the classroom and picked out a seat. A minute later Ms. Trudeau walked into the room. Everyone became silent and the triplets' mouths dropped opened.

"Why that's..."

"Shush, quiet Jonathan," Mikaia quickly said.

"Good morning class. My name is Tique Trudeau. I'll be your Science teacher for the first hour, then your Math teacher for the second. I'm looking forward to getting to know each of you this year. As you know I just moved to Opportunity, but I've taught for several years and should be able to help you with the entire curriculum."

That's our Tique! Jonathan eagerly sent to Nicholas and Mikaia. *What is she doing here?*

She's a teacher, isn't she? Nicholas transferred

back.

I know that, but here, at Lowe? a puzzled Jonathan replied.

I don't understand either, Nicholas added, *but I'm glad she's here. Not only is she a good teacher, but that means one more of the Master Inventor's followers is in town!*

Let's listen to what she's saying and then get together later to figure this out, suggested Mikaia.

We could ask her at the end of class, transferred Jonathan.

And what are you going to tell our friends? Please go on ahead because the three of us have to talk to Ms. Trudeau in private. thought Mikaia.

I've got it, not a good idea. Let's talk to her later, replied Jonathan.

"And in math we'll be doing statistics, probability, and analyzing data along with numerous other mathematical operations," Tique said and started passing out science and math books.

At the end of science class as they were leaving, the triplets looked over at Ms. Trudeau who looked at them, smiled, and winked.

"She certainly is nice," said Marie as they headed up the hallway.

"I think hers may be my favorite class," added Larry.

"Now for P.E.," said Will.

"I don't understand why we have to take P.E.

when we are already spending twenty hours a week practicing and playing football," replied Jonathan.

"That's a good point, Jonathan," agreed Nicholas. "Maybe we should ask Mr. Edwards that."

"Maybe we should form a committee," suggested Mikaia.

"Why would you want to be on a committee about football and P.E.?" asked Jonathan.

"Because if we're going to be practicing cheerleading for ten hours a week, plus jump around at all the games, then we certainly don't need to attend a P.E. class too," said Mikaia.

"But I get knocked down in football!" said Jonathan.

"And I can knock you down right now, if you want," Mikaia replied back.

"I think he understands now, Mikaia. Sometime soon we'll form a committee of everyone who participates in sports teams representing our school and talk to Mr. Edwards," Nicholas suggested.

"Yeah, I can live with that," said Jonathan as they all hurried towards their respective locker rooms.

To their delight, Mr. Lombardi divided the boys into two groups. One group would do various athletic activities while the other group would be made up of the football players who would practice their plays for football and get ready for the scrimmage after school.

Mikaia found that her P.E. teacher, Ms. Flits, didn't much care if some of the girls were on the cheerleading team or were Olympic track stars. They all were going to do every activity she could throw at them.

Out on the football field Nicholas was able to catch up with North and tell him that everything would be all right between the Hawkins and Phil and Pete. He had also asked Ashlee if she would mind inviting North to her jet skiing party at Lake McClure since he really didn't have many friends. Just as Nicholas thought, Ashlee felt it would be a good idea, especially since she was even beginning to think he was all right. North was very pleased to be invited and spent most of the scrimmage smiling as he knocked players down to make holes in the line.

Jonathan continued to tackle everyone but Nicholas, since he was the only one that blocked his mind and was able to anticipate Jonathan's moves.

"That Ms. Flits is something," Mikaia said as the three of them waited at the flagpole for their ride. "I think she must have been in the Marines."

"Why the Marines?" asked Jonathan.

"I don't know. Maybe it was the anchor tattooed on her arm or the crossed swords on her lower left leg. I guess I'll have to look at that P.E. class as conditioning for soccer."

Chapter Fifteen

A Great Idea

"Hey kids," the triplets heard Dad say as he pulled up. "How'd everything go?"

"You'll never guess who our Science and Math teacher is," said Jonathan.

"As I recall it's a Ms. Trudeau? Am I right?"

"You're right, but her first name is Tique," replied Jonathan.

"Tique? That's strange. Isn't that the name of your teacher at the old school?"

"Not just the same name, but the same person," stated Nicholas.

"Why she must be a hundred and fifty years old!" their dad said.

"Yeah, but as you know, Dad, since she helps the Master Inventor and hasn't spent much time on earth, she only grows older when she's here. So she looks like she's only in her late thirties," explained Mikaia.

"Do you know why she's teaching at your school?" he asked.

"We haven't had a chance to talk to her alone, but we will," replied Nicholas.

"One other thing, Dad. It's about Willow," said Nicholas.

"Oh yes, I've seen her in the ice cream shop."

"We found out yesterday that she is half Miwok and has spent a lot of time in Yosemite," continued Nicholas.

"That means that we might have even seen her when we were there, that is before we knew her," their dad replied.

"Our friend, Will, knows a lot about her. Her father, Paul Brown, is the manager of the grocery store. Her mother comes from generations of Miwoks and her maiden name is Hay. We think Willow's great-great-grandmother was Mary Hay, the lady we met in Yosemite in 1886. Her family was driven off of the thirty acres behind us that Pete Rider now owns," Nicholas explained.

"That's a strange coincidence, but many Miwoks do still live in the area," their dad replied.

"But it's also a coincidence that that is the same property that Mitch Steffini has been asking about," Mikaia added.

"It could be that something is going on or maybe not," their dad replied.

"I think we'd better look into it further," said Jonathan.

"And where do you think we should start?" asked Mikaia.

"I think we should bump into Mitch Steffini. He probably doesn't know I can read minds. If we ask him the right questions I may be able to find out what he's up to," suggested Jonathan.

"Brilliant idea," Mikaia shot back. "Now if we can only figure out where he hangs out."

"I know where he is," said their Dad.

"How do you know?" asked Jonathan.

"I just saw him coming out of the grocery store. He'd been talking to Mr. Brown and I heard him say he was going over to the Café and Grill for a late lunch."

"Do you know Paul Brown?" asked Nicholas.

"I do, and he just introduced me to Mitch Steffini," their dad replied. "You've got to remember, this is a small town."

"Do you have time to let us drop in at the café?" asked Jonathan.

"Sure, we just passed it a minute ago. I'll turn around and let you out. I think I'll check at the bank with Harold on a land matter and meet you back here."

The triplets headed for the café and looked through the window.

"He's inside, sitting by himself at a table, reading some papers. Let's go in and join him," suggested Jonathan.

"We can't seem too pushy," said Mikaia. "Let's get the table next to him and order soft drinks. Then, we'll try to get his attention. Since Nicholas remembers so much about the land stuff and since you need to concentrate on his thoughts, let's let Nicholas lead out."

"Sure," replied Nicholas. By now Jonathan was already through the door and nearing the table.

The triplets sat at the table next to Mitch and ordered cokes. Mitch was in deep concentration. Even though the triplets talked rather loudly, he kept his focus on his papers. Finally, Nicholas decided to speak up.

"Haven't we met recently?" Nicholas said loudly as he leaned towards Mr. Steffini.

Mr. Steffini turned slowly and looked up. There was a blank expression on his face.

"Yes, I believe we have. You're the Frazier triplets. I just was introduced to your Dad a few minutes ago," he replied.

"Isn't your office in Mariposa?" asked Nicholas.

"That's where I do most of my business, but I also have clients all over the county."

"We've recently seen you several times around town, so you must have a client here," mentioned Nicholas.

"You're very perceptive. I am doing some work for a client."

"We've heard you're interested in certain land around Opportunity," Nicholas commented.

"I often help with real estate transactions."

"We've been studying the history of the area and have been particularly interested in land ownership, from the early Miwoks through the early nineteen hundreds."

Nicholas noticed that wrinkles appeared on Mitch's face when he made his last statement about the land. He may have struck a nerve, so he decided to continue.

"We actually have been buying some of the old deeds and bank ledgers from the eighteen hundreds at the antique store. Jonathan likes to collect historical documents," Nicholas continued as Mitch just stared.

"We've also been interested in the Miwoks and their presence in Yosemite and Opportunity," Nicholas said. Again he noticed a slight wrinkling on Mitch's forehead."

"Then I'd have to say you have been very busy, and so am I," Mitch said.

He got up and placed some papers back in his briefcase. He looked at the triplets for a moment.

Nicholas finally decided that he needed to say something. "It was nice seeing you again."

Mitch finally spoke, "And I'm sure it will happen again," He headed for the door.

"Talking to that guy is like talking to a statue," said Nicholas. "Actually, I think a statue has a better personality."

"Well, Jonathan, since Nicholas couldn't get anything did you?" asked Mikaia.

Jonathan looked a bit puzzled, like he was trying to put things together in his mind.

"Actually, I did. But I think Mitch knows that I can read minds. He kept fighting me and trying to keep me out of his thoughts. So I kept concentrating as hard as I could and I did get a few things."

"Okay, what did you get?" Mikaia finally asked.

"He is working on a land deal and it has something to do with the Native Americans and Paul Brown. He's working on some kind of business deal with them and Pete's orchard land is part of it," Jonathan replied.

"Pete's thirty-acre orchard, the Native Americans, along with a business deal," Nicholas repeated.

"There's got to be one more piece of the puzzle that pulls it all together.

"Hey guys, let's get going," their dad said as he stood at the door.

Mikaia laid some money on the table. Then they hurried out and got into the Odyssey.

"I know I'm missing something," Nicholas mumbled as he got in.

"Missing what?" asked their dad.

"We got a chance to talk to Mr. Steffini, but it was like talking to a wall. Jonathan had trouble reading his thoughts," stated Nicholas.

"But," Jonathan interjected, "he is working on some kind of deal that involves Pete's orchard land and it has to do with some kind of business with the Native Americans."

Dad quickly pulled over and stopped the car.

"What's the matter, Dad!" asked Mikaia.

"I can't believe that I hadn't figured this out before. The missing word is gambling!"

"Gambling?" said Jonathan.

"Yes! In California, as in some other states, Indian tribes are allowed to operate casinos on their tribal land. Early Indian treaties with the U.S. government gave them special recognition and ownership of their land," Dad exclaimed.

"I've got the final piece!" Nicholas shouted. "The Native Americans, in this case Mary Hay's family, once owned Pete's thirty acres. Fred Rider actually stole it from them. If Mitch and the Hays can prove it was stolen from them and belonged to an Indian family, they could get it recognized as tribal land. If that happened, they could build a casino right next to the old school and in our backyard!"

"You've got it, Nicholas, that's it!" their dad said. "And there is still one more problem. I've heard of tribes buying land next to theirs and getting it recognized as tribal land too. If there was a large casino to be built right next to the old school, I'm sure the school board would want to sell the old school land. Obviously, they could never build a new school a few feet from a casino. I wonder who would make the best offer for that land?"

"The casino owners," Jonathan said, "and that's the end of the old school and the time machine. That ground would be dug up and stabilized for a parking lot or something!"

"No wonder Mitch is so focused on helping his clients. Not only can he make a lot of money with them, but he can make Cryptic happy at the same time!" added Mikaia.

"Well, custodians of the old school, now what are you going to do?" Dad asked.

"Think and ask a few more questions," said Nicholas.

"But can you stop it?" their dad asked.

"We know it gets stopped somehow because when we took a field trip three months ago to Opportunity in 2019, the old school was still here," Mikaia reminded them.

"That's true," Nicholas said. "But if we can travel in time and change history who's to say Cryptic wouldn't do it? So we'd better put on our thinking caps!"

As they drove towards home Jonathan sighed and said, "And I was hoping they'd make the old school a park or museum someday."

"Bingo!" said Mikaia. "I think you just found the answer, Jonathan."

"I did?" Jonathan replied.

"If we could get the school district to give the old school to the city or county for a museum and park, then it would be awfully hard for anyone to build a casino right next to it!" said Mikaia.

"Let's make it even harder for them. If we can get Pete Rider to donate his thirty acres to the city or county for a park, and with the school board doing the same, it would be almost impossible for them to succeed," Nicholas added.

"What if Pete can't afford to do that, even if we asked him?" Jonathan said.

"He could say he would take a low bid on his land, if the offer came from the county to turn it into a park. Then the community could have fund raisers to buy it. With a growing community, a nice park and museum near town would benefit everyone," answered Mikaia.

"Remember when Ms. Ivy asked Bo for a donation for Opportunity's Gold Festival that went towards schools and parks?" asked Nicholas.

"Yeah," said Jonathan, "Bo said that since Terry had agreed to donate, he would."

"If necessary, they could use that money to help buy the land," Nicholas added.

"Now you kids are really thinking! I like all of that!" said their dad as he stopped the car.

While they walked towards the house Nicholas said, "We're going to have to assume that getting the land and building a casino is what Mitch is trying to do. We can't tell anybody that except maybe Pete. Even if we're wrong, starting a movement to make that area into a park and museum is a great idea. It would save the old school and the cavern with the time machine."

"It seems to me like the three of you have some people to contact in order to get things moving," said Dad as they entered the house.

The triplets filled their mom in on the first day of school. Then they told her all about the casino possibility and their plans to organize a movement to build a park and museum. She felt that the people she'd met in town would really like that.

"By the way, Dad, Mr. Edwards said we could bring cell phones to school, if we only used them before and after school," mentioned Mikaia.

"And in case of an emergency," added Jonathan.

"Your Mom and I will have to think about that," their dad replied as the triplets went to Mikaia's room to work out a plan.

"We'll have to work fast before Mitch can make his play for the land," said Mikaia.

"I can identify several key people whose support we're going to need," said Nicholas.

"The first one is Pete Rider," replied Jonathan. "We've got to see how much he's willing to give."

"Yes, he's key," Mikaia replied. "Next should be Mr. Dewey, the Superintendent of The Foothill Unified School District. When we met with the school board to get them to keep that old school because of all its history, he was very supportive."

"Don't forget Bill Peters is our friend and the Mayor of Opportunity. We'll need the city's support and he'll know of other key people we should contact," Nicholas added.

"If the city can't afford to help we may need to meet with the County Board of Supervisors," said Jonathan.

"How do you know about them?" asked Mikaia.

"I read that chapter last year in our social science book about city, county, and state governments," he replied with a smile.

"I thought you skipped that one," said Mikaia.

"Naw, it had a lot of neat pictures of people doing all kinds of stuff."

"You read it because of the pictures?" asked Nicholas.

"Sure, that's why they put them there, to get a guy's attention."

"Apparently it works," was all Mikaia could say.

"Yes, we should contact the county and even the historical society," added Nicholas.

"Do they have a historical society in Opportunity?" Mikaia asked.

"If not, we could ask Mom and Dad to start one!" Jonathan suggested.

"One person we haven't mentioned who knows a lot about Opportunity is Harold," said Nicholas. "If we go back into town, we could see both Harold and Bill at the bank."

"Great place to start," agreed Mikaia. "I'll see if Mom or Dad could drive us, if not, there's always our bikes."

"And I'll call the bank to make sure they're both going to be there. After all that running in the scrimmage today I don't want to ride my bike all the way into town only to find them gone," said Jonathan.

"Good idea," replied Nicholas as Jonathan and Mikaia took off down the stairs.

After a few minutes Nicholas heard Jonathan yell up to him, "It's going to be bikes, but both Harold and Bill will be there for a little while longer. We need to leave in five!"

A few minutes later the triplets were speeding down the hill towards town. They made a right at the intersection and peddled towards the bank.

"We came down that hill in record time!" said Jonathan, who was breathing deeply.

"I didn't know we were keeping track," Mikaia stated as they leaned their bikes against the front wall of the bank.

"Yep, twelve and a half minutes," he replied proudly. "Our second best was thirteen and a half last month."

"And how many minutes did it take for Mom to drive us to school today?" Mikaia asked.

"Six and a half, that is when the car actually started moving and then stopped in front of the school. You didn't think I'd know?"

"Knowing you, Jonathan, I shouldn't have doubted. Anything's possible," replied Mikaia.

"School's an important one. I want to know exactly when I have to wake up in order to get there just at the right time," Jonathan added as they walked into the bank.

"Great, you made it," Bill Peters said shaking each of their hands. "Follow me to my office. Harold is waiting."

Harold stood and greeted them as they entered. "You three sure keep busy," he said with a smile.

"Actually, a short vacation would be nice. With school and football starting I don't think that's going to happen...and now all this," said Jonathan.

"Okay, now what does 'all this' mean?" asked Mr. Peters.

"We felt that both of you should know what we think Mitch Steffini is up to," replied Mikaia. "It's going to take a lot of people to stop him, but if we succeed the reward will be great!"

"Does it have to do with his checking on Pete Rider's thirty acres of land by the old school?" Bill asked.

"Definitely," said Nicholas. "We think he's linked up with Paul Brown whose wife is Ellie Brown-Hay. Ellie is the great granddaughter of Mary Hay whose father once owned that property until 1874. That's the year Fred Rider, Pete's grandfather, shot her father and ran her and her mother off the land because he didn't like Native Americans. Mary and her mom went back to Yosemite to live with their Miwok tribe. Fred then recorded that he paid Mr. Hay one dollar for the land and took over their property."

"Yes, we know the story," commented Harold.

"The key is the word 'casino', and that's where the Brown-Hay's come in," Nicholas added.

There was a long pause before Bill Peters jumped up.

"You're kidding me!" said Bill. "You think they're going to try and take over the thirty acres by proving it was a theft, and that Ellie Hays still owns it? Then they'll claim it as Indian land and build a casino?"

"That's what it looks like," answered Jonathan..

"The problem is that it just might work. That would make the old school and the land inappropriate for a new school. More than likely the school board would sell the land," Bill reasoned.

"And guess who's in line to buy it?" added Jonathan.

"The group that Mitch and the Browns get to fund an Indian casino!" Bill replied.

"Then goodbye to the old school and its history, and goodbye to the cavern and time machine below it, and hello to our new next door neighbors!" Nicholas exclaimed.

"If what you say is correct, this would have a profound effect on the whole community, the whole county," Harold replied.

"No more nice small town. Here comes the big stores, traffic, sanitation expansion, more police, firemen, hotels and all kinds of people, some of whom won't be concerned about taking care of our community," Bill said as he shook his head.

"Some people might want a casino. Land values would probably go up along with the increased building and stores. That would mean more jobs for people. The only problem is that anybody who wants a job in Opportunity already has one, so the new jobs would bring in a lot of new people," added Harold.

"All that may have to be left to the voters," Nicholas interjected. "We're interested in saving the old school which means we have to save the thirty acres."

"We do have a plan," said Jonathan.

"Well, let's hear it," Bill said.

"We want to save the old school by turning it into a museum. It is one of the oldest buildings in town and had the most effect on our early citizens. If we can get the city or county to turn it into a museum, then it would be safe," replied Jonathan.

"I for one like that idea, but the school district owns it and that doesn't stop building on the thirty acres next to it," Bill noted.

"True," said Mikaia. "We'll need to talk to Superintendent Dewey and the School Board about donating it. If they can't afford to, then we can ask for donations to buy it and do fundraising like the Gold Festival."

"That's a possibility. There are some community development funds available and I'm sure the county historical society would be very interested in helping," Bill said. He leaned back in his chair and looked up.

"In order to have a nice museum we'll need to get the thirty acres next to it. Obviously, if Mitch gets hold of that land, the casino investors working with the Native Americans could offer a lot more for the old school land than we could. But if we got the thirty acres we could make it into a park with all kinds of recreational activities for the community," said Nicholas.

"And that sounds terrific!" Bill said. "We really need that. But we still don't have the land."

"Since Pete Rider is a friend of ours..." Nicholas started to say.

"Pete Rider is a friend of yours! Pete Rider?" Bill asked in disbelief.

"It's a long story, but he's come around a lot," answered Nicholas. "We could talk to him and see if he would donate the land for the park. If he can't afford to do that, then we could have groups who would benefit, help us fundraise."

"You've really got this planned out," Bill replied, "and I like it. It just might work."

"The key is Pete Rider," said Harold. "If he donated the land to the city for a park, that would make it more difficult for Mitch to get it designated as Indian land."

"That's why we have to keep our plan quiet and why we need to talk to Pete before Mitch makes his move," explained Nicholas.

"As always, I'm very impressed by your ability to see a problem and find a way to turn it into a benefit for someone, in this case, the community. At the same time you'll be stopping Mitch from having the Followers gain more influence in the community," said a pleased Harold.

"Harold," asked Jonathan, "you don't think that Paul and Ellie Brown-Hay are Followers?"

"Probably not. We've been friends for a long time. If Paul's working with Mitch he's probably doing it to right a wrong that happened many years ago. As a business man, it would be a good deal for him and his family if he could pull it off. By the way, you may want to try the Café in twenty minutes."

"What do you mean?" asked Mikaia.

"Don't you want to talk to Pete Rider?" Harold asked.

"Of course," replied Mikaia. "You may not know this but Pete not only likes to go to the Cafe for a morning cup of coffee, but he also gets his late afternoon cup there.

"Then we're on our way," replied Jonathan.

"Harold, you'll never guess who our new science and math teacher is," mentioned Mikaia.

Harold thought for a moment then began to smile as he said, "I guess Tique Trudeau."

"How'd you know?" asked Jonathan.

"Because I encouraged her. Since her teaching skills aren't being used much by the Master Inventor and since she is a great teacher, I helped her apply for the job at Lowe."

"But won't she grow older now?" Nicholas asked.

"That she will, but since she likes teaching so much she's willing to shorten her life to do it," replied Harold. "Many people make big sacrifices for things they love."

"I'll make a few calls to some key city council members whom I can trust," said Bill. "Then I'll talk to Allison Buck, the President of the County Historical Society, who happens to be my neighbor."

"And I'll check with the Browns to make sure this is what they're planning," Harold added. He stood up as the triplets left the room.

Chapter Sixteen

Implementation

"Man, things sure do happen fast around here," Jonathan noted as they pushed their bikes towards the Café.

"It sounds like Bill and Harold are supportive of our plan. I hope the rest of the community feels the same, especially Pete!" shared Mikaia as they looked through the window of the café.

"Bill was right. He's sitting at the counter. There are only a couple of other people in the café. Let's get the counter seats next to him," suggested Nicholas.

The triplets went in and took the seats next to Pete.

"How are you doing?" asked Nicholas as Pete looked up.

"Fine, now that Sam is going to pay the thousand dollars deductible I have to pay on my car to get the insurance money," Pete replied. "And I have to admit, I did enjoy the way he squirmed as he tried to figure out what happened."

"We have a favor to ask you, at least something

for you to think about. It does involve saving the old school and the time machine and would cost you a lot of money," said Nicholas.

"So far it doesn't sound too promising," Pete replied.

"We need your word that our talk is confidential," added Nicholas.

"That I can do."

"After our last talk about Mitch Steffini's interest in your land, we think he's trying to take it from you. He's going to claim your family stole it from the Hays in 1874, and then get it registered as Indian land. With that he'll then work with the Brown-Hay family to get funding for a casino," Nicholas said as Pete quickly sat up.

"Why that snot-nosed little pencil pusher," Pete said. "I'm sorry! The idea of them making my family look bad and gaining all that money off the land really burns me."

"The money is just part of it. If he succeeds it would destroy the old school and the cavern with the time machine, and that's our main concern," replied Nicholas.

"However, if you donated the land to the city or county for a park and we could get the school district to do the same with the old school for a museum, it would make it much more difficult for them to get your land."

"That sure would put a different twist on things...a museum and park," Pete said as he took a sip of coffee.

"Donating the land for a park would partly serve as a way of righting a wrong and give your family back some respect if this information gets out. It also ruins some big plans the local Followers have of getting back into Cryptic's graces," added Nicholas.

"You sure have a way with words for being so young. I do owe you three an awful lot, and I'd very much like to do something as well to pay back a few Followers. Besides, I have enough to live on around here and if I donate the land, I'll probably get a good tax write off...You've got a deal!" Pete said as he shook hands with Nicholas, then Mikaia and Jonathan.

"I'll check with Bill Peters at the bank tomorrow and see what I have to do. Bill is both the banker and the Mayor, so this should be real easy. By the way, here's my private number if you need to talk to me." Pete handed Nicholas his card.

"That went way better than I'd hoped," said Nicholas as they left the café.

"Pete's still Pete, but he's come a long way and does want to help," replied Mikaia.

"Since we're only a few blocks from the school district office, why don't we ride over and see if Mr. Dewey can meet with us?" suggested Jonathan. "If he can't, we can always make an appointment for later tomorrow after school."

"Good thinking," Nicholas replied. "You really want to get this thing going."

"Actually, I didn't like the idea of having to ride

250

our bikes up and down that hill again so soon unless we really had too."

"That's a good reason too, I guess," said Mikaia.

A few minutes later they were walking through the district office doors when they heard a familiar voice.

"Nice to see the three of you again," Miss Ivy, the Superintendent's Administrative Assistant said enthusiastically. "How was orientation?"

"We were quite impressed with the orientation and our teachers," replied Mikaia. "We're all glad we moved here."

"And we're glad you did," she replied. "Now what can I do for you?"

"We need to talk to Mr. Dewey for a moment, if he's available. There's nothing wrong. We have an idea we'd like to share with him that would benefit the community."

"He is in, and I'm sure if he's not too busy, he'd be more than willing to meet with you. He still talks about your speeches at the June school board meeting. Let me check."

Miss Ivy disappeared down a hallway. A moment later she reappeared and waved at them to come. They followed her into a large office as Mr. Dewey rose from his desk to greet them.

"It's a pleasure to see you again. How can I be of service?" he asked.

"We've been doing some thinking about how we could help make Opportunity an even better place," said Nicholas.

"I'm always open to ways of improving our education and community. Please go on."

"You know how much we want to save the old school and its history," Nicholas continued.

"You made that clear at the school board meeting and convinced nearly everyone that it should be saved."

"Now we're thinking that we could not only save it forever but make it a place that would give even more back to the citizens."

"Sounds good so far," commented Mr. Dewey.

"We'd like to see it made into a museum which represents the past as well as our present history," Nicholas said as Mr. Dewey leaned forward.

"A museum for the community, I like the idea. But I don't think the school district can afford to just donate the land. We do have to build additional rooms and we are short of money."

"The other part of this would be making the land next to it a park to meet all our recreational needs. That would include sports fields that the school district could use," Nicholas added.

"That would certainly help. Now we have to drive south to the Mariposa County Park for a lot of our events," Mr. Dewey said as he listened attentively. "But that land is owned by Pete Rider."

"Yes, that's true, but we've discussed it with him and he's willing to donate all thirty acres to the city or county if they use it as a park," replied Mikaia.

"That's hard to believe. Mr. Rider is going to donate...his land?" Mr. Dewey asked in disbelief.

"He's changed a lot more recently and really wants to do things for the community," Mikaia added.

"A large park next to the old school museum, would be a perfect match. Having the recreational fields nearby would be of great benefit to the district. There are still a lot of money issues and agreements that have to be solved over building and preparing all of this. I would certainly be one who'd want to move forward. You have my support. I'll need to talk to the school board members and see how they feel about this possibility. Donating the school land could be a problem."

"We also felt that the community would be so supportive of the idea that many people and organizations would be willing to donate or raise money to buy the old school and its property and improve the park," Nicholas concluded.

"And you came up with this all by yourselves?" he asked.

"Yes, we really want to see this land preserved for the benefit of the community," answered Mikaia.

"You three really amaze me. I've never met sixth graders with your wisdom and maturity."

"Thank you. We're just like others who want to help and make things better," Mikaia replied.

"All I can say is I wish there were more youngsters like you. I'll let you know as soon as I can what I find out."

"Thanks for listening and being willing to help," said Jonathan. The triplets waved goodbye to Miss Ivy and climbed onto their bikes for the ride home.

"So far it looks like everyone's for the idea and even wants to help," commented Jonathan as they peddled up Highway 49 through town.

"It's hard to pass up a community park and museum. I think that everyone would want to have them as part of their community," Mikaia replied.

"I can," said Nicholas. The others suddenly realized what he meant.

They arrived home a short time before their mother was going to serve dinner.

"You three must have been pushing some buttons on the park and museum idea," Mom said as they walked in.

"Why's that?" asked Jonathan

"Because I have received two calls for you. One is from Harold and the other from Mr. Peters. I left their numbers for you on the hall counter.

The triplets hurried back into the entrance hall and picked up the phone numbers.

"Do you or Jonathan want to call?" asked Nicholas looking at Mikaia.

"You've got the numbers, you can make the calls," Jonathan replied.

"They sure were quick in getting back to us. I hope its good news," commented Mikaia.

"I'll call Bill Peters first," Nicholas said as he

dialed his number.

"Hello, Mr. Peters? This is Nicholas Frazier. Yes, we did talk to Pete Rider. He said he would donate his land. You already knew?...He called and he's going to meet with you tomorrow morning...Great!...You've called most of the city council members and they like the idea and they want to see if the city can do it?...Fantastic...Oh, Allison Buck, from the historical society...She said they've been hoping something like this would happen and would love to help with the museum?...Yeah...We were able to see Mr. Dewey late this afternoon...He was very supportive but doesn't think they could outright donate the old school because they need the money...Yes, he is checking with school board members and said he'd get back to us...Yes, everything is looking good...Thanks for letting us know so fast...Goodbye!"

"Did you hear that?" asked Nicholas.

"We sure did. That's great," said Jonathan.

"It looks like we've started an avalanche of activity! Now, let's see what Harold found out," Mikaia exclaimed as Nicholas dialed his number.

"Hi, Harold, this is Nicholas. What were you able to find out?...You talked to Paul Brown at the store. He said that Mitch came to him with the idea of trying to prove the Riders illegally took the land from his wife's family...Then he sweetened the deal by telling him he could claim it as Indian land and make a bundle on a casino...He said that Mitch told him he already had investors?...Why did he tell you all of this?...The Hays have been friends with your family for three generations...He's not pushing the idea, just being a businessman to see what might happen...It's Mitch that's doing all the work...Yes...Pete will donate the land and Mr. Dewey liked the idea but, the district probably couldn't just donate the school...Yes, we'll move forward fast. Talk to you later," Nicholas replied.

"Harold said that Paul Brown mentioned that Mitch had evidence that showed that Fred Rider took the land by force and was going to bring his evidence forward in the next few days," reported Nicholas.

"So, we were completely right," said Jonathan.

"It looks like we were right on everything except that Paul and his wife Ellie didn't bring this up. They preferred to leave that piece of history alone...until Mitch came along," added Nicholas.

"Yeah, waving money around that would destroy the old school and cavern!" said Jonathan. "Now what?"

"Now we've got to do an end around play," said Nicholas.

"Great, I'll tackle him as he passes the line," Jonathan replied.

"That's not what I have in mind. We need to get around Mitch and score before he can stop us," responded Nicholas.

"You mean let everyone know about a possible park and museum and get their support before Mitch can gather support for a casino?" asked Mikaia.

"You've got it, but we'll need permission from Pete before we can make the land donation public. We also need to let people know we have the Mayor and Superintendent's support," Nicholas added.

"You're really good at putting these details together," said Jonathan.

"A human calculator," Mikaia added with a laugh as Nicholas smiled. "When we were little kids, you'd always rather read the little label on the toy than play with it."

"So, how do we let everyone in Opportunity know about this?" Nicholas asked.

"I'd put it in the paper. That's how we found out a lot of historical things about Opportunity," suggested Jonathan.

"The Opportunity Journal...that reporter we met at the river...Deena French!" said Mikaia.

"Bingo!" said a smiling Nicholas.

"You were already thinking about that, weren't you?" asked Jonathan.

"It did make sense since everyone reads our local paper and we know Deena," replied Nicholas.

"Then tomorrow after school we'll pay her a visit at the newspaper office," suggested Jonathan.

"Since we'll be at school most of the day, we'll ask Mom to call for us and make an appointment for the afternoon. Before we talk to Denna, we'll call Pete for his permission to tell her about his donation," said Nicholas.

"Sounds like a plan," Jonathan replied.

They each headed to their own rooms to work on the English assignment Mr. George had given them.

Tuesday morning they were up early anticipating another full day of school and activities. Mikaia asked their mom if she would call Denna for an appointment and then pick them up after practice and drive them there.

At school everyone was excited about their first day and came dressed in new clothes. Almost everyone brought backpacks in which to keep their books and school supplies. When Mikaia and her mom had bought a backpack as a birthday gift for Marie, they had also picked up new ones for the triplets.

The triplets didn't get a chance to talk alone with Ms. Trudeau, but Tique did smile and wink again at each of them several times.

Thursday was going to be their first football game so the boys each practiced hard after school in preparation. Jonathan continued to tackle anyone near him and Nicholas continued to break through the line and mostly avoid Jonathan's tackles. Mikaia, along with Ashlee and Marie, had a good practice with the cheerleading team as they prepared for their Thursday after school rally performance and the football game that followed.

Mr. George gave his English Class a quiz on the homework he'd assigned with Mikaia and Nicholas each receiving a score of 93%. Jonathan kicked back in his desk and smiled as he received 100%.

They all met up at the flagpole after practice.

"You either studied hard for a change or you read Mr. George's mind to get the 100% on the quiz, Jonathan," said Mikaia.

"Well, he read all the questions to us as we went along and each time he would think of the right answer. What was I to do? Not pay attention?" asked Jonathan.

"I guess I can see your point, but it seems like cheating," replied Mikaia.

"Let me ask you this. What if I had a photographic memory, which most people don't have, instead of being able to read minds. Is that cheating because I had that special gift?" asked Jonathan.

"I understand what you're saying," noted Nicholas. "I guess if you have a gift you should use it."

"See Mikaia, Nicholas thinks it's okay," replied Jonathan.

"I still think you need to be careful...and still be sure you study," cautioned Mikaia as the Odyssey pulled up.

"Hop in!" said their mom, "I talked to Mrs. French and she can see you right away at the Journal."

"Thanks Mom," replied Nicholas. "May I borrow your cell phone for a moment?"

"Sure, it's in my purse."

Nicholas dialed the number from the card Pete had given to them. The phone rang several times before he answered.

259

"Mr. Rider, this is Nicholas Frazier. Did you meet with Mr. Peters this morning?...It's a go?...You're going to donate the land to the city?...Fantastic! We're on our way to talk to Deena French at the Journal about the park and museum. Is it okay if we mention your donation?...We really think people should know what you did for the community. Okay, we will, thanks," said Nicholas.

"Things are going well. Pete's got the donation started. The city council members Bill talked with are very supportive of the city taking on the challenge. Pete actually felt a bit embarrassed about his donation, but finally said it would be all right if we told Deena. So, everything's looking good," Nicholas finished explaining as they pulled up in front of the Journal.

"I'll wait for you out here. This is your special project," said their mom.

Deena met them at the door.

"It's nice to see the three of you again. I understand from your Mom, Cathy, that you need to talk to me about something regarding the community?" she asked. They followed her to a small office that had a nice view of the town.

"Yes," Mikaia said, "and we appreciate your being able to see us on such short notice."

"At a newspaper most of my work is on short notice," Deena replied with a smile. "Now what do you have for me?"

"We've been talking to some people in town about

Opportunity having its own park and museum. We haven't been here long, but we really feel our city needs these things. This summer we've had fun fixing up the old school and playground so we and others can enjoy it. So, we're sort of leading a movement to make the old school into a museum and the land around it into a park for the city," explained Mikaia.

"That's an exciting idea. People have talked about doing something like that before, especially since our town is growing," replied Deena. "But that takes a lot of planning, money, and work."

"I think we've been able to get everyone started already," Nicholas added.

"You can say that again," exclaimed Jonathan.

"What do you mean?" Deena asked as she took out a pen and note pad and started writing.

"We've already talked to Mr. Peters and Mr. Dewey. They both want to help. Mr. Peters has the support from the city council to make a park and museum a city project.

Mr. Dewey is talking to the school board members about a way they could afford to make the old school part of it."

"That's fantastic," replied Deena as she kept writing.

"And best of all, Mr. Rider is in the process of donating his thirty acres next to the old school to the city for park and recreational fields," Mikaia added.

"This is amazing. You've got something going that others have worked on unsuccessfully for years."

"Oh, also, Mrs. Buck, from the County Historical Society, said that they'd be willing to help with the museum any way they could," added Nicholas.

"This is a great story and good for the community. Everyone could benefit from this, the schools with more sports facilities, our families, preserving our history, everyone."

"That's what we had hoped. We'd just like to see things move as fast as possible so it can start being enjoyed," shared Jonathan.

"I really appreciate what you're doing and sharing all this with me. I'm going to make a few phone calls, then quickly interview a few people and get this news out!" an excited Deena exclaimed. "Do you mind if I take your picture, you know for my records?"

"Uh, no, I guess," Nicholas said. He looked at Mikaia and Jonathan while Deena pulled a camera out from her desk.

"Then just stand by the wall and I'll quickly...Okay, now all smile!" she said as the camera flashed. "Great picture," she added looking at her view screen.

"Well, thank you. We appreciate your time," said Mikaia as they stood up to leave.

"No, let me thank you for your time. You three are full of more surprises than any fifty people I've met before," Deena replied. "I'll be talking to you soon!"

The triplets got back in the Odyssey and told their mom what had happened. As they passed the grocery store they saw Mitch Steffini going in.

"I hope this puts an end to Mitch's plans for the town and the need to bring up some bad things from the past," stated Nicholas.

"Me too," said Jonathan. "What would be great is if everyone started working together on this project and it really united the town."

When the triplets got home they completed their chores then attacked the homework they'd been given by Mr. George and Tique. They decided to go to bed early and get some needed sleep. Since he couldn't sleep, Jonathan decided to read through some of the old documents in his collection.

The triplets' days seemed to keep getting longer and their responsibilities more demanding. Yet, they each knew they had done their best and were trying to live up to the values and expectations of the Master Inventor.

Chapter Seventeen

A Community United

"Hey, kids, come on down!" Dad called up the stairs to the triplets who were just waking up.

"What's the matter Dad, are there more spiders in the garage?" Jonathan yelled back down with a laugh.

"No, you're on the front page of the Opportunity Journal! And Jonathan, you're holding a spider!"

"I'm what?" Jonathan called out as he was halfway down the stairs.

As the triplets came into the kitchen they saw their dad sitting at the table holding up the newspaper.

"Frazier Triplets Working to Get City a Park and Museum!" read Dad. "That's the headline on the front page, along with a nice picture of you and an article by Deena French," he continued. "Sorry, Jonathan, I was only kidding about the spider."

"Wow, that Deena works fast," said Mikaia as they looked over their dad's shoulder. "She even has quotes from Bill Peters and Mr. Dewey."

"Great article, kids," said their mom. "From what I read this whole thing is moving so fast

Opportunity's bound to have a park and museum in no time. In the article, Deena even refers to you three as 'dynamic and selfless community leaders working for the betterment of Opportunity'. You're almost at hero status...again. You three always keep amazing us."

"We didn't do it for publicity, Mom. We did it to save the old school and its powers and to keep Opportunity a good place to live," said Mikaia.

"I know that, dear, but it's nice to see that others appreciate the work you've been doing even though they don't know the half of it," she replied.

"I guess so," Nicholas said as he kept reading the article.

"She even said some nice things about Pete Rider. His donation was key to making the park and museum a possibility," said Jonathan.

"It looks like you timed this well," Dad mentioned. "It would be almost impossible, if not very embarrassing, for Mitch Steffini to step forward now and state that he and the Browns are going to try and take the land and build a casino."

"That's what we'd hoped," said Nicholas as they all sat down for some breakfast.

The triplets decided to ride their bikes to school. They knew that would be their main form of transportation most days and wanted to get used to riding with their backpacks on. Besides, the school had a safe bike compound in which to lock up their bikes.

When the triplets got to school they were met by their friends who were all excited about knowing someone on the front page of the Journal. They thought that a park and museum were exactly what Opportunity needed.

In their first period social science class Mr. George recognized them for their civic activity. He used their approach to getting a community moving on an important issue as a lesson on how anyone, no matter what his age, can help a community make positive changes. The triplets were slightly embarrassed, but their friends thought it was a lot of fun.

When they got to Ms. Trudeau's science class, the triplets finally got a chance to talk to Tique when the school had a practice fire alarm. On the way out to the back field the three of them visited with her. She reinforced what Harold had told them about her reasons for wanting to teach again. She didn't realize she'd have them in her class until she saw their names on her class lists a couple of days before school. She was pleasantly surprised when she did, since now she could spend more time with them. Tique said she would still 'critique' them at the old school when they returned from a field trip that used Midst.

As the triplets were walking towards the gym they saw Arnold approaching. They had seen him at school a couple of times but didn't have any classes with him.

"Looks like you've got your name in the papers

again," he said as he approached.

"Yeah," Nicholas replied, not knowing where Arnold was going with his comment. "When we talked to Deena French at the Journal we were only interested in getting things moving on a park and museum. She made us sound much more important than we are."

"Well, I have to say I like the idea. We don't have much to do around this town. A park and museum would help a lot," said Arnold. The triplets just stood there for a moment realizing that Arnold had just made the first positive comment they'd ever heard him say.

"We appreciate your support," Nicholas replied. "Maybe you could help. The community's going to need a lot of people working together to pull this off."

Arnold looked at the triplets, then with a slight smile said, "Yeah, maybe I can help. It might be fun." He turned and headed towards class.

"Man, where did that come from?" asked Jonathan.

"Beats me," said Nicholas.

"Maybe Arnold's tired of isolating himself by being so negative. I haven't seen him hanging around with anyone since North left him," expressed Mikaia.

"It would be nice if he put his energy towards helping instead of being a butt," Jonathan said as Nicholas and Mikaia looked at him.

"A butt?" Mikaia said. "You haven't used that word for a long time."

"That's because that particular word has only applied to Arnold since we met him."

"Then what if he actually does start helping?" Mikaia asked.

"Then he could move from a 'butt' to a possible 'buddy'," Jonathan replied.

"You've sure got a lot of things figured out...in your own way," said Mikaia as she headed for the girls' locker room.

When Nicholas and Jonathan walked into the boys' locker room, they were met by North.

"I just want to say I'm glad you got good news coverage for that great idea," he said as he approached.

"Thanks, North," said Jonathan.

"The three of you deserve it. I don't think the community really knows all the things you've done to help."

"We've not done much," replied Nicholas.

"You may not know it, but a lot of us are aware of just how special you three really are. We've kind of put things together. People won't say anything to you about it, so I thought I'd just let you know."

"Thanks for telling us," Nicholas replied. "Hey, we just bumped into Arnold. He seemed even friendly."

"I've noticed that too. I still don't want to hang around with him, but I think he's making an effort to be a nicer person. Don't forget, you can count on me, as always, to open up the line for you tomorrow at our game with Oakwood, Nicholas," North said.

"I'll take all the holes you can make," Nicholas said with a laugh as they headed in to prepare for tomorrow's game.

After practice the triples caught up with each other at the bike compound.

"I could sure use some ice cream," Jonathan said, "you know, for the added energy we're going to need for tomorrow."

"Jonathan," Nicholas said, "you really don't need an excuse to convince us that an ice cream would be a good idea. Just the fact that we ride our bikes by the ice cream shop is a good enough reason to stop."

"That's right," Mikaia replied. They got on their bikes and rode towards town. When they went by the bank they noticed Mitch Steffini. He had just gotten out of his car and waved at them to stop. They slowed down and wheeled their bikes up to where he was standing.

"I'm man enough to admit when I've been out played. I'm not sure how you three do it, but you're very effective. That doesn't mean I'm giving up, just trying a little harder," said Mitch.

"We're not in competition with you, Mr. Steffini," Mikaia replied. "We're just doing what we think is best for the community."

"Best for the community or your mentor?" he asked.

"Actually, best for both," Jonathan replied.

"Either way, I still plan to rile things up around

here by letting folks know that the land their new park may be built on was stolen from the Indians."

"That certainly won't be good for the community," replied Nicholas.

"At least it will put a couple of aces in my hand for my next play," he replied with an actual smile.

"I don't think it will help at all," Jonathan said. He laid his bike against a wall and reached into his backpack.

"What do you mean by that?"

"Do you have evidence that Fred Rider's thirty acres is Indian land?" Jonathan asked.

"What do you take me for, a fool? Of course I do. I have a copy of the county record that shows Fred Rider took Mr. Hay's land from him and his family for one dollar after he shot him and ran his family off."

"How long do Native Americans have to own a piece of property for the government to recognize it as Indian or tribal land?" Jonathan continued as Nicholas and Mikaia tried to figure out what he was up to.

"Tribal land is land they've resided on for years, usually going back for generations. Why do you ask?" replied Mitch.

"Because I believe I'm better at doing homework than you,"

"How so?" a now puzzled Mitch asked.

"This is a copy of a page from an old Bank of Opportunity ledger I bought at the antique shop. On

May 10, 1874, the ledger shows an entry for a dollar purchase by Fred Rider for thirty acres of land owned by Mr. Hay."

"That just verifies what I found in the county record." Mitch replied with a slight smile.

"True, but an earlier entry into the ledger, dated January 2, 1874, shows Mr. Hay purchasing, for two hundred dollars, the same thirty acres from a Mr. William Lowe. That's Harold Lowe's grandfather. So unless you can prove that Harold is an Indian, Fred Rider's land was only owned by an Indian family for four and a half months. Here's a copy of that page for you," Jonathan said with a big smile. He handed the paper to Mitch who just stared at it. "You'd better check your sleeve for another two aces," Jonathan added.

Mitch seemed totally caught off guard.

"Don't think you've beaten me. You'll see me again. Right now I have business in Mariposa," Mitch said getting back into his car.

"You were great! Jonathan," said Nicholas. "How'd you figure all that out and why didn't you tell us?" he asked.

"I couldn't sleep last night so I read through some of my historical documents and I came across the ledger. Reading them usually puts me to sleep right away. But then I saw the January 2nd entry and I put things together. Fred's land never was Indian land except for a short time. It belonged to William Lowe. So even if Fred Rider took it dishonestly, it could never be considered tribal or Indian land for the purpose of building a casino."

"I'm very impressed," said Mikaia, "but why didn't you tell us what you'd found?"

"We were all so busy reading the newspaper and getting ready for school I just plain forgot. I made a copy of the ledger page to show you and left it in my backpack. I guess it's a good thing I did."

"You can say that again," replied Nicholas. "I think you just stopped the one thing that could keep the park and museum from being built."

"That's good to know," replied Jonathan. "Now let's get some ice cream."

The triplets pushed their bikes down the block to the Ice Cream and Candy Shop. They saw Willow behind the counter as they walked in.

This could be difficult, Nicholas messaged to Mikaia and Jonathan, *since we just ruined the chance for Willow's family to make a lot of money.*

You're right, we need to be careful what we say, conveyed Mikaia, *okay Jonathan?*

All I want is a double chocolate chip, he shot back.

"Congratulations!" Willow yelled as she saw them. "Finally, someone got this city to do something right for the citizens!"

"You mean you like the idea of a park and museum?" asked a surprised Jonathan.

"Of course, this way everyone wins. I, for one, don't like to see every inch of Opportunity developed.

When I read that you started a movement to build a large park, I was very happy. I want to help in any way I can."

"I'm just curious how your parents feel?" asked Nicholas.

"Oh, at first they thought of a different use for the land, but when they heard that Mr. Rider had donated it for a park, for everyone to use, they were very pleased."

"Then they're no longer trying to form a business relationship with Mr. Steffini?" continued Nicholas.

"That man? He tried to talk them into all kinds of things, but they never felt he was being honest with them. They kept saying he didn't have a pure heart. No, they told him this morning that he was on his own," Willow said while she scooped up a double chocolate chip, a double mint chip and a single rocky road.

"Who are those for?" asked Jonathan.

"Why for the three of you, of course. Aren't these your flavors? I mean until we get the green frog flavor back?" Willow said with a laugh.

"You bet!" said Jonathan as he took his cone. "I still can't see how you can remember everyone's favorite."

"Maybe, I just remember yours, Jonathan," Willow said softly as Jonathan started to blush. "By the way, your ice cream is on me today."

"Why would you pay for our ice creams?" Nicholas asked.

"Because of your leadership in getting this community finally moving on a great project and because you probably saved my family from reliving some painful history," she replied.

"If I'd known that helping people got me free ice cream, I would have started helping more long ago," Jonathan said.

"Actually, Jonathan, that's just one of the benefits for helping," replied Mikaia.

"I know that," stated Jonathan using his tongue to stop a chocolate chip from dropping from his cone.

"Thanks again," Mikaia said. "We appreciate it."

"Remember, if there's anything I can do to help, let me know," Willow said as the triplets left the shop.

"Wow, Willow was excited about the park and museum," said Jonathan.

"Remember what Mary Hay, Willow's great, great grandmother told us when we traveled back to Yosemite in 1886?" asked Mikaia.

"Yes, she said that the things the Great Spirit gave to them they shared, and that they just took what they needed so others could have what they needed," said Nicholas.

"Good memory," said Jonathan. "The Miwok Native Americans shared everything back in those days."

"From what I can see the Miwoks, meaning Willow's family, still do, since the park land really belongs to them," Nicholas replied while he climbed onto his bike for the ride back home.

"Hi, you three, how did school go today?" their mom asked.

"Everything went fine, Mom," said Mikaia.

"And we all got free ice cream again. This time Willow paid for it since she likes the park idea," said Jonathan.

"Don't forget to tell Mom what you did," mentioned Nicholas.

"What did Jonathan do?" asked Dad as he came into the kitchen.

"Nothing real important," he replied.

"Not real important!" said Mikaia. "By finding the bank ledger that showed that the Brown-Hay's only owned the thirty acres for several months, you pretty much stopped Mitch Steffini. When you proved it wasn't Indian land, you drove him right out of town."

"Now nothing stops us from having a new park and museum," said Nicholas.

"Sounds kind of important to me," said their dad. "Good job! Because of you three, in the last couple of days this whole community has come together."

"Speaking of getting together, Bill Peters called and wants to meet with all of us after school on Friday. He said it has to do with the museum and park," said Mom.

"Sounds fine with us," replied Mikaia looking at Nicholas and Jonathan.

"Then I'll call him back and let him know," said their mom. "By the way, dinner will be ready around six, and I believe it is Jonathan's turn to wash the dishes."

"Man, around here a guy can go from being a hero to a pot scrubber in no time at all," replied Jonathan.

"At least we got free ice cream today," reminded Nicholas.

"True, that sure helps. At least it gave me the energy to get started on my homework, especially all the math problems Tique assigned. I thought she would take it a little easy on us."

"Just like Halo, she's preparing us for the future too," mentioned Mikaia.

Upon leaving the triplets, Mitch Steffini, had not gone directly back to his office in Mariposa. After making a couple of phone calls, he drove to Frank Hawkins' trucking company. Both Sam and Frank were waiting in the storage shed when he walked in.

"I thought you had all of this under control!" said Frank angrily. "We even told Cryptic about our plan to destroy the old school and build a casino. He liked the idea and said it was our last chance. Now you've blown it for all of us!"

"Those triplets turned the tables around on us. If I go forward now, without the Brown's support, I'll get nowhere. Besides, everyone's so excited about a park that if I even brought up a casino as an alternative, I'd never get another client in Opportunity," replied Mitch.

"But we have to do something!" said Sam. "If we don't we're toast!"

"I don't know what you can do. I plan to stay put in Mariposa. There are a few active Followers there that I can help. That should get me back into Cryptic's good graces."

"I for one, plan on taking long haul loads up and down the east coast for some time," replied Frank. "Cryptic will have to find me, if he really cares to."

"Well, you're not going on your own! I got you started in this trucking company and I still own twenty five percent. I'm going to take those runs with you. I don't want to be anywhere near Opportunity for a while when Cryptic comes a calling! Evelyn can handle the hardware store," said Sam.

"Then grab your things, cause I'm out of here," Frank said heading towards the door.

The triplets had dinner then quickly returned to their homework, except for Jonathan.

He spent some time scrubbing and drying dishes before he was dismissed to his room to finish his homework.

Later that night Nicholas tossed and turned in his bed. He pulled the covers up when he felt freezing cold and then kicked them off when he began to sweat from the heat. Finally, he just lay still realizing he couldn't move at all. As he began to gasp for breath, he heard a voice calmly say, "You will simply disappear into the smoke and the ice." The next thing he knew, he was wide awake.

Chapter Eighteen

The Game and Rewards

When the triplets came into the kitchen to grab a quick breakfast, they saw their dad looking at another front-page headline that read "Frazier Kids Create a Storm!"

"We didn't start any kind of storm," said an upset Jonathan.

"No, Jonathan, what Deena French is saying is good. The storm you started was getting everyone excited about a park and museum for the community. It seems that everyone wants to help," said Dad.

"In that case, I guess we did," Jonathan replied as he poured himself some cereal.

"Looks like some more good press," said Mom.

"I sure wish she'd stop. It gets embarrassing." said Mikaia.

"You three have just become a symbol for what's good in the community. You pull people together and make them feel they want to make things happen too," said their dad.

"If it keeps getting me free ice cream, I'm all for it," said Jonathan while he put his lunch into his backpack.

"Can you pick us up after the game?" asked Nicholas.

"Sure," replied their dad. "Mom and I both plan to be there to support you...and the cheerleaders."

"Then you'll see me knock those Oakwood players all over the place," said Jonathan.

"I don't know, Jonathan, Calvin says they're as big as high school players."

"What do they feed them at that school, raw meat? Well, if they're that big I can at least make them wobble when I bounce off or maybe grab an ankle and trip them."

"We know you'll all do your best. We'd better go if you want a ride today. I have a breakfast meeting in town," said Mom.

"I'm ready," said Jonathan.

"Me too," replied Nicholas.

"Just a second," called out Mikaia as she made one last trip to her room to get her cheerleading pom poms.

When they arrived at school everyone was excited about the rally and game. The spirit committee, along with the cheerleaders, had decorated the school and the gym with banners and posters urging the team to beat Oakwood. Even the teachers got caught up in the excitement. Most of them wore the blue and gold school colors.

Mr. George reminded the class that their family history reports were due the next day, while Tique gave the class a short quiz on the math problems she had assigned. Nicholas and Mikaia each missed one of the ten problems. Since Tique sat at her desk working on something else, reading her mind didn't help Jonathan. He still managed to get seven of the problems right, although he did use the excuse that he was busy washing dishes while his siblings had more time to study.

The school day had been shortened by half an hour to allow for the rally. At the final bell, everyone headed for the gym to get a seat. The music was turned up and the cheerleaders, including Mikaia, Ashlee and Marie, did an energetic dance routine to a song from the movie "High School Musical". Everyone stood up and applauded which made the cheerleaders jump around even more.

The Principal, Mr. Edwards, made a speech about how great the first week had been as he urged the team to beat Oakwood. He then brought to the microphone the football coach, Mr. Lombardi, who introduced each player. As Nicholas and Jonathan were introduced, much to their embarrassment, a lot of the students not only applauded but stood up as well. After a cheer routine in which the whole student body got to participate, the rally was dismissed to the bleachers by the athletic field.

The cheerleaders got the crowd excited as the teams ran onto the field. Everyone kept chanting, "Go Lowe, beat Oakwood!" while Mr. Lombardi gave the team some last-minute instructions. The coin flip was won by the Lowe captain who chose to receive.

The kickoff was fielded by Larry on the twenty-yard line. He made a great run back before being tackled on the thirty-five. The ball was hiked to Calvin who flipped the ball out to Nicholas who was following North, his right tackle, through the line. He gained twenty yards as the home fans cheered.

The next play was a short pass across the middle to Larry, who cut in front of the defensive back to make the catch. Again, there were cheers as they moved the ball forward ten more yards.

On the third play Larry cut across the middle again with Calvin faking a pass to him but instead throwing it twenty yards down field to Nicholas who'd quickly left his defender behind. Nicholas pulled in the ball and ran the next fifteen yards for the touchdown. The fans jumped to their feet and his excited team members patted him on the back

Lowe's kickoff was run back to the twenty-five-yard line. On their first play, the running back followed his left guard and tackle through the line only to be hammered by Jonathan who had quickly run forward. With a gain of four yards Oakwood tried the same play again to the right. Again, the runner was met by Jonathan, along with Will, and both hit him on the thirty-two-yard line.

On their third down, the Oakwood quarterback dropped back for a surprise pass to his left end, who had managed to break free from the line and angle towards the side line. The ball was released and floated towards the receiver only to be picked off by Jonathan at the last minute. Then he made a twenty-five-yard run back before being tackled by Oakwood's quarterback. Again, the fans jumped to their feet.

The offensive line took the field as Calvin called a running play for Nicholas who again followed North through the right side and into the end zone. Mikaia and the cheer leaders screamed and the Lowe fans were on their feet again.

By the time the game ended Nicholas had scored three touchdowns and Jonathan on defense scored one with another interception and run into the end zone. The final score was 35 to 7, a strong victory for Lowe. Lowe had gained two hundred and ninety yards while Oakwood had managed a mere one hundred and twenty. Jonathan complained that the only reason Oakwood had scored one touchdown was because he was tripped by the Oakwood receiver he was defending just before the receiver made the catch. The backfield official had taken a tumble and missed seeing the penalty. But it still was a big victory for Lowe.

"Man, Nicholas, you were crazy out there. You cut around players like an antelope," said Calvin.

"Thanks, Calvin," replied Nicholas. "North broke some great holes for me and my legs just wanted to run."

"You took it to the end zone. I just knocked the first couple of players aside for you," added an excited North.

"You were like a bulldozer out there, North," Coach Lombardi said patting him on the back. "And Jonathan, you were like a missile that hammered everyone! I lost count of your tackles!" the coach added. He called the team together and congratulated them on how well they had played.

By the time Nicholas and Jonathan had left the locker room to meet their parents, their team members were already referring to Nicholas as the 'Antelope' and Jonathan as the 'Hammer'.

As North passed by to meet his dad, Nicholas yelled out, "Hey, great game Dozer!"

North turned and gave him a thumbs up sign along with a big smile.

"You two were everywhere in that game," said their mother.

"You should have seen how excited Ashlee and Marie were when you scored," said Mikaia. "If their shoes hadn't been tied, they would have jumped right out of them. I kind of hope you don't score as often next game. I don't think I can scream that much again."

"You both played a very smart game and your team is strong in all areas," said their dad.

"Fortunately, the hard work is worth it," said Jonathan, "but you're not going to convince me that the ice cream didn't help."

"I don't think any of us would be successful at doing that," Mom replied as they drove home.

Once home, their dad barbecued some steaks for

dinner in celebration of their victory. Their mom had made a large fresh apple pie for the occasion along with mushroom sauce for their steaks. After dinner each of the triplets was presented with a gift.

"What are these for?" asked Mikaia.

"They are 'just because' gifts," Mom replied.

"Just because of what?" Jonathan asked.

"Just because we love each of you," said Mom.

"And also because of all the things you've done for the Master Inventor and others over these last few months," added Dad.

"You didn't have to buy us gifts," replied Nicholas. "We would have done all that anyway."

"Let's not get carried away. Gifts are a great thing to receive!" enthused Jonathan. "Besides, you're never supposed to make a gift giver feel bad."

"That's true, Jonathan," his dad replied.

"So, let's open them," Jonathan said. He picked up the one with his name on it and began to unwrap it. To his surprise he found a stack of old documents and newspapers.

"Thanks to Bo at the antique shop, we were able to find you original copies of a variety of old documents regarding California's early history," his dad said.

"Hey, a copy of the San Francisco Chronicle that has the front-page story of the 1906 earthquake and fire! And here's one about the discovery of gold at Captain Sutter's Mill in 1848!...and a bunch more," exclaimed Jonathan.

"We thought you'd like those for your historical document collection," his dad said.

"I sure would! Thanks!"

By now Nicholas had picked up his present and was shaking it.

"Why don't you just open it?" asked his mom.

"I'm just making the surprise last longer by trying to guess what it might be," Nicholas replied and he finally decided to find out. As he carefully opened the package he found three bottles that were rolled up in bubble wrap.

"This is great! I've wanted this bottle for my collection for a long time, but I couldn't afford it. It's a rare old medicine bottle from a mining camp that had been brought from the east coast. The other two are old whisky bottles used by civil war soldiers. These are valuable too! Thanks Mom and Dad."

"You're welcome," his mom replied

"What did you find, Mikaia?" Dad asked as she pulled the paper off of her gift.

"This beautiful old doll," she replied while she held it up for a closer look. "It's small and a bit worn, but I can tell it was well loved."

"You're right on that," said her mother.

"Bo found this especially for you. It's a lot like the one your grandparents gave to you several years ago that made you want to start your doll collection," her dad said.

"Yes, dear, it was the actual doll of a girl about your age, who brought it with her on her wagon trip to California in 1853. We do know the girl's name was 'Sara' and she had named the doll 'Katrina'. The story is that her family fell upon hard times when they arrived in California and had to part with a lot of their things, including her doll," said her mother.

"That's a sad story, but I'm going to give it the loving home it deserves," said Mikaia as she rocked it in her arms.

"These were very thoughtful gifts," said Nicholas.

"You can say that again," replied Jonathan pulling up a copy of an original Mexican land grant dated 1842.

"And my doll is so precious. I couldn't have asked for a more special gift, thank you both," added Mikaia.

The next morning the triplets were off and running again to get to school on time. Their mom reminded them of the meeting they had with Bill Peters at the bank after school. Since it was Friday, Mikaia had carefully placed their family history report in her backpack. She didn't want to turn it in late to Mr. George, especially since they'd finished it a week ago.

When they arrived at school everyone was still talking about their big victory over Oakwood. Jonathan was careful to reply that the Oakwood team wasn't as big as everyone had said, and that's what made it possible for him to tackle everyone. Of course he didn't mention that he could read minds. Nicholas even had Mr. George referring to him as "Antelope" with a laugh and then heard almost everyone calling North "Dozer," as he simply smiled.

Candy L'Heur, Mikaia's cheerleading coach, praised the girls for how well they had performed the routines which had gotten the crowd so involved in the game. She even talked about having the team work towards competing in the state cheerleading championships in May.

Nicholas found Ashlee nearby everywhere he went.

Jonathan glanced several times at Marie during class as she coyly flipped her hair from her eyes and smiled.

Friday just seemed to fly by for the triplets. Before they knew it, they were standing by the flagpole waiting for their parents when Ashlee approached them.

"Don't forget my beach party at Lake McClure tomorrow at eleven," she said.

"We'll be there," replied Nicholas.

"Is there anything we could bring?" asked Mikaia.

"Just your beach towel, sun lotion, and swim suits to use on the jet skis. You'll probably get pretty wet riding them. Everything else will be provided by my family."

"Great! We'll see you then," replied Mikaia when her parents drove up.

When they parked in front of the bank, they saw Mr. Dewey walk in.

"This looks like an important meeting," Dad said

as they approached the door.

The receptionist greeted them and walked them back to a large meeting room. When they went in they saw Mr. Dewey talking to Bill Peters and Harold. A lady, who was introduced as Allison Buck from the historical society, was seated near the window.

"I'm glad all of the Frazier family could be here," Bill said shaking hands with each of them as Harold winked at the triplets.

"You three have caused quite a commotion in Opportunity. I've never seen this community come together on a project like this before. Let us bring you up to date on what you started. You already know that the city council voted to take on the park and museum project. We have some community development monies we can use on both. Jud Day and Henry Lowe have volunteered their time to design the plans for the park," Mr. Peters said.

"That's really nice of them!" said Mikaia.

"What about the money for the old school and property?" asked Nicholas.

"The school district is selling the old school to the city for half its value," replied Mr. Dewey. "We will then enter into an agreement with the city which allows our schools to use the recreational fields. Phil Steward made a donation to the city which covers the total amount they owe to the school district for the old school."

"Mr. Steward paid for the old school, to save it?" asked Jonathan.

"Yes, he said something about owing this community a lot," said Mr. Dewey.

"We're organizing a city-wide committee to oversee the total park and museum project," said Mr. Peters. "Pete Rider and I are going to be Joint Chairs of the Committee."

"Mr. Rider is going to Joint Chair?" a surprised Mikaia asked.

"The key to this whole project was when you three got him to donate the land. Since he made that donation, we asked him to help oversee it. He said he'd be honored to," replied Mr. Peters. "Mr. Dewey and Harold Lowe will also be on the committee. We'd all like the three of you to serve on it too, as representatives of the Middle School," Mr. Peters continued. Nicholas quickly looked at Mikaia and Jonathan who both transferred back that it was fine with them.

"We'd be pleased to be on the committee," replied Nicholas. "Do you have a high school representative yet?"

"No, not yet. Do you have someone in mind?" Mr. Peters asked.

"Yes," replied Nicholas, "a senior named Willow. She's the daughter of Paul and Ellie Brown."

"She's a smart and mature young lady, and a good student," Mr. Dewey added.

"I think she'd be a great choice," Mr. Peters said, "but will she do it?"

"She told us a couple days ago at the ice cream

shop she'd be willing to help in any way she could," mentioned Jonathan.

"Then why don't you three invite her to join us?" asked Mr. Peters.

"We'd be glad to," replied Mikaia.

"We've asked Mrs. Buck to chair the sub committee on making the old school into a museum," Mr. Peters said smiling at her.

"And I'm thrilled to do it," said Mrs. Buck. "It's interesting that you bring up Willow's name since I've asked her mother, Ellie Brown, to be on the museum committee and head up the section we plan to have on the Miwok. She's already gathering up all kinds of Native American artifacts and even a collection of baskets her famous grandmother, Martha Hay, had loaned to the Rider family."

"Mr. Rider still had her great grandmother's basket collection and gave them back to Ellie?" asked a surprised Nicholas.

"That's what we understand," replied Mrs. Buck. "Bo Flanders, who now runs the antique shop, also volunteered to gather local antiques for the museum. I've asked him to serve on the museum committee too."

"Boy, everyone has really come together," said Mikaia.

"And even Phil Steward, besides donating the money to buy the old school, volunteered to head up the mining section of the museum since he's a mining engineer," replied Mrs. Buck.

"One more thing may interest the three of you," Harold added. "Evelyn Hawkins called today and said that the hardware store would contribute the entire playground equipment for the park."

"Evelyn Hawkins said that, like in Sam Hawkins wife?" Jonathan said again just to double check what he'd heard.

"You've got it," Harold replied with his usual calm smile.

"I think this whole town is amazed at what you started just four days ago. It makes me proud to be Mayor of Opportunity and it makes me proud to be able to call the Fraziers my friends," Bill Peters said as Mr. Dewey, Mrs. Buck, and Harold nodded in agreement.

"No doubt about it now," Dad said as they got into the Odyssey. "The park and museum are a reality. Within the next two years it should be mostly completed...thanks to the three of you."

"We just gave it a jump start," said Nicholas. "Obviously the whole community had wanted something like this for years."

"You're right, but you three did start it," he replied.

"I still can't believe that Pete donated the land and is now co-chair of the committee," said Jonathan.

"What about Phil Steward donating the money to buy the old school from the school district for a museum, and then volunteering to coordinate the mining section?" added Nicholas.

291

"My favorite is Evelyn Hawkins donating the money for the park playground. That's going to cost a bundle!" said Mikaia and Jonathan began to laugh.

"What's so funny?" Nicholas asked.

"I wonder if Sam even knows he's paying for all that yet. He and Frank are halfway to New York by now!" added Jonathan and they all began to laugh.

"It looks to me like you've just about worked your way out of a job," said Dad.

"How's that?" asked Jonathan.

"Because from what I can see there aren't any Followers left in Opportunity! The last one I know of was Mitch Steffini, and he's hiding in Mariposa."

"That's right," agreed Mikaia. "What do we do now, retire?"

"I'm sure Cryptic will be finding new recruits or sending some of his stronger Followers to Opportunity, at some point. Evil has always been around to tempt people," shared their dad. "Besides, as custodians of the old school and now the old museum, you still have things to learn and field trips to take."

"Yeah, I guess we'd better check with Harold, or Halo, before we pull back on our responsibilities," replied Jonathan. "I will still do anything he asks, except maybe cut back on ice cream."

Chapter Nineteen

Fire and Ice

Everyone slept in on Saturday. The triplets didn't have to meet Ashlee at the lake until eleven. When they finally came down for breakfast, their mom had fixed Eggs Benedict and homemade cinnamon rolls.

"This is a great breakfast," said Jonathan. "How many cinnamon rolls can each of us have?"

"Try to hold it at two, Jonathan. They are quite large. Besides, from what you told me Ashlee's family is preparing all kinds of food for you at the beach."

"You're right, Mom. I probably should leave some room," Jonathan said as he picked up his second roll and added extra butter and frosting.

"I'm really looking forward to the party. I've only ridden a jet ski a couple of times at Lake Tahoe," said Nicholas. "We're so excited we've already got our swimsuits on under out clothes."

"That goes for all of us," added Mikaia. "I'm also looking forward to hanging out with our friends."

As their dad dropped them off at the lake he told them he'd be back around four. They each grabbed a backpack, towel and sun lotion and headed down toward a large canopy the Wilson's had set up near the shore.

Calvin, Marie, and Larry were already there, helping Mr. Wilson get the jet skis ready. Will and Brad arrived just after the triplets, as did North.

The Triplets looked out over Lake McClure.

"Hey, it's Antelope and Hammer, along with the new cheerleader," yelled Calvin laughing. "Why don't you guys grab Will and Brad and help us move these jet skis?"

"We're on it!" Jonathan called back as he and Nicholas trotted down the shore.

When North appeared Nicholas yelled, "Hey, Dozer, we could use your back too." North waved and headed towards the group.

They got the jet skis off of the trailer and into the

water. Mr. Wilson started each one after making some last-minute adjustments.

"They're all filled up and ready to go," Mr. Wilson said.

He quickly reviewed with everyone how the controls worked.

"Be sure you're wearing one of these life jackets," he added as Calvin, Larry, and Marie hopped on.

"Jonathan, why don't you get on the back of mine?" suggested Marie as she smiled and flipped her hair from her face. Jonathan took one look at her twinkling eyes, smiled, grabbed a jacket, and jumped on. Within a moment they were flying across the still water at high speed, with Calvin and Larry alongside.

"It was really nice of you to invite us today," said Mikaia to Peggy Wilson.

"It was Ashlee who wanted an end of summer and start of school party with her friends, and we were happy to do it. Besides, we get to jet ski all the time," replied Mrs. Wilson.

"You sure have put out a lot of food," Nicholas observed. "Are more people coming?"

Mrs. Wilson laughed as she said, "No it's just the eight of you. From past experience I've learned how much a few of Ashlee's friends can eat. Besides, we owe you for helping find her a few weeks ago when she was lost in Yosemite. Ashlee still thinks you three did a lot more than just find her tracks."

"Man, those things really move," yelled Calvin as he brought his jet ski in for Will to try.

A moment later Larry, Marie, and Jonathan returned. Mikaia and Will climbed on one. Nicholas climbed on the other only to find that Ashlee had jumped on behind him.

"It's okay Nicholas, I'll hold onto you tight," she said while Nicholas turned up the throttle and headed out into the lake.

It was a beautiful, warm day. The sky was a brilliant blue. Even with all that, there were very few people enjoying Lake McClure's cool water. After an exciting ride, they all returned to the beach to eat the lunch that Mrs. Wilson had prepared.

"I'll race you to the other side," Jonathan said to Nicholas as he took a big bite out of his sandwich. "If I win, you get to clean the spiders out from now on."

"What if I win?" asked Nicholas.

"Then I'll keep knocking down spiders and take your turns at washing dishes for the next month!"

"Go for it, Antelope!" encouraged Calvin.

"It's a deal," replied Nicholas. "I'll take the blue one."

"Fine with me. I think the red jet ski is faster anyway," replied Jonathan.

He laid his sandwich down and walked towards the shore.

"Mikaia," said Jonathan, "why don't you come along as the judge, so you can let Nicholas know when I beat him."

"Sure, I've only soloed on those once today. It's about time I gave it another go," replied Mikaia as she ran down and climbed on the yellow jet ski.

"Be sure to let us know who wins, Mikaia," called out Ashlee.

Then they heard Mikaia yell out, "Ready, set, go!"

Water shot everywhere as the three jet skis took off with a roar. About a block out, their friends could see that the boys were virtually even while Mikaia followed a bit to the side.

When they sped towards the far shore Nicholas began to pull ahead. Jonathan quickly adjusted and leaned down even lower on his jet ski to cause less wind resistance. As the race continued they noticed that a low cloud of smoke, probably from a campfire on shore, was beginning to make it difficult to see. Within a minute or two Nicholas began to slow down. Jonathan and Mikaia pulled up next to him.

"I can't see the shoreline," said Jonathan. "What is that stuff?"

"It smells a bit like smoke to me, but not as strong," Nicholas replied.

"I say the race is a tie and we work our way back," said Mikaia.

"I'm with you on that," replied Nicholas.

"It's getting really hot out here!" Jonathan said and used the sleeve on his t-shirt to wipe his forehead.

"You can say that again," added Nicholas.

"Look to our left!" said Mikaia, "It looks like flames are coming up out of the water!"

"We're either involved with a weird phenomenon

or we're about to receive a visit from Cryptic!" concluded Nicholas.

"And I was having a perfect day!" Jonathan asserted as the flames drew closer and hotter, and then began to surround them.

"You didn't happen to bring the small 'golden rule bell' did you?" Nicholas asked Jonathan, "the one that drives Cryptic away?"

"Of course I did, but it's in my backpack!" he replied.

"Then we'd better think fast or we'll all have to jump into the lake in a minute to keep from getting toasted!" said Nicholas.

"Let's just sign and pop over to the nearest shore until this passes. No one will see us do it," yelled Mikaia.

Now the hot winds were blowing harder and making it difficult for them to hear.

I'm all for that, replied Nicholas as he switched to telepathy. *On three and we make the sign,* he added.

On three, they all tried to put their hands together, but couldn't remove them from the handles of their jet skis.

Not this again! said Jonathan. *I can't get my hands off the jet ski!*

Neither can I! Mikaia replied. *Let's slowly move our jet skis in the same direction and see if we can't get out of this,* suggested Jonathan.

Good idea, but we don't know how deep the flames are. We could end up getting burned or having our jet skis explode from the heat, Nicholas replied as they all began to catch the scent of burning sulfur.

The heat was almost unbearable when they saw a figure forming in the flames in front of them.

This doesn't look good, said Jonathan as he yanked hard trying to free his hands from the jet ski.

"Fancy meeting the three of you here," the triplets heard while the form took the shape of a man wearing a dark suit and tie with a pearl white long-sleeved shirt. "I was hoping I could catch you somewhere all alone. What a perfect place for us to visit...if only for a moment," the voice continued softly as the wind calmed down.

"Cryptic!" yelled Nicholas. "Now what's your game?"

"You should know by now, Nicholas. I've warned you several times. But in case you mere children have forgotten, it's called 'fire and ice'! Many, who have doubted my powers, have simply disappeared into them."

"You're just a poor loser because we've managed to change your Followers to the good or chase them out of Opportunity!" Jonathan yelled back.

"That's just a small portion of it, Jonathan. You've also embarrassed me and doubted my powers, even to the point of thinking you were my equal."

"We know we can never be equal. Your evil will always creep back in somewhere no matter what we do as long as selfishness and hatred exist in the

299

world," said Mikaia angrily.

"At least you understand the great advantage I have over you in recruiting Followers. But I grow weary of this conversation, as I grow weary of you."

"So where's your ice, big man?" yelled Jonathan.

What are you doing, Jonathan? transferred Nicholas.

I'm burning up! If he's going to kill us I much prefer the ice!

Right, Great idea! sent Mikaia. *Do you have any ideas about getting us out of here?*

"Oh, yes, the ice. I almost forgot!" Cryptic called out a little louder.

Immediately, the flames subsided. The triplets could hear a cracking sound as the surface of the lake began to freeze around them. The air turned from hot to cold and they felt frost begin to form on their hair and eyebrows.

Good going, Nicholas decided to send to Jonathan.

"This is a last goodbye. In a moment you will freeze solid. Your weight will flip your jet skis over and you'll fall through the ice and drown in the water below. Your friends will think it was all a tragic drowning accident," Cryptic said with an evil grin.

The triplets felt the cold breeze as it slowly drained their lives from them. But in the wind, they heard a soft but steady voice saying, "You have the power of love in your hearts and goodness in your souls. Use your mind to focus this upon your tormentor, for those are the only things he can never destroy. Focus, focus..." the voice kept saying. The triplets focused their minds and stared into Cryptic's eyes.

At first Cryptic stared back with the same evil grin. Then he began to blink, first just a little, then a lot. His smile turned to a frown as his face began to reveal an uncertainty that the triplets had seen only once before. He looked confused. He tried to break his eyes free from the triplets, but his were fastened to theirs. Frost appeared on his hair and face, as the cold wind began to blow stronger in his direction.

Suddenly, three of his tall Apprentices appeared, wearing red suits and ties and the same pearl white long-sleeved shirts as Cryptic. They moved forward towards the triplets as if to block and break the visual hold the triplets held over their Master. But their features turned frosty at an incredible rate, as their bodies seemed to turn to ice. With a surprised look frozen on their faces, the red ice they had become shattered like glass and fell onto the surface of the frozen lake.

The triplets kept their focus, as Cryptic's angry and icy form began to float backwards. The ice that held them to the lake's surface began to crack, making the tingling sound of wind chimes. The frost and ice on their bodies began to turn to water, and for the first time they could move their hands.

Cryptic kept floating backward, disbelief filling his eyes. The last thing the triplets heard from Cryptic was a weak "How?"

Jonathan replied with shout, "Because sooner or later good will always wins out over evil, Mr. Ice Cube!"

With Jonathan's last words, Cryptic disappeared.

The triplets just sat still on their jet skis. Their bodies were warming up since the ice on the lake's surface was almost gone. Even the hazy smoke began to lift allowing them to see the shoreline.

"That was too close!" exclaimed Nicholas.

"I don't ever want to go through that again," added Mikaia.

"That was Halo's voice, wasn't it?" Jonathan asked.

"He always said he liked to use the wind as his messenger," replied Nicholas.

"I have to admit he does have good timing," commented Jonathan.

Looking thoughtful, Mikaia said, "I believe the Master Inventor just gave us another power."

"Maybe we've had the power of good over evil all along and just didn't know it," suggested Nicholas.

"I wish Halo would just come out and tell us these things, before we get all frozen up," replied Jonathan.

"He probably wanted us to learn about this by ourselves," said Nicholas.

"I think we'd better get back," said Mikaia. "Everyone's going to be worried about us since we've been gone so long."

"What are we going to say?" asked Jonathan.

"They probably saw the smoke, so let's just say we stopped and waited until it cleared," suggested Nicholas.

"That would be the safe thing to do," agreed Mikaia. They started their jet skis and headed back towards the south end of the lake.

"Who do we say won the race?" Jonathan yelled out.

"I'll tell them it was a tie," yelled back Mikaia.

"How can you race several miles and get a tie?" yelled back Jonathan.

"Stranger things have happened than that, Jonathan," Nicholas yelled.

Jonathan rode another couple hundred feet before he yelled back, "You can say that again!"

As the triplets approached the shore everyone ran down to the water.

"Are you all right?" Mr. Wilson called out.

"We're fine," Mikaia shouted as they slowed down and drifted in.

"When we saw that large cloud of smoke appear right where you were heading, we got worried. We still can't figure out where it came from. We called the forest service but they had no reports of a fire," said Mrs. Wilson.

"Since we couldn't see the shoreline, we just stopped and drifted while we waited for it to lift," explained Mikaia.

"That was very sensible," said Mr. Wilson.

"Sorry we took so long," said Nicholas. "Now

whose turn is it?"

Larry quickly raised his hand and said, "I'll take a spin." Nicholas hopped off and Larry climbed on. "By the way, who won the race?"

"It was a tie," said Mikaia.

"How in the world could you get a...hey, there's something cold in here," Larry said as he reached down and pulled out a long piece of ice."

"Please let me see that," said Mr. Wilson. He looked at the ice carefully, then at the jet ski.

"I've never seen that happen before on these things," he said puzzled.

After he found a few more pieces on the other two jet skis, he sat on each and started them up.

"They're running fine. That's sure strange. I guess it's okay to take them back out," he said scratching his head.

Within a moment Larry, Calvin, and North, shot off down the lake. Everyone could hear North yelling, "Yahoo!"

"You did have us worried, Mikaia," said Ashlee as they sat down under the canopy and drank some bottled water. "But I knew whatever it was the three of you would be all right. I think you can handle anything. I just wish I knew more about you."

"Since we're all friends and plan to hang around together a lot, there will be plenty of time for you to figure it all out," replied Mikaia with a smile and Ashlee smiled back.

Right at four the triplets' father appeared. He

joined them on the beach for a few minutes and thanked the Wilsons for taking the triplets jet skiing. After a few goodbyes, they drove home.

When he asked, the triplets told their dad that they'd tell him how the day went when they got home, so their mom could hear it too. When they arrived home, they sat down in the kitchen and filled their parents in on all that had happened.

"You must have all been quite scared," said their mom.

"A little," replied Nicholas, "but somehow we knew that we'd be all right."

"Because of the powers you have?" their dad asked.

"Partly," said Mikaia, "but also because we knew that Halo and the Master Inventor were looking out for us."

"I just wish Halo would fill us in on things a little more before we have to learn them the hard way," complained Jonathan.

"I think that's where trust comes in, knowing that someone is looking out for you even when you don't see him," replied their dad.

"Yeah, there's still so much more to learn," said Jonathan.

"There always is," replied his dad.

Made in the USA
Middletown, DE
29 September 2021